ANTIDOTE TO VENOM

ANTIDOTE TO VENOM

FREEMAN WILLS CROFTS

WITH AN INTRODUCTION BY
MARTIN EDWARDS

THE BRITISH LIBRARY

This edition published in 2015 by
The British Library
96 Euston Road
London NW1 2DB

Originally published in London in 1938 by Hodder & Stoughton

Copyright © 2015 Estate of Freeman Wills Crofts
Introduction copyright © 2015 Martin Edwards

Cataloguing in Publication Data
A catalogue record for this book is available from the British Library

ISBN 978 0 7123 5779 1

Typeset by IDSUK (DataConnection) Ltd
Printed and bound by CPI Group (UK) Ltd, Croydon, CR0 4YY

AUTHOR'S NOTE

THIS book is a two-fold experiment: first, it is an attempt to combine the direct and inverted types of detective story and second, an effort to tell a story of crime positively.

I should like to express my gratitude to Mr. E. G. Boulenger (Director of the Aquarium and Curator of Reptiles in the Zoological Society's Gardens, London) for his kindness in reading my script and advising on matters connected with the Zoo.

F. W. C.

CONTENTS

CHAPTER   PAGE

INTRODUCTION   7

I.   VENOM: IN THE FAMILY   11

II.   VENOM: IN THE OFFICE   23

III.   VENOM: THROUGH THE EYE   36

IV.   VENOM: THROUGH THE AFFECTIONS   46

V.   VENOM: THROUGH THE POCKET   59

VI.   VENOM: IN SOCIETY   69

VII.   VENOM: THROUGH SURROUNDINGS   82

VIII.   VENOM: THROUGH TEMPTATION   98

IX.   VENOM: IN ACTION   113

X.   VENOM: THROUGH FALSEHOOD   123

XI.   VENOM: THROUGH MURDER   137

XII.   VENOM: THROUGH DECEIT   151

XIII.   VENOM: THROUGH THE LAW   163

XIV.   VENOM: IN THE MIND   177

XV.   VENOM: IN THE PRESS   189

XVI.   VENOM: IN THE CONFERENCE   203

XVII.   VENOM: THROUGH INTERROGATION   217

XVIII.   VENOM: IN THE WORKSHOP   230

XIX.   VENOM: FROM THE RIVER   240

XX.   VENOM: THE RECKONING   252

XXI.   VENOM: THROUGH DEATH   263

XXII.   VENOM: THROUGH THE TONGUE   273

XXIII. VENOM: THE ANTIDOTE   284

INTRODUCTION

Antidote to Venom is an ambitious and unusual detective novel, first published in 1938, during 'the Golden Age of murder'. The author, Freeman Wills Crofts, was widely regarded as one of the leading crime writers of the day. T.S. Eliot was among his many admirers, while Raymond Chandler, who could be grumpy about traditional detective stories, called Crofts 'the soundest builder of them all', although he added the caveat: 'when he doesn't get too fancy'.

In the years before he wrote this book, Crofts had been experimenting with his detective fiction, trying to escape from the predictable. He was well known for his meticulous story construction, and his murderers regularly fashioned for themselves seemingly unbreakable alibis, only for those alibis to be dismantled by Crofts' painstaking police officers. But starting with *The 12.30 from Croydon*, which appeared in 1934, Crofts began to vary his approach, producing an 'inverted story', in which events are seen at first from the perspective of the culprit.

Antidote to Venom, which Crofts described as 'a two-fold experiment', takes this method a stage further. The story benefits from an unusual setting – a zoo in the Midlands – and the central character is George Surridge, eminently respectable director of the Birmington Zoo. George's marriage to Clarissa is far from happy, and due to a combination of her demands and his own gambling habit, he is short of money. He has an affluent, elderly aunt in poor health, and finds himself wishing that she will hurry up and die, so that he can inherit. When he starts a relationship with an attractive widow, his need for funds becomes acute, and seasoned mystery readers presume that Surridge will murder his aunt. However, Crofts cleverly confounds expectations with a series of cunning plot twists.

Readers of Golden Age whodunits expect ingenuity, and Crofts delivers, not only with the murder method, but also with story structure. The first aspect of his experiment was the combination of the 'inverted' narrative with an account of 'direct' investigative work conducted by Crofts' usual detective, Chief Inspector Joseph French of New Scotland Yard. Although Birmington is far from his home ground, a stroke of bad luck for the guilty sees French becoming involved. He encounters a *modus operandi* so complicated and original – the zoo background is highly relevant – that Crofts supplied explanatory diagrams for the reader's benefit.

Before this book appeared, Anthony Berkeley and other leading writers had begun shifting the focus of crime fiction away from the cerebral puzzle and towards the psychological study of character. Although Crofts was an instinctive traditionalist, he responded to the mood of the times, and adjusted French's approach accordingly: 'The psychological argument could never be ignored. In fact, the older French grew and the more varied his experience became, the more weighty he found it.' And Crofts went further, and attempted something quite daring, and (so far as I know) unique in the work of leading detective novelists. As the story develops, it becomes clear that questions of morality and religious faith are at its heart. In Crofts' terms, this was 'an effort to tell a story of crime positively'.

Freeman Wills Crofts (1879–1957) was born in Dublin, and at the age of seventeen, he joined the Belfast and Northern Counties Railway. He worked his way up to the position of Chief Assistant Engineer, but by then he had already embarked on a new career as a detective novelist, and his books sold so well that at the age of fifty he was able to retire to Surrey, and concentrate on writing full time.

The Cask, Crofts' first detective novel, appeared in 1920, the same year as Agatha Christie's *The Mysterious Affair at Styles*, and made rather more of a splash than Hercule Poirot's debut. Four years later, Inspector French was introduced in *Inspector French's Greatest Case*. The title suggests that Crofts did not intend him to be a series character, but French's doggedness suited him perfectly for complex investigations, and he was described by one commentator on the genre as 'the first great policeman in the business'. Crofts said that French is 'decent and he's straight and he's as kindly as his job will allow'. His key characteristics are 'thoroughness and perseverance as well as a reasonable amount of intelligence…' He was, Crofts added, 'a home bird, and nothing pleases him more than to get into his slippers before the fire and bury himself in some novel of sea adventure'.

In his unfussy, unglamorous diligence, French mirrored his creator. Crofts was a quiet, serious and well-liked man who was entirely unaffected by his popular success. He became a founder member of the Detection Club, formed by Berkeley in 1930, and contributed to some of the Club's 'round robin' mystery stories, including the collaborative novel *The Floating Admiral*.

Religious faith meant a great deal to Crofts. He wrote *The Four Gospels in One Story* as 'a modern biography' for the benefit of lay people, and introduced a moral dimension into novels such as *Fatal Venture*, where he trains his fire on greed in business. He became enthusiastic about the work of the Oxford Group, which insisted that military armament alone would not solve the rapidly worsening international crisis of the late Thirties; the Group became known as Moral Rearmament in the year of *Antidote to Venom*'s first publication.

The central image of this novel is venom, both literal and metaphorical, and the final chapter delivers an explicit message about the 'antidote' to sin. In using the form of a detective novel for evangelical purposes, Crofts was pushing the boundaries of the genre. Most readers will, I suspect, conclude that his experiment with structure is more successful than his portrayal of a criminal's redemption. Even so, his bold inventiveness deserves respect. *Antidote to Venom* is an intriguing and original mystery, and its republication after many years of neglect is most welcome.

Martin Edwards
www.martinedwardsbooks.com

CHAPTER I

VENOM: IN THE FAMILY

GEORGE SURRIDGE entered his study shortly before seven on a cold night in mid October. He was in an irritable frame of mind, the result of an unusual crescendo of small worries. It had been one of those days on which everything had gone wrong, the last straw being provided by an aching tooth which had gnawed itself into his consciousness through all that he did. He had meant to go down town and have it seen to, but one thing after another had cropped up to prevent him. With more than usual pleasure he had been looking forward to this half-hour of relaxation before dinner.

But even now the tendency persisted. As he glanced at the fire his brow darkened. It had been allowed to go down and the room was cold. How many times, he asked himself savagely, did that confounded girl need to be told to have it burning up brightly when he came in? Why couldn't she do what she was asked? His hand strayed towards the bell, then desisted. What was the good? If he said enough to make any impression on her she would leave and then there would be hell to pay with Clarissa. He glanced at the wood bucket. For a wonder there was something in it. Irritably he raked the coals together and threw on a couple of blocks. Then crossing the room he poured himself out a stiff whisky and soda.

He carried the glass to his arm-chair, and picking up the evening paper which he had brought in with him but laid aside, he sat down with a grunt of relief.

He turned to the financial pages. Stocks were dropping, and considering the state of the country, he didn't see why they should. There was talk of another slump and the idea frightened him. For money meant a good deal to George Surridge. As it was he was hard up, and if things grew worse his position might become really serious.

He was a man of rather undistinguished appearance, of the type which would inevitably pass unnoticed in a crowd. Of medium height and build, he was neither markedly well or ill favoured in face. His hair, of a medium shade of brown, was greying at the temples. His forehead was perhaps his best feature, fairly high though not broad, but his mouth was weak and his eyes a trifle shifty. He looked tired and worried and old for his age, which was forty-six.

But though he seemed to be bearing his share of trouble, a casual acquaintance would have said he had little reason to grumble. He held a good job. George Surridge was Director of the Birmington Corporation Zoo; and the Birmington Zoo was claimed by Birmington people as the second zoo in the country: smaller perhaps than London—though not a whit inferior—but larger and better than any other. This post gave him a good social position in the city, an adequate salary and free occupation of the comfortable house in which he was now seated, not to speak of coal and these logs—which had now burst into a blaze and begun to give out heat—as well as the electric current which was lighting his reading lamp.

It was certainly a snug enough post, and unless he made some serious break, secure. The work also was congenial. He loved animals and they seemed to recognise in him a friend. So far none of them had ever turned on him or shown temper when he was with them. On the whole, too, he got on reasonably well with his staff. If his relations with his wife had been equally satisfactory he might have been more content, but unhappily these left a good deal to be desired.

He settled down comfortably with his whisky and news-paper. This little rest should help him, and by dinner time he should be feeling normal.

He was not, however, to be allowed to enjoy his relaxation. He had read for a few moments only when the door opened and his wife entered. She was dressed for the street and had evidently just reached home.

Clarissa Surridge was a woman striking enough looking to attract the eye of the casual passer-by. Tall, and with a presence, her well cut clothes accentuated the lines of her fine figure. Her pale oval face had good features, though a discontented and rather unhappy expression. In spite of her make-up—usually much too lavish for her husband's taste—little lines appeared on her forehead and at the corners of her eyes, while streaks of grey marked her dark hair. Now she looked upset and annoyed and George saw that he was in for trouble.

"Oh, you're home?" she began ungraciously, then continued in a hard unsympathetic voice. "The car's broken down again. I thought I'd never get back. Either the car's done or Pratt doesn't know how to manage it."

George's heart sank. The car undoubtedly was old. It had been a good Mortin in its day, but of course five years was five years. It was certainly shabby, though the engine was sound. Recently he had had a re-bore and he had also got a new battery, tyres and other fittings. It really wasn't too bad.

"What's the matter now?" he asked, with an unpleasant accent on the last word.

Clarissa closed the door, not too gently, and advanced into the room. "I've just told you. What are you going to do about it?"

"Nothing. The car's all right." He glanced down at his paper as if he had closed the subject, then looked up again. "What went wrong?"

"How do I know? I'm not a mechanic." Her voice indicated with uncompromising clarity that the subject was anything but closed.

"Well, what happened?" went on George impatiently.

"It stopped." His wife warmed to her subject as she proceeded to develop it. "I had just set down Margaret Marr at a shop when it stopped: there in King Street in the middle of the traffic. The police came over and a crowd gathered while it was being pushed into the kerb. I don't know when I felt such a fool."

"What has Pratt done about it?"

"I don't know what he's done about it and I care less. What I know is that it's the third time it has happened in a couple of months."

George Surridge jerked himself about in his chair. Really women's notions were the limit. "Rubbish," he said shortly. "Every car goes wrong occasionally."

"Well, as I tell you, it's gone wrong once too often. I give you warning I'm not going on with it any longer. Why, it's six years old if it's a day."

"Five."

"It's the same thing. When are you going to get a new one? I've spoken about it often enough."

"Speaking about it won't provide the money. I've told you I can't afford it at present."

"What nonsense! You have plenty of money. If not, where has it all gone to?"

George lifted his paper again as if to read, then once again dropped it. "You would have all that painting done. Only for that I might have managed it."

If this was meant as an olive branch, it failed in its purpose. Clarissa's eyes flashed angrily and her voice took on a more bitter tone. "Oh, my fault, of course. That painting! Why, it's *years* since anything was done. And your committee friends wouldn't move, though it was their liability. I suppose they have no money either."

"They thought they had done enough for one year with the new electric wiring."

"Yes, tear the place to bits and then leave it like that! I'd like to know how I was to have my friends in if the house was like a pigsty?"

This touched a sore spot and George reacted accordingly. "*I* could do without them all right," he declared grimly, and as the thought of his grievances grew, he went on with a rising inflexion. "Here I come home after sweating all day for you and your house and I want a little peace, and there's never a minute I can call my own."

"And what about me?" Clarissa retorted. "Do you think I do nothing all day? Haven't I got this house to run—on half nothing? And you grudge me a little relaxation."

George Surridge all but laughed as he compared this picture of his wife's existence with the reality. Actually she lived her own life among her own friends, keeping her own council, and using the house as a sort of inferior hotel, of which, owing to its unfashionable situation, she was slightly ashamed. "A little relaxation?" he retorted. "Hang it all, don't be an utter fool. Look here," he felt he had spoken improperly and was sorry, but could not bring himself to apologise, "forget what I said. Let's have a quiet evening for once in away and I'll see what I can do about the car."

Clarissa smiled maliciously. "If you had wanted a quiet evening you shouldn't have invited your aunt to dinner."

"Oh hell! I forgot about her."

"Not my friends this time."

George waved his paper irritably. "We have to do it, as you know very well. If she thought she didn't get proper attention, she's quite capable of altering her will."

"She'll perhaps see through your affection and do it in any case." Swinging on her heel, Clarissa left the room, while George sat on before the now dying fire, gazing gloomily into the cooling embers.

The scene with his wife had not unduly upset him. Unhappily he had grown accustomed to such an atmosphere, as for many years it had been the normal one existing between them. There were indeed few subjects they could discuss without heat, and not infrequently recriminations were much more bitter than on this evening.

His thoughts travelled back over the path his steps had so far followed. He had been lucky as a youth. He had had good parents, a comfortable home, an excellent education and enough money to enable him to choose his career. He had always loved animals, but at first the idea of becoming connected with a zoo had not occurred to him. He had taken his degree in veterinary surgery, intending to set up in one of the hunting counties. Then a small mischance had given a new twist to his ideas.

Driving to the wharves in Antwerp on his return from a holiday in Germany, a slight collision with another car had caused him to miss his boat. With some hours to spare before the next, he had naturally gravitated to the Zoo. In passing through the gardens he had observed on an office door the inscription, "Bureau du Directeur." The idea that here was his life's work leapt into his mind and his first care on returning to England was to make an appointment with the Director of the London Zoo to ask about possibilities.

Luckily or unluckily for him, it happened that at that very moment the Director was in need of a junior assistant. He took to his visitor personally, and was pleased not only with his obvious love for animals, but the fact that he was a qualified veterinary surgeon. To make a long story short, he offered him a job, which was instantly and rapturously accepted.

Young George Surridge's heart was in his work and he gave satisfaction. In six years he was promoted twice, and at the end of ten he found himself second in command and his chief's right hand man.

Then he fell in love.

It happened that some months before his last promotion George was sent on business to the house of a Mr. Ellington, a City magnate who lived in St. John's Wood. This gentleman had a tiny aquarium stocked with rare fish small in dimension but spectacular as to shape and colour. He was anxious to extend his collection and had consulted George's chief on the project. George's job was to view the site and assist with expert advice.

Ellington found the young man interesting and kept him to tea. There George met Mrs. Ellington and her two daughters. Clarissa, the elder, he admired immensely, though no thought of love at that time entered his mind.

The progress of the new aquarium involved further visits and George gradually grew more and more intimate with the family. He soon learned that both daughters were engaged, Clarissa to an artist and Joan to an officer in the Guards. The artist he detested at sight, privately diagnosing him, with a callous disregard to the purity of metaphor, as a weedy gasbag.

As time passed, in spite of his quite genuine efforts to prevent it, he found his admiration of Clarissa growing into a very real love. He was honourably minded and he felt he should avoid the house, but the job still required his presence, and when Clarissa asked him to wait for lunch or tea, as she often did, he had not the strength to refuse.

So matters dragged on for some time and then, just after George's promotion to the position of Chief Assistant, there came a fresh development. Clarissa and the artist had a terrible quarrel. George never knew what it was about, but it ended in Clarissa breaking off the engagement.

George at first was stunned by the possibilities now opening out before him. Just as he had obtained his new job and reached a position in which he could afford to marry, the girl he had so hopelessly loved had become free. He scarcely dared to think that she would accept him, owing to the difference of their social stations. However, after waiting for a reasonable time he took his courage in both hands and proposed. To his surprise she accepted him, and a few months later they were married.

Then for George there set in a period of disillusionment, which grew more and more heartbreaking as the weeks passed. Clarissa before marriage had cheerfully accepted all the disabilities which he had warned her would result from what, in comparison with her previous life, would be straightened circumstances. Her acceptance had, he was sure, been perfectly honest, but she had not realised to what she was agreeing. When, for example, she found they were travelling second class on their honeymoon to Switzerland, she had frowned, though without remark. And when at Pontresina they had gone to a comparatively primitive hotel with small rooms and without private baths, she had been a little short. It was not, he felt sure, inconsistency on her part. It was simply that she had never before in her life travelled otherwise than in the lap of luxury.

This question of money was not referred to between them, but it loomed larger and larger in his thoughts and it spoiled his pleasure. Rightly or wrongly, he felt Clarissa was looking down on the entertainment which he was able to provide, and he grew correspondingly awkward and distant in manner, a change to which she reacted unhappily. At the same time there began to grow up in his heart a sense of grievance against her. She had money of her own, but she never offered to share the financial burden. At first he clung to the view that this was to spare his pride, and he certainly would have felt affronted if she had offered to pay for the holiday. But he did think she might occasionally have said: "Look here, let's go halves in this," or sometimes have paid for the occasional special excursions they took, some of which were quite expensive.

Though he sincerely tried to make excuses for her, this money question spoiled their honeymoon, and both were glad when they set their faces homewards. Often afterwards he thought that if he had been honest with her and told her directly of his difficulties, a happy understanding might have been reached. But his pride stepped in and prevented him.

When they reached London and set up in what was to her a tiny and rather inconvenient house, this bar to their happiness remained. It was true that Clarissa did now spend money on their establishment, but he gradually found that it was only on things which benefited herself, not on those they used jointly. They settled down, however, as well as do a great many other married couples. Outwardly they were amicable enough and they avoided the bitter quarrels that separated some of their friends. But they had little real fellowship. George's love for his wife gradually died, and he began to ask himself whether she had ever felt any at all for him.

When they had been married some eight years, George obtained one of the plums of the zoological world: the director-ship of the Birmington Zoo. A new house among new surround-ings and the breaking of certain old ties might bring about that reconciliation and companionship for which he so much longed. From every point of view he was delighted at the prospect and he moved to the Midlands with enthusiasm.

Once again he was disappointed. Though from a professional point of view the change left nothing to be desired, the effect on his home life was bad rather than good. In the new city Clarissa missed her friends. Moreover she did not particularly take to the Midlanders. With her metropolitan standards she was inclined to look down upon them as provincials. They quickly sensed her feeling and their welcome grew less friendly. Clarissa became lonely and unhappy.

This is not to say that she did not make friends. Both she and George made a number, but the process proved slower than it need have done.

In Birmington, as in Switzerland and London, the question of money tended to prevent real good fellowship developing between husband and wife. As director, George was now in receipt of a much larger salary than formerly, as well as a free house, rates, and other perquisites. If Clarissa had been content with their former scale of living, it would have greatly eased his position, enabling him to insure and to save against a rainy day, as he wished. But with the larger salary her demands grew greater, and while they lived in a better way, it took almost the whole of the larger salary to do it.

In that ten years of life at Birmington, relations between the couple had slowly deteriorated. At times George felt he absolutely hated his wife. They still had had no direct breach, but he could not be blind to the fact that one might occur at any moment.

He felt old and dispirited, did George Surridge, as he sat on in his study gazing morosely into the dying fire. A sense of futility oppressed him, a sense that nothing he was doing was worth while and that much he was occupied with would be better left undone. Besides the unhappiness of his home, another matter, even more serious, was preying on his mind. He had been idiotic enough, for sheer amusement and relaxation, to get into a gambling set at the club. He had lost, and was losing, more than he could afford, and yet he didn't want to stop playing. The men he met were a pleasant crowd, indeed they seemed to him at times the best friends he had. He saw, however, that he must break with them, for the simple reason that he couldn't afford the continued drain on his pocket. This he had realised for some months, yet when they invited him to join them he had not had the strength to refuse, telling himself on each occasion that this time he must win, and that if he did, never again would he touch a card.

His thoughts swung round into a familiar channel. If only his old aunt would die and leave him her money! She was well-to-do, was Miss Lucy Pentland, not exactly wealthy, but obviously with a comfortable little fortune enough, and she had on more than one occasion told him that he would be her heir. Moreover, she was in poor health. In the nature of things she could not last very much longer. If only she would die!

Surridge pulled himself up, slightly ashamed of himself. He did not of course wish the old lady any harm. Quite the reverse. But really, when people reached a certain age their usefulness was over. And in his opinion she had reached and passed that stage. She could not enjoy her life. If she were to die, what a difference it would make to him!

Thoughts of her reminded him that she was probably at that moment on her way to the house. The evening would be trying. She was a little deaf and was hard to entertain. Thank goodness she liked to go home early.

Finishing his whisky, Surridge went upstairs to change for dinner.

CHAPTER II

VENOM: IN THE OFFICE

SHORTLY after nine next morning George Surridge left his house, which stood, screened off from the public by a belt of Scotch firs, in a corner of the Zoological Gardens, and walked along the private path to his office in the adjoining lot. This also was separated from the public by vegetation, though here in the form of a privet hedge. The office stood on raised ground, and from the chair at his desk George could see over the hedge and the flower borders down the main walk of the Gardens, which ran wide and straight right across the area to the entrance gate. From a casual inspection of the crowds on this walk, together with a glance at the hands of the clock on his chimneypiece, long practice had enabled him to form a close approximation of the turnstile records, and therefore of the important matter of the day's takings.

With his customary "Morning, Harley," to the clerk in the outer office, and "Morning, Miss Hepworth," to his secretary in her little ante-room, George entered his private room. It was well furnished and comfortable. A roaring fire blazed up the chimney, and the tidyness of the books and papers and the spotless cleanliness of the windows and furniture showed that George could command attentive service. On the blotting pad on the large flat desk stood a pile of opened letters, with to the left a newspaper and a couple of periodicals. After a moment before the fire George sat down at the desk and pressed a button. Miss Hepworth entered with her pencil and pad and in silence took her place at a small table close by.

She was a rather baffling sort of girl. Always neatly dressed and competent looking, though not exactly a beauty, she was reserved to the verge of actual hostility. To George she was a complete enigma. He never could tell what she was thinking about, if indeed she ever did think of anything but her work. Whether she admired him or hated the sight of him he had no idea, and while he didn't particularly care, he would have been interested to know. But she was an admirable machine, and to her he owed a great deal of his clerical efficiency.

Methodically he began to work through the letters. Here was one from Messrs. Hooper of Liverpool, trying to excuse themselves for having supplied mouldy nuts for the monkeys and certain birds, and offering to accept a slight reduction on the price. "Not a bit of it," Surridge commented. "They can take their damned stuff away and send more, or else they can do without our custom. There's illness enough as it is among the monkeys."

He passed over the letter, knowing that in due course a document would be laid before him beginning: "With reference to your communication of 15th inst., I regret to inform you," and so on. When Miss Hepworth had first come she would have inserted the words "esteemed" before "communication," and "duly to hand" after "15th inst.", but he had managed to break her of these. He could not, however, make her alter the sweep of her gambit, nor even get her to substitute the word "letter" for "communication."

The next letter was from the Liverpool agents of the Purple Star Steamship Company, and read: "We beg to advise you that we are expecting our s.s. *Delhi* to berth in the Ambleside Dock, Liverpool, at 7.0 a.m. on Friday morning, 24th inst. with the two elephants consigned to you, and referred to in our LST of 7th inst. We shall be obliged if you will kindly arrange to take delivery as soon after that hour as possible."

This matter George had already dealt with. Transport of elephants through England was rather a job. They were too big to send by rail, and it would have cost a considerable sum to fit up a road lorry to take them. The elephants would therefore have to walk the hundred odd miles to Birmington. They would take it in easy stages and he had arranged for sheds for them to sleep in each night. Two Indian keepers had travelled with them, and he was sending his own man, Ali, with a couple of assistants to render help in case of need.

A number of letters covered ordinary routine matters. In these food bulked large. Coarse meat for the larger carnivora was easy to obtain, but in the winter the large amount of green food required for the vegetarian creatures was more of a problem. The quantities of certain articles of diet were enormous. Fish ran into some dozens of tons per annum. Each king penguin alone ate some dozen herring every day, and on occasion would take twice this number at a single meal without turning a feather. Eggs, bread, milk, fruit, all ran into astronomical figures, and all must be of good quality and quite fresh. The catering department was in itself a full time job, and George had an assistant to carry on the routine work. But all new or large contracts he supervised himself.

Then there were letters from people who wanted to get rid of pets—or rather of creatures which had been pets—and thought the Birmington Zoo a suitable dumping ground. Adolescent bears were frequently on offer. Bought as small and enticing balls of fur, they had the drawback that they grew, eventually becoming an embarrassing and overwhelming charge. People who brought home monkeys from abroad and who had their most cherished possessions torn into shreds, or were bitten to the bone, came to the opinion that a monkey in the Zoo was worth two in the hand. Other people wrote asking questions about animals: "My daughter has been given a pair of Belgian hares. What do you consider their most nutritive diet?" With all these and many more, George dealt quickly.

After the letters there were interviews. Keepers came in with reports on all kinds of matters, mostly in response to a call, but occasionally on their own initiative, if they considered their business important enough to go before the "Chief." The health of various sick animals was discussed, as well as methods of dealing with tantrums or notions which others had taken. Repairs to buildings were noted, with ideas for alterations or improvements. The gardener had a scheme for next year's planting and touched on a vexed question of some standing: whether or not the gravel walks should be replaced with asphalte. Gradually George built up his list of the points to which he must give special attention during his daily inspection, which was now shortly due.

"That all?" he said at last.

"John Cochrane is waiting to see you." Miss Hepworth's tone held a distinct reproof that he should have forgotten the interview.

But George had not forgotten it. This was one of those cases he loathed dealing with, and now he braced himself for an unpleasant ten minutes. "Send him in," he directed and there entered a small wiry man of about fifty, with a sallow face and downcast expression.

Cochrane was a night watchman and had been employed for some six years. He was a good average man, sober and careful, and until the present matter arose, George would have said quite reliable. Up till now he had never been "before" George, but had done his work unobtrusively and, so far as was known to the contrary, well. Unhappily, in this paragon a yellow streak had now been discovered.

It happened that a week earlier Surridge had been up in London and had missed his usual return train. Instead of reaching Birmington at 11.0 p.m. he did not arrive till 3.0 in the morning. It also happened that either because of there being more passengers than usual or fewer taxis, he found himself able only to share a vehicle, and that for only part of his way home. Half a mile from the Zoo he got out, intending to walk the rest of the way.

As he turned a street corner he all but ran into a man who was coming to meet him. The man quickly put his hand over his face. But he was too slow: George had recognised him.

"What are you doing here, Cochrane?" he asked. "Have you got leave from duty?"

Cochrane was so much taken aback that he could scarcely speak. Then he admitted that he had left his work without either obtaining leave or putting someone else in his place. George suspended him and told him to call and see him next morning.

The man's statement next day seemed straightforward and George believed it. He said his wife was ill and had been ordered medicine every four hours day and night. She could not get it for herself and during the day he had been able to attend on her. For the night he could not afford a nurse, but he had paid a neighbour a few shillings a week to look after her during his turn of duty. On the previous night the woman had been called unexpectedly from home. As soon as he had heard of this he had tried to get a substitute, but without success. He had decided, wrongly, he now admitted, to slip home in the middle of his nine hours watching, give her her medicine, and return as quickly as possible. He lived within a couple of miles of the Zoo and did not expect to be absent for more than an hour at the outside.

George was distressed about the affair, but the more he thought over it, the more serious the fault appeared. He saw that as director he could not consider the man's home circumstances, but only his duty to his employers. If fire had broken out the results might have been disastrous. Not only might there have been heavy financial loss, but dangerous animals might have escaped and people might have been killed. He told Cochrane that he would consult his Chairman on the matter, but that he had no hope that the latter would agree to his being kept on, and that he ought to look out for another job.

George had taken the trouble to find the doctor who was attending Mrs. Cochrane to check the man's story. It proved to be Dr. Marr, a friend of his own, who lived close by. Marr confirmed the details of the case.

"I'm sorry if he's going to lose his job," the doctor went on. "Though he's a man I don't personally get on with—bad manner, you know—the family is decent. Mrs. Cochrane is a really good sort of woman and the son and daughter are doing well. The daughter's in service with the Burnabys: you must have seen her scores of times, and the son has a fairly good job at a garage."

The Burnabys, father and daughter, also lived close to the Zoo and were friends of the Surridges. Surridge had often noticed the maid, and now that his attention had been called to the matter, he saw that she was like her father. His own feeling was that after a week's suspension Cochrane might be re-started, but when he discussed the affair with his chairman, Colonel Kirkman, he found him adamant. A man who had so abused a position of trust could not be kept. If the medicine were so important,

Cochrane's course was obvious. He should have seen his immediate superior and had proper arrangements made for his relief.

"We're not unreasonable people," Kirkman went on. "If he had asked for leave he would have got it. I don't see, Surridge, that you can possibly keep him. The Committee wouldn't stand for it." Cochrane had remained suspended since the incident, and it was to pass on this verdict that George had now asked him to call.

The interview was even more unpleasant than George had anticipated. Cochrane took the news badly. He spoke very bitterly, but George couldn't help himself.

"I'm sorry, Cochrane," he concluded. "When you think the thing over you'll see that I have had no alternative. There's some money due to you, and if you go to Mr. Harley you'll get it. And I may say that if in a private capacity I can help you to a job, I'll be glad to do it."

The question of the man's successor would have to be settled without delay, but he decided to postpone it for the moment, as Renshaw, his chief assistant, was waiting to accompany him on the daily inspection.

The Zoo was in process of transformation from the old-fashioned arrangement, in which the houses of the various exhibits were massed together with small barred pens attached to each, to a modern layout, with larger areas for the animals, reproducing as far as possible their natural surroundings. An adjoining estate of twenty acres had recently been added to the old four-acre park, and the new houses were being built and the animals moved into them as finances permitted. George was very keen on this work and had infected the staff with his enthusiasm.

The main walk already referred to, still however remained the centre of interest. On its right were five blocks of buildings containing respectively the elephants, certain large cats such as pumas, jaguars and cheetahs, the tigers, and the lions. Behind these houses was an area of garden with three pools, for polar bears, penguins and seals. At the other side of the pools were seven more houses, for snakes, small Indian animals, small monkeys, large monkeys, camels, dromedaries, and rhinoceroses respectively. The arrangement was like a D, where the five houses along the walk were represented by the vertical line, the pools by the central area, and the other houses by the curved back. Of these latter, the snake-house was nearest Surridge's office at the top of the D, and between the monkey-houses—that is, halfway round the curved side—there was a small private door leading out to an adjoining road. This was not used by the public and was always kept locked.

It was Surridge's custom to begin his inspection with the snake-house, work down the curved side of the D, and so on to the other houses. The collection of snakes was extremely good, one of the best features of the Zoo. There were two immense anacondas, constrictors not far from twenty-five feet long and each capable of swallowing a small sheep at a meal. There were English adders, and the dreaded puff adders from South Africa. There were brown snakes, black snakes, green snakes and yellow snakes, whip snakes, cobras and rattle snakes. There were a pair of ringhals, appalling reptiles which can shoot a jet of poison from ten feet away, unerringly reaching their victim's eyes, as well as many harmless and beautifully marked creatures. All seemed to Surridge in good condition. Whether there was something that suited them in the air or soil of Birmington, or whether their health was due to the care of their attendant, Keeper Nesbit, Surridge did not know, but he secretly believed that Birmington had more success with its snakes than any other zoo in the world.

It was for this reason that the Burnabys, with whom the dismissed watchman's daughter was in service, had come to the district. Burnaby had been professor of pathology at Leeds University, from which position he had recently retired. During the latter part of his life he had specialised on the use of snake poisons in treating various diseases, and he had been looking forward for years to the time when he could retire and write his *magnum opus*, the book descriptive of his researches, which would make him famous. Wishing to continue his investigations, and knowing the reputation of the Birmington Zoo for its snakes, he had asked George for special facilities to experiment with his collection, and these George, with the approval of his committee, had granted. The old man had thereupon bought a house close by, fitted up a laboratory, and with his daughter to keep house for him, had settled down to work. He had even been granted keys to the snake-house and some of the cages, as well as to the private side door, which latter saved him a long walk round through the main entrance.

Surridge and Renshaw passed on to the small Indian animals and from them to the monkeys. Here things were not so satisfactory as in the snake-house. A lot of monkeys had been ill lately with something like flu. A marmoset and a lemur had died, and one or two others seemed in an unsatisfactory way. Both men were worried about the affair.

"If there's not an all round improvement by the end of the week I'll wire for Hibbert," Surridge said, referring to the calling in for consultation of the chief medical officer attached to the London Zoo, a matter which they had already discussed. "No reflection on you, of course. But I think we should have a second opinion."

"I should welcome it," Renshaw agreed.

They passed on, continuing their round, dealing with the hundred and one matters which in a place of such size are continually arising. Then Surridge returned to his office, and for the hour still remaining before lunch, settled down to get out his monthly report for the next meeting of his committee.

For some years he had given up going home in the middle of the day, lunching instead down town at his club. Ostensibly this was for the sake of his business: to keep in touch with the other men of the city and be *au fait* with what was going on. Really his motive was quite different. The society of his wife had become a strain and he was glad of any excuse to avoid being with her. He believed she also liked the arrangement, partly for the same reason as his own, and partly because it left her freer and saved trouble in the house.

Presently he left the office to walk the half mile or more to the club. He usually went with a man named Mornington, an artist who lived near the Zoo and whose work, being carried on exclusively at his home, left him in need of the society of his fellows. But to-day there was no sign of Mornington, and George went on alone.

As he walked his thoughts reverted to his own circumstances. The question of money was growing more and more pressing. He would have to do something about it, something drastic. He could give up his play of course, but he didn't want to do that unless it proved absolutely unavoidable. It was not so much for the excitement of the gambling, though he enjoyed that, as for the companionship. An even more important reason was that he now owed a considerable sum. If he stopped playing he would inevitably have to find that money, whereas a run of luck on one evening might clear him. This had occurred already on three separate occasions, on each of which he had won back a pretty considerable amount. There was no reason why the same thing should not happen again. If, and when, it did, that would be the time to stop.

Then there was his aunt's legacy. He did not know what she was worth, but it must be several thousand: say seven or eight thousand at the most moderate estimate. And at her death he would get most of it—she had told him so. What, he wondered, would his share amount to? After death duties were deducted and one or two small legacies to servants were paid, there should be at least five thousand over. Five thousand! What could he not do with five thousand? Not only would it clear him of debt, but he could get that blessed car for Clarissa as well as several other things she wanted. They could take a really decent holiday; she had friends in California whom she wished to see, and for professional reasons he had always wanted to visit South Africa. In countless ways the friction and strain would be taken from his home life. And all this he would get if only the old lady were to die! Last night she had looked particularly ill; pale like parchment and more feeble and depressed than he ever remembered having seen her. Again he told himself that he didn't wish her harm, but it was folly not to recognise facts. Her death was the one thing that would set him on his feet.

It happened that the first person he saw in the club was Dr. Marr. Marr was a man of about fifty, tall and spare, with a look of competence and a kindly smile, which when it broke out transformed his rather severe face, making it radiate good will. He was a general favourite, particularly, George had heard, among his panel patients.

George had often compared their lives, which in most respects were a complete contrast. Marr was happy at home: Margaret Marr was one of the salt of the earth. He had a big

practice and seemed to have plenty of money, though George
in fairness admitted that he worked for it. Also he held certain
official positions, including that of police doctor for the district.
He never lunched at the club when he could avoid it, preferring
his home to all other places upon earth.

"Unexpected seeing you here," Surridge greeted him.

"I know," returned the doctor. "I'm lunching Ormsby-Lane.
Down from London for a consultation. What's the best news
with you? Have you sacked that poor devil Cochrane?"

They talked over the case for a few moments, while George
wondered how he could introduce the subject of his aunt,
whom he knew Marr attended. He had to be careful about what
he said. It must not look as if he were thinking too much of the
old lady's money.

Then Marr himself gave him an opportunity. "I didn't see
you last night at Cooper's lecture on his Sinai excavations," he
observed. "Interesting stuff and fine pictures."

"I should have liked to go," George returned, "but I couldn't.
We had the aunt to dinner: Miss Pentland, you know."

"Oh, yes. I was out seeing her a couple of days ago."

George hastened to improve the occasion. "I hope it was
only a social call? She seemed a little tired last night, though not
exactly ill."

The doctor shrugged. "Well, she's getting on in years, you
know." He paused, shook his head, then changed the subject.

George's heart gave a leap. Marr, he knew, was if anything an
optimist, and such a remark in such a connection could surely
mean only one thing. Her doctor also thought Lucy Pentland's
health was failing. George longed to press for more definite
information, but while he was weighing the pros and cons the
opportunity passed. Marr interrupted himself in the middle of a

sentence. "There's Ormsby-Lane," he exclaimed. "Excuse me, old man, I must go and meet him."

Lunch passed without further incident, and after a chat in the smoking-room, George returned to his office. Frequently he had to pay calls in the city at this hour, and twice a week he played a round of golf, but on this occasion there was no such engagement and he walked back with the artist, Mornington.

There was plenty of work to keep him busy all the afternoon: reports, statistics, estimates to be prepared, technical articles in the journals to be read. Also he was doing a paper for the Zoological Society on the effect of environment on animals in captivity, and he wanted to arrange the notes he had already collected.

In spite of this, he could not keep Marr's remark, and particularly Marr's gesture, out of his mind. From an optimist they certainly did look significant. Marr, he would stake his life, thought badly of his patient. And he, George, was medically no fool. In qualifying as a vet he had learnt a lot about human ailments. He could see for himself that quite unmistakably the old lady was going down the hill…

And that would mean—five thousand pounds!

CHAPTER III

VENOM: THROUGH THE EYE

DURING the following week George had the stroke of luck at cards for which he had been hoping. On two successive nights at the club he had won: enough to meet his immediate difficulties and a little more. For the time being his financial crisis was over, though cynically he told himself that before long it would recur. He had been to see his aunt, and to his secret delight—which he tried unsuccessfully to hide from himself—her break-up seemed to grow more and more imminent. Incessantly he wondered how long she was likely to last, though always he pulled himself up with the reminder that he did not really wish her harm.

In the Zoo he had been a good deal worried about the epidemic among the monkeys. Three more animals had gone down with it and another had died: a valuable old gibbon from Siam which the Zoo could ill afford to lose. It was a serious matter, upon which drastic action must be taken. George had rung up Hibbert, the London Zoo vet, only to find that he was from home. He had then put through a similar call to Edinburgh, this time with more satisfactory results. Mr. M'Leod, their medical expert, the secretary replied, would leave for Birmington by the first train. He had experience of a similar outbreak among the monkeys of his own Zoo and would bring a serum which had proved efficacious in that instance. He believed it would effect a cure in this one also.

On the afternoon on which he received this news George had a very nasty headache, and when he had finished his essential work, he decided to relax until it was time to go to the station to meet M'Leod. A stroll round the grounds, looking at the visitors always rested him. It amused him to notice how like the people were to the animals and the animals to the people. They did the same things, obviously from the same motives, though the people tried to hide these motives and the animals didn't. Usually, he thought, with a rather bitter smile, in any such comparison the animals had the best of it.

His eyes passed from one visitor to another and then rested on a woman who was standing watching with an amused smile the evolutions of the penguins, as they swam and dived and made a great fuss over nothing very apparent. She was what is expressively called "easy to look at." She was perhaps a little below medium height and had a comfortable well rounded figure, dark hair and a sensible competent kindly face, not at all beautiful, but full of personality and charm. She was extraordinarily well dressed: indeed, it was this which had first attracted George's attention. As far as he could see, her clothes were neither fashionable nor expensive—they were not at all what he had been told was smart—but there was a suggestion of extreme daintiness and good taste which he considered more telling than either.

He stood looking at her for some minutes. What restfulness there was in that face! He wondered if he might speak to her, then after a momentary hesitation he went over.

"You're interested in the animals?" he said with some diffidence. "I'm the director here and I've been watching you. You look as if you felt more than mere idle curiosity."

"Oh, but I do," she answered, and he couldn't remember when he had heard so delightful a voice, low pitched and soft and musical, so different from the nasal squawks of most of Clarissa's friends. "I love them. I don't believe the people who say they have only instinct. I'm sure they have their own thoughts and weigh things up and take decisions, just as we do."

"I know it," he declared. "I've seen it again and again. Do you know the story of the polar bear who baited a trap for umbrellas?"

She smiled delightfully. "I'm sure I don't. What is it?"

"The bear acquired an umbrella complex; he wanted to collect them and break them up. It's believed that someone poked him with an umbrella and that started it. However, his problem was how to get people to put their umbrellas within his reach, and he solved it in a tremendously ingenious way. He put a bit of fish on a ledge above his head, almost, but not quite out of his reach. Then when a likely umbrella hove in sight, he sat up and ogled the fish, whining and pretending he couldn't reach it. The kind-hearted spectator realised the trouble and reached in with his umbrella to poke the fish down. There was a whirl of fur and the umbrella departed this life."

She laughed; a rich gurgling whole hearted laugh of amusement and enjoyment: to Surridge an entrancing sound. "Lovely," she exclaimed, "but I'm afraid you're pulling my leg."

"I didn't see it myself," he admitted, "but I've heard it's perfectly true. But whether or not, you're right about animal's reasoning powers. I remember the case of a wolf," and he went on to tell a number of anecdotes of the creatures under his care.

She was a fascinating person to talk to. She really listened for one thing, and when she did speak, it was to make some witty comment or ask some really understanding question. It was a long time since George had spoken to anyone so sympathetic. "Would you care for a peep behind the scenes?" he went on presently, and when she enthusiastically agreed, he spent a delightful hour showing her that side of zoo working which is usually hidden from the public.

It was perhaps inevitable that a good deal of their talk should become personal. He learnt something of her tastes and was thrilled to find them very similar to his own. They liked the same kind of music, and though she knew much more of literature than he, so far as he had followed her they had the same favourites. They were at one in a love of travel, of mountains and of Italy. In a word, George enjoyed their chat more than anything he had experienced for a long time.

He wondered who she was and where she lived, but to his veiled and tentative questions she returned blandly unilluminating replies. Presently she said she must go, and though she thanked him for his attention, she was vague about paying a further visit.

As George Surridge went to the station to meet M'Leod he sighed. What a woman! What grace, what sympathy, what kindliness! He could not help comparing her to Clarissa. If only he had a woman like this to confide in, to share his joys and sorrows, what a different life he would have led and what a different man he would be!

She had not gone an hour till he bitterly regretted not having given her his own name and asked hers. Done in that open way, he now felt that she would have responded. Always that had been his failing—through indecision or timidity to miss his opportunities. By the time he decided on his action and screwed up his courage to the sticking point, it was too late: the moment had passed.

For a time his duties put all other matters out of his mind. M'Leod proved a pleasant and competent man. He examined the monkeys with immense care, and said the disease seemed the same as that with which he had already dealt, in which case his serum would probably prove efficacious. With considerable skill he administered it. He was staying over till next day, and Surridge took him to the Club for dinner and on to a show at the city's principal theatre.

But when at last George Surridge got to bed, thoughts of the woman he had met took possession of his mind to the exclusion of all else. He pictured her as he had seen her, so charming and restful, so elegant in general effect, so dainty in such matters as gloves and shoes, so clear complexioned and healthy looking, so easy and graceful in her movements. What humour and intelligence there was in her expression, what vitality in her eyes, what kindliness in her smile! Never had George been so impressed by a casual encounter.

Next day as he moved about on his lawful occasions, the memory of the meeting remained as a sort of background to all he did. An intense longing to see the woman again was growing up in his mind, and vaguely he began considering plans for finding her.

As during the forenoon he carried out his daily inspection, he met Professor Burnaby coming out of the snake-house. Burnaby was a tall, lean old man with a high forehead and the clean-shaven, clean-cut features of the thinker. He peered at Surridge shortsightedly through his thick spectacles, then hailed him.

"You're coming round this afternoon, I hope," he went on in a thin, high-pitched voice. "It's going to be a great occasion for the house of Burnaby."

Surridge now remembered that there had been an invitation for himself and Clarissa to a cocktail party to mark the engagement of Joyce, the old man's only daughter. He had intended to plead another engagement, but really there was no reason why he shouldn't go, and he answered pleasantly that he was looking forward to it.

Burnaby, who was very well off, lived close by in a small but charming house in some half acre of well-laid-out grounds. The road ran at the back of the house and at each side were the tiny estates of neighbours. In front was the glory of the little place: well kept sward sloping gently down to the River Choole, here a broad and sluggish stream. The grounds were separated from the actual water by the old towpath only, now practically unused. On the farther bank was one of the municipal parks, with its background of evergreen shrubs and fine trees. Houses were all but invisible from the grounds, and save for the occasional sight of strolling citizens at the other side of the Choole, it was hard to realise that "Riverview" was not far from the centre of one of the largest towns of England.

When George had finished at the office, he found it was time to start for the party. Calshort Road, in which the Burnabys lived, ran along the side of the Zoo and into it opened the small private door behind the monkey-houses, already referred to. George let himself out through this door to find Dr. and Mrs. Marr passing. They also, it appeared, were going to the Burnabys.

"Didn't expect to meet you here," the doctor greeted him. "I thought cocktail parties were an abomination in your eyes?"

"I met Burnaby to-day and he asked me specially," George answered. "He's been civil to me and I thought I'd better come."

"But you've been so good to him about the snakes," Mrs. Marr put in. "Only for you he would never have been given permission to carry on his experiments."

"Oh, I don't know. He's trying to do something pretty useful."

"What is it exactly?" Mrs. Marr asked. "I know he's doing a book on snakes, but what particular point is he working on?"

"Cancer," her husband answered briefly. "You know that injections of venom cure hæmophilia and other diseases, and he's been trying if it will kill the cancer cells."

"The professor's very clever, isn't he?" Mrs. Marr went on. "I think it's marvellous that he's still working at his age. He must surely be nearly eighty?"

"Seventy-four, I believe," Surridge replied. "I know because he had to give his age when applying for leave to conduct his experiments."

"He looks older. I don't know what he'll do when Joyce goes away. I'm delighted about Joyce: she's a splendid woman and she's had a pretty dull time looking after him. She well deserves some happiness and I hope she'll get it."

"The old man will get a housekeeper," Marr put in.

"He'll have to, unless he has some other relative we've never heard of. That Lily Cochrane's a good girl, but she's too young to keep house for him."

As she spoke, Mrs. Marr knocked at the door which they had now reached, and a moment later George was being greeted by Joyce Burnaby and her fiancé Alex Tansley. Joyce was a woman of about forty, with a calm dependable-looking face and clear straight-forward eyes; Tansley, a pleasant but ordinary looking man of about her own age.

Quite a number of people from the little world of the Birmington University were there, as well as some of the neighbours and leading citizens. Most were known to George, but as it happened, he found himself wedged into a corner with one of the few men he had never seen before. To his surprise he discovered that this was a relative of Burnaby's, a nephew.

"I didn't know he had a nephew," George declared. "By the way, my name is Surridge, and I've got to know your uncle fairly intimately since he came to live here. I'm in charge of the Zoo and I meet him in connection with his snake serum work."

As George said this he noticed that his new acquaintance treated him to a strange and rather searching look. He felt as if he were being somehow weighed up: as if the stranger were anxious to know what manner of man he was. He was about to remark on it jokingly, when the other looked away and answered quietly: "I know your name. I've heard my uncle speak of you. Mine, by the way, is Capper, and I'm a solicitor in Bursham. I know my uncle is very grateful to you for the facilities you have given him to carry on his work."

They continued chatting for a few moments, during which time Capper's manner remained completely normal. But the more he saw of him, the less George took to him. He was certainly not too prepossessing in appearance. A man of some five and forty, he was short and stout, with a very narrow and almost entirely bald head and close set eyes of a rather too extreme shrewdness. His features were good, but his expression was sly and his movements somehow suggested those of a snake.

Capper, however, appeared to be a favourite of Burnaby's, for George heard the old man speaking to him in an almost affectionate tone.

It was some time before George himself had an opportunity to talk to Burnaby, but presently he managed to get near him.

"I haven't seen you to congratulate you on the engagement," he said pleasantly. "I'm delighted on Miss Burnaby's account, but sorry on yours. I'm afraid you'll be a little lonely when she goes away."

The old man rubbed his thin hands: a characteristic gesture. "I shall be indeed: terribly lonely. However, I'm so glad for

Joyce's sake that I don't mind about myself. She's been so wonderfully good. I just can't say, Surridge, what I owe to her."

"I can well understand it."

"She certainly deserves some happiness, for it's been pretty dull for her here. But I think she's going to get it. You've met Tansley?"

"Yes; a nice fellow."

For some moments they discussed the engagement, and then George politely turned to the old man's work. "How are you getting on recently?" he asked. "It's some time since I heard."

Burnaby shrugged. His manner lost its slight exuberance and he spoke as if he was facing disappointment.

"Well, it's rather slow. I'm doing a new set of experiments which I hope will be more successful. That, by the way, reminds me that I want some more venom. I'd like to take it from one of the king cobras. Nesbit has promised to give me a hand. You've no objection, I suppose?"

George, as a matter of fact, had an objection, though he didn't say so. This taking of venom from large snakes was dangerous work. They were so extra-ordinary quick. One person gripped their neck in a sort of tongs and thus theoretically immobilised them, while another either allowed them to bite a sponge or other absorbent article, or abstracted the venom direct from the tooth with a Pravaz syringe. But though the principle was good, it didn't always work out in practice. It wasn't easy, for example, to grip the neck securely without injuring the snake, and only a little carelessness would enable it to strike before capture or to escape from its pillory. However, Nesbit, the keeper, was an able man and could be depended on to take every precaution. Besides, the original permission given Burnaby by the Board specifically covered the operation.

"You use guinea-pigs for your tests?" George went on, for something to say.

"Not recently," Burnaby returned. "I've been using mice for some time for the preliminary experiments and guinea-pigs only for final confirmation. Mice are cheaper and easier to get."

"It's quite a big trade, isn't it, producing animals for experiment?" asked Capper, who was standing close by and had heard Burnaby's remark.

Burnaby agreed. "One feels sorry for the little creatures," he went on, "but what is one to do? By the way, Surridge, have you met my nephew, David Capper? I owe him a lot. He's the most wonderful amateur mechanic and wood-worker, and he's made me many an intricate piece of apparatus for my work which I never could have got otherwise." He turned to Capper. "Mr. Surridge has been very kind to me about the snakes, David."

When a little later the trio broke up and Burnaby drifted away to speak to other guests, George saw that once again Capper was regarding him with that same appraising, questioning look that he had observed before. This time he was going to speak, but Capper forestalled him by suddenly turning away to greet a lady who was passing. George had no further chance to put his question, but during the remainder of the evening the man's conduct remained a puzzling and slightly disturbing recollection.

CHAPTER IV

VENOM: THROUGH THE AFFECTIONS

FOR some couple of months after the Burnaby's reception time passed uneventfully for George Surridge. Once again some unexpected luck at poker recouped the greater part of his losses and left him in easier, if still precarious, circumstances. His relations with Clarissa remained much as usual: if they were not happier, they were not visibly worse. On the other hand, things at the Zoo were better. The elephants had arrived in good condition and had proved great acquisitions. The disease among the monkeys had ceased and there had been no more deaths. They had received some rare and greatly prized small cats from Indo-China: creatures which not even the London Zoo possessed. The rebuilding was going on satisfactorily and the new watchman in Cochrane's place was doing well.

But though George's position was temporarily easier, he was still very short of money. If only, he thought for the hundredth time, he had his aunt's five thousand! Nothing less than a sum of this magnitude would put him permanently right. A few pounds at poker was well enough; it would meet gambling debts and immediate necessities, but to obtain the fundamental improvement his circumstances needed would take something very different.

With intense though hidden interest he had noted the change in Miss Pentland's health, and he had been a little shocked at his own disappointment when he found it was not deteriorating as rapidly as he had hoped. That she was ill he felt sure; her face had the drawn pallor of disease. And she was, he thought, getting weaker, though so slowly that there seemed no promise of an early inheritance.

Invariably at this stage George reminded himself that he did not wish the old lady any harm. But as the days passed, his disappointment at her continuing strength changed to actual dismay. More than anything he had ever wanted, he longed for that money.

Then one night a dreadful idea shot into his mind. She was ill and very old: she must die soon. If her death was too much delayed—could it not be—accelerated?

George was filled with horror when he realised just what he had been thinking. Why, that would be—he could scarcely bring himself to frame the word—that would be *murder*! Good God, how dreadful! Hastily he banished the thought.

But in spite of all his efforts, it came back. It grew, not less hateful, but more familiar. He toyed with the idea, wondering how such a thing might be done, then again assured himself with vehemence that nothing in heaven or earth would ever induce him to be guilty of such a hideous crime.

Still the horrible suggestion lurked in the recesses of his mind. ...

The next afternoon it happened that George had business at the other side of the city, and when it was finished he took a bus back. As he sat down he glanced indifferently round. Then a hand seemed to grip his heart. There, just opposite him, was the woman whom he had shown round the Gardens, and whose image had ever since remained in the background of his thoughts.

The meeting was so unexpected that for a moment he couldn't move. Then, recovering himself, he leant forward.

"I wonder if you remember me?" he asked diffidently. "We met some weeks ago at the Zoo."

"Of course." She smiled in a conventional way and he was thrilled to notice the colour deepen in her cheeks. There was a vacant seat beside her. With pounding heart he took it.

"An unexpected pleasure," he went on as lightly as he could. "I have often hoped you would come back to take another look at our mutual friends."

"I wanted to," she answered, and he found that her voice was infinitely more moving and delightful even than he had supposed. "But I've not been able. I don't live here, you know."

"I hope you'll manage it," he went on. "After you left I remembered I had not shown you our photographs. We've got some quite decent ones. There's one I should think must be unique: of Tommy—you remember Tommy, the lion?—springing across his cage. It's rather fine."

She smiled and her eyes lit up with interest. "How did you manage to get that?"

George warmed to his subject. "A fluke really," he declared, going on to talk about the intricacies of animal photography. "But I can't explain it in a few seconds." He paused and glanced out of the window. They were just about to leave the centre of the city. "I wonder if I might be very daring? I was just going to have some tea. Will you be extraordinarily kind and join me?"

He waited as if the retention of his job were at issue. Then a surge of delight passed over him as she answered: "That would be nice. Thank you, yes, I'll come."

They were near what he considered the best restaurant in the city and he installed her in a secluded alcove. It was early and they had the place practically to themselves. George felt absurdly nervous: he couldn't understand what was the matter with him. He particularly wished to be easy and offhand, though pleasant in manner, but he knew himself to be addle-headed, tongue-tied and as self-conscious as a boy in his teens. On many occasions he had mentally rehearsed conversations with her, but now all these fled from his mind. He could think of nothing but the most inane platitudes, and even these he pronounced hesitat-ingly and without conviction.

But marvellously she didn't appear to notice it. Her lips formed themselves into a slow smile which turned his heart to water, while she spoke to him as if he were a normal human being, almost indeed her equal. Her soft low-pitched voice fell upon his ears like distant music. He was so moved that it took all his resolution to maintain his rôle of casual acquaintance.

Presently the subject of the Zoo animals palled and, without deliberate intention, they began to talk of themselves. He told her that he was married, believing it not only right to do so, but wise. On her part she was equally frank.

Her name, it appeared, was Nancy Weymore, and she was a widow. Her husband had been a doctor in Worcestershire, and had built up a large and lucrative practice when he developed sepsis from an infected cut and died in great pain. Then she had endured a further shock. It transpired that he had been living almost entirely upon income and had saved but little money. As she had none herself, she had therefore to find a job. She had been lucky in getting one as model in the fashion department of one of the big Birmington shops. Unfortunately, owing to a reconstruction, she had recently lost this job, and for the last three months she had been acting as companion to an invalid lady living in the country near Neverton, some dozen miles from Birmington. The old lady, she said, was a dear and she was very happy with her.

She did not tell all this to George in a breath. It came out bit by bit as they talked. Some of it, indeed, he grasped only by putting two and two together. Now that it had been suggested to him, he noticed that her clothes, while still conveying the impression of extreme neatness and good taste, appeared older and more worn than on their first meeting.

She seemed lonely and glad of the chance of talking, and their tea dragged out for nearly an hour. Then she said it was time for her bus and that she must go. He wanted to see her off, but she would not allow that.

"But I may see you again?" he implored as she collected her things. "There is so much I want to tell you."

She demurred, though he thought not very decisively. An inspiration seized him. "Have you ever been on Orlop Hill?" he asked.

She shook her head.

"Then you must come," he declared firmly. "Orlop Hill is our chief beauty spot and no one can appreciate this country who has not been there. It's an escarpment of the Peak District and you can see the hills of that area to the north and to the south this great plain. There's a road for cars to near the top, and from there it's only a short walk to the beacon."

"It sounds delightful," she said, doubtfully. "How should we manage it?"

"Drive, of course," he returned, excitement at the prospect swelling up within him. "I'll call for you at Neverton with the car. It's in the same general direction as Orlop and won't be much out of the way. Only on account of the short evenings we'll have to start early to get the view."

She didn't seem very keen on the idea, but at last she gave in and a meeting was arranged. On Wednesdays and Saturdays George played golf, and on the following Wednesday he undertook to call for her instead.

It was not till he was in bed that night that the real significance of the step he had taken began to knock for admission into George Surridge's mind. He did not wish to think of it, but he could not help doing so. What exactly had happened to him?

Had he fallen in love with this woman, and if so, what was he proposing to do about it? If he went on with this friendship, how would it end? Would it mean the break-up of his home and the loss of his job?—in other words, his ruin?

He knew that on the grounds of expediency, as well as morality, he should not proceed with the affair, but when he pictured Nancy Weymore as she had appeared seated beside him in the restaurant: when he remembered what she had said and recalled the tones of her voice, he felt that if necessary he would risk all and every consequence to see and hear her again.

Fortunately it was not necessary that he should risk anything. He could meet her without fear of any resultant disaster. This drive on Wednesday would commit him to nothing. In itself it would be a quite ordinary excursion without any special significance, and they could part at the end of it as they had met, mere acquaintances.

But when he considered the matter further, George found that it was not quite as simple as he had supposed. He usually took a bus to the golf course, leaving the car for Clarissa. He couldn't get the car without letting her know why he wanted it, and he didn't feel like telling her a direct lie.

He saw, in short, that he would have to hire a car. Here was more expense. He could scarcely make ends meet as it was, and to take on a further outlay was the last thing he desired. However, that couldn't be helped. At least he needn't be afraid of the garage people talking: in the interests of trade they would keep their own council.

He need not be afraid either, of being seen on the Orlop Hill. At this time of year it would be as deserted as the Sahara. They could not go to a restaurant because none would be open. He would have to take tea with him. He could not very well use flasks from home, as Clarissa might notice their absence. It would be better to buy one of those tea outfits and have it filled at an hotel. Still more expense, confound it! However, he felt he was now too far committed to draw back.

Next day after lunching at the Club he went to a garage where they specialised in the hiring of cars, and arranged for an N.J. Gnat to be ready on the Wednesday. At an adjoining shop he bought a tea box—it cost him nearly three pounds—and left it in an hotel with the necessary orders. All this made him feel excited and upset. He oscillated between trepidation over the step he was taking and an almost unbearable eagerness for the time to arrive.

At length it did so. He woke that morning with the impression that something of overwhelming importance was about to happen, and sprang out of bed to look at the sky. Thank goodness, it was going to be fine. He dressed as in a dream and carried out his morning's work like an automaton, his mind full of what was coming. Gone were his fears and regrets. For that morning at least he would not have changed his position with any man in England.

His plans functioned without a hitch. He went as usual to the club for lunch, leaving early on the plea that he had to pay a call in the country. The Gnat, shining as if it had just left the makers' hands, was ready for him, as was also the well-filled tea-box. With the box in the rear and soft rugs on the seat beside him, he drove out of Central Square in Birmington, taking the road to the north-east.

He was annoyed to find that nervousness was again overtaking him, and that the nearer he came to Neverton, the worse it grew. Nancy had indicated that she would walk out along the road to meet him, from which he concluded that she did not wish him to call at her employer's house. He began now to worry about all sorts of things: whether he could be on the wrong road and so miss her, whether he could ever be as witty and interesting as not to bore her, whether she would enjoy the excursion. But no longer did he consider possible untoward results of the acquaintanceship: by now he could not see beyond the present.

At last, some mile before he reached the village of Neverton, his heart was set fluttering by the sight of a figure on the road ahead. Yes, it was she: a new Nancy Weymore in a tweed coat and skirt, a felt hat and tan brogues. Charming as she had looked in her town clothes, he thought she looked even more ravishing in these. He pulled up.

"I'm not late, I hope?" he said, anxiously. "You've come a long way."

"I was just going to say how punctual you were," she answered as she got in and settled herself beside him. "What a delightful car! New, surely?"

"Borrowed, I'm afraid," he returned, smiling. "The family bus is in use to-day."

To have as much time as possible on the Orlop, he drove quickly. The needle oscillated between forty and fifty, occasionally touching sixty, and, for George did not wish to risk being stopped, rigorously dropping to twenty-eight in controlled areas. The road soon began to ascend, and then as it wound higher and higher, they exchanged the fertile and populous plain, first for outlying farm-houses surrounded by pastures, and finally for the open moor. Presently they reached the summit and George drew into a parking-place where the road turned down a long gentle slope between two hummocks.

"The beacon's up there," he said, pointing to the higher of the little peaks. "It's really not far. Are you game?"

"Rather," she nodded. "What a perfect place! I had no idea there was anything like this in the neighbourhood."

"Wait till you see the view from the top," he advised. "Shall we have tea up there, or wait till we get back to the car?"

She smiled entrancingly. "Tea in this wilderness? Are you a complete wizard?"

He showed her the case. She gave a little cry of satisfaction. "That was all that was required to make it perfect," she assured him. "But I think we'd better wait till we come back. Don't you?"

He would have been delighted to have had it anywhere or nowhere, at that moment or never, but all he said was: "Right-o. Then shall we start?"

A rough path had been beaten by many feet over the coarse grass and scrubby heather of the mountainside. There were no trees and they could see the curving contours of the ground stretching away into the distance, the dark green broken here and there by the browns and greys of outcropping rock. Little runnels of water crossed the path and a more vivid colouring in the grass showed boggy patches. The air was sharp and clear and exhilarating, and the thin yellow sunlight, streaming nearly horizontally, threw dark shadows everywhere.

They reached the top after a short climb and stood gazing round them. Nancy breathed a soft "Oh!" and to hear that sound more than recompensed George for all the trouble and expense of the outing. It was indeed a splendid panorama which lay before them. As George had said, the view to the north was of mountains, peak rising after peak with dark valleys between, while southwards lay the plain, with the white streak of the road they had come by, winding down backwards and forwards and getting narrower and narrower, till eventually it disappeared in the haze of the low-lying ground.

Climbing in the comparatively low temperature had been pleasantly warm, but the wind at the top proved a different matter. They did not wait there long. After gazing for a few minutes in one direction after another, Nancy said she was cold and they began the descent.

Up to this everything had gone on in a perfectly normal way, and had Clarissa herself been there she would have seen nothing to which she could possibly have taken exception. But as they climbed down the rough track something happened which changed the whole character of the expedition.

Stepping on a small stone where a little stream flowed across the path, Nancy's foot slipped. She splashed into the water and would have fallen had not George leaped forward and caught her in his arms.

He had not intended that their little excursion should be anything but a pleasant meeting between acquaintances, but he had not reckoned with a situation of this kind. The contact swept away his caution and paralysed his powers of resistance. For a few moments he stood motionless, then with a hoarse cry of "Nancy!" he crushed her to him and covered her face with kisses.

At first she struggled. "No, no, no," she gasped, trying to escape from his arms. But presently she became quiet and then, slowly, she turned to him and threw her arms round his neck.

When he released her both stood as if dazed. Then she gave a little moan. "Oh," she cried, "we shouldn't have done that. It was so pleasant, and now we've spoilt it all."

"We've spoilt nothing, Nancy," he returned. "We love each other. This was bound to come."

She shivered. "Oh, no," she repeated, "we shouldn't have done it. We were wrong. We must forget it."

He turned down the hill. His heart was still pounding, but he controlled himself and spoke quietly. "We can never forget it. This is too big a thing to forget. It's fundamental."

She began to walk by his side. "No, we must forget it. It can't come to anything but unhappiness."

"It has happened," he returned doggedly. "Nothing can change it, and we can't forget it."

She looked more troubled. "Your wife," she said, softly. "You know you told me——"

He shook his head impatiently. "That can't affect it. I have never—" he hesitated as if for a word, then went on, "I have never—felt for her—as I do—for you."

She made a gesture as if to stop him, but she didn't speak and they walked in silence to the car. In silence she got in, merely shaking her head when he murmured something about tea. "Let us go back," she said at last. "We must think what is best to be done."

This time he drove slowly, letting the car for the most part coast down the long hill. His mind was in confusion. He did not know what to suggest. Already he was beginning to realise the two outstanding features of the situation: first, that he loved this woman as he had never before loved anyone, as he had not known that anyone could be loved, and secondly, that to proceed further with the affair would mean complete disaster. Not only would there be the terrible break with Clarissa, which he could face, but also entire financial ruin through the loss of his job, which he didn't see how he could.

Lost in thought, he drove steadily on till an exclamation from Nancy told him that they were approaching Neverton. "Stop," she warned him. "I must get out here."

"But we've settled nothing," he returned, as he drew in to the side of the road.

"It's been settled for us," she declared, "by circumstances. It will be misery if we don't see each other again, but it'll be greater misery if we do. We must part: now."

George felt that in theory she was right: they would have to part. But not then: at least not finally. "We can't," he insisted, "just say good-bye like that, as if we were strangers and I had casually given you a lift. It may be that when we have thought things over we shall decide you are right and that we shall have to part. But we can't do that unless we are absolutely sure there's no other way. No, Nancy, I'm not unreasonable, but I can't agree to that. We must meet again to settle what we're going to do."

She was against it, but he was firm and at last she gave way. One further meeting she would agree to, but no others: and there were to be no letters. Finally it was arranged that on that day week— the first date that Nancy could manage—they should repeat their drive to Orlop. Wondering how he could exist for a whole week without seeing her, George drove back to Birmington.

That week dragged in a way he had never before experienced. He thought it would never come to an end. Fortunately, their secret remained intact. He had prepared a plausible story of a business visit to a neighbouring town for use in case of need, but he was relieved to find that this was not required. No questions were asked, and he was satisfied that no suspicions had been anywhere aroused.

On the next Wednesday he repeated his preparations. He hired the same car and had the tea box filled at the same hotel. He drove out to near Neverton, picked up Nancy, and went on to the hills. They had a walk, came back to the car, had tea, and returned as before.

In one way it was the most thrilling afternoon George had ever spent, and in another it was the most unsatisfactory. It was thrilling, wonderful and delightful beyond belief, because he was with Nancy. Alone with her he was completely happy. All he wanted was that time should stand still, and that they two could go on for ever just as they were. She, he believed, felt the same: complete and absolute bliss in a present which ruled out all disturbing thoughts of the future.

It was this powerful urge, to enjoy what they could while they could, that made the afternoon at once delightful and unsatisfactory, because when it came to an end it found them with the question of their future still undecided. Nancy urged a final parting, though not nearly so strongly as she had on the first occasion. He was for another meeting, this time definitely to settle the matter. In the end she once again allowed herself to be persuaded.

As a result there happened what, had they been in a normal frame of mind, they could easily have foreseen. At their next meeting they came no nearer to a conclusion, and a further excursion was arranged. So gradually they formed a habit. Every Wednesday afternoon, and often evenings in between, they managed to meet. And the more frequently they discussed their final parting, the further the decision receded from both their minds. These successive meetings began to form a continuous present, and future problems were more rigorously excluded than ever from their thoughts. Trouble might be coming, but why go out to meet it?

CHAPTER V

VENOM: THROUGH THE POCKET

NOW George Surridge began to learn what so many who had embarked on a similar experiment had discovered before him: the extreme difficulty of living a successful double life.

He knew perfectly well that the longer he continued his stolen meetings with Nancy Weymore, the more certain ultimate discovery would become. So far they had had extraordinarily good luck, but sooner or later they would meet someone they knew, and that for him would be the end.

There were so many danger points. The Orlop Hills were deserted in winter, but spring would soon come, and with every week the area would grow more dangerous. They would have to go somewhere else, but he could think of nowhere that would be safe. And it was not only their destination which was perilous. He might be seen—perhaps from another car—when picking Nancy up. While on the road they might break down, or worse still they might have an accident and be brought into court.

Then there was the devilish way in which people pressed enquiries, apparently for no object except idle curiosity. Someone might say to George, "I missed you from golf on Wednesday," to which even the vaguest and most general reply might lead to disaster. If he excused himself for that day only, someone else might point out that he had not had his game for quite a lot of Wednesdays. If on the other hand he said he had business at the London Zoo every Wednesday, some fool might say: "I go to London on Wednesdays also. What train do you travel by?" George saw that nothing that he could invent would be final. Always some further question would be possible which might do the damage.

But the danger from outside acquaintances was as nothing compared to that from his wife. How easy for the wife of some other golfer to say to Clarissa: "John misses your husband so much on the golf course." Then there were his colleagues at the Zoo. They golfed and drove about in cars. What might they not see?

Such were but a few of the sources from which ruin might come, but they were by no means the most perilous. What he feared even more was the enemy within the gates. He himself was deteriorating in certain ways. He was growing nervy and suspicious. Apart from Nancy his sense of dissatisfaction and futility was growing, and it made him irritable and absent-minded. More than once he had caught Miss Hepworth stealthily regarding him with an excited interest. She suspected something, the vixen! He must get rid of her. But how could he? She was an efficient secretary and to trump up an excuse for sacking her would only be to give himself away.

There was still another source from which disaster threatened: the most deadly of all. This fear oppressed George more than the others because of its inevitable nature. Discovery might result from some unfortunate accident, but from this enemy there was no escape. If only he were to carry on long enough as he was doing, ruin would come whether there was an accident or not. It was as certain and as unavoidable as death itself.

The source was finance. Before Nancy had come into his life he was spending rather more than he could afford: now he was spending a good deal more. There were all sorts of small expenses, each unimportant in itself, but the total amounting to a substantial sum. George was getting almost desperate. He was beginning not to pay bills, to forget tips, to decline any outlay he could possibly avoid. But cheeseparing was not going to be sufficient. He knew beyond the possibility of doubt that he could not go on as he was doing for long.

With growing frequency his thoughts turned towards his aunt, Lucy Pentland. If only he could get that money that was coming to him, not at some time in the distant future, but now! Not only would it remove this ghastly financial worry, but it would mean greater safety in every way. With more money he and Nancy could take better precautions. She could give up that wretched job of hers and go and live in decent surroundings in some place in which he could visit her. A tiny cottage somewhere with a garden and roses on the porch! He grew almost sick with desire as he thought of it. And it might become a possibility—if Lucy Pentland were to die.

George knew that her death could be brought about. He had heard, for example, about parcels of explosives being sent through the post which, on being opened, blew their recipients to pieces. He had pictured every step which would be necessary to carry out such a scheme, and he saw that it could be done with absolute safety. He had read of the introduction of poisonous pills or medicine into the victim's bottle of tonic. That would not be so easy, but it would be possible. There were various ways. . . .

But only in imagination of course. Obviously there could be nothing serious in these ideas. George didn't pretend to be a saint, but he drew the line somewhere. He knew that he could never do anything to hurt anyone. Murder? No, no! Hideous thought! He didn't mean it for a moment.

Yet Lucy Pentland's death would solve all his problems. He *must* ask Marr about her. But again, he dare not.

If George had been a little more introspective he might well have wondered why he dare not ask Marr. As nephew he naturally ought to show an interest in his aunt's welfare. What was it that made him shrink from the enquiry?

Then one day an event took place which seemed at first to be entirely unconnected with George and his affairs. It proved however to be of fundamental importance to his subsequent actions and fate, as well incidentally as providing the information about his aunt's health he had so greatly desired.

On that day as he stepped on to the road at the Zoo gates on his way to lunch Dr. Marr drove quickly past in his car. He looked grave and as he passed he made a gesture of concern to George. A little knot of men, evidently discussing something serious, looked at the car and nodded. George went across to them.

"It's Miss Burnaby, sir," one of the group answered. "Knocked down by a car not ten minutes ago. They've taken her home."

"Is she badly hurt?"

"They think she's dead. She could scarcely be anything else. The wheel crushed her chest."

In spite of his preoccupation, George was a good deal upset. He had met Joyce Burnaby scores of times and had formed a sincere liking for her, and of course, owing to her father's work at the Zoo, he knew him very well indeed. A terrible thing for them both! The poor woman just about to be married, with a prospect of happiness she seemed up till then to have missed. If she really were dead, it would be a dreadful shock for the old man. He had come to depend so completely on her, and so far as George knew, he had no other relative except that unpleasant nephew, Capper. And Capper couldn't take a daughter's place.

As George considered these matters he was walking rapidly to *Riverview*. A few people were standing outside the door and a policeman with a note-book had evidently been taking statements. George went up to him.

"I'm a friend of the family," he explained. "Can you tell me what has happened?"

The policeman noted George's name and address and then told what he knew. It appeared that Joyce Burnaby had met her fate exactly as had so many hundreds before her. She had stepped too quickly out from behind a bus, failing to see a car which was coming in the opposite direction. The driver had done his best, but he couldn't save her. She was believed to have been killed instantaneously. The doctor was then with her and they would soon know definitely.

George murmured a reply and walked into the house through the open door. At first he could find no one, then Lily Cochrane appeared, trembling and with a face like chalk. He beckoned to her.

"I came to see if I could do anything," he explained. "Where is the professor?"

She answered him, he thought, eagerly, as if relieved to divide the responsibility. "He's very strange, sir: sort of dazed. He just sat down after they brought her in and I can't get him to speak or move."

"I'll see him," George told her. "It'll be a terrible shock, of course, but he'll be all right presently."

The girl nodded. "He's in the study, sir."

George went to the study. Old Burnaby was sitting in his chair, staring vacantly out of the window. He did not move as George came up.

"I called to see if I could do anything," George repeated. "I've just heard this moment."

Professor Burnaby made no reply. He slowly turned his head and for a moment looked dully at George, then faintly shook his head and resumed his fixed stare out of the window.

George felt the old man would rather be alone, but he looked so shaken and frail that he scarcely liked to leave him. He decided to get Marr to see him, and sat down to wait till the doctor should come downstairs. Burnaby took no further notice of him. Once or twice his lips moved, but George could not make out what he was saying.

A few minutes later he heard Marr on the stairs and went out. "Well?" he asked, in a low voice.

Marr shook his head. "Instantaneous," he returned, also speaking softly. "A fractured skull and crushed—" He swept his hand diagonally across his chest. "At least there was no suffering."

"I think you should have a look at Burnaby," went on George. "He seems pretty hard hit."

"Where is he?"

"In there."

Marr disappeared into the study and George hung about the hall, discussing the affair in low tones with the policeman. He did not like to go till he had heard Marr's report. This, he thought, would end the old man's research. After such a shock he would never have the stamina to continue work. And how much better it would be for all concerned if the work did stop! George had never liked all the handling of the snakes. He had feared an accident: either that someone would be bitten or that a snake would escape. It would certainly be an ease to his mind if Burnaby never again entered the reptile house.

Presently Marr reappeared. "He'll be all right," he pronounced. "I've told him to go to bed and I'll send a nurse to see that he does it."

"Who's going to look after things for him?"

"There's a nephew, a solicitor named Capper. I've 'phoned for him. He can make the arrangements and the nurse can stay for a day or two."

"There'll be an inquest?"

"Oh yes. But it'll be formal. It seems to have been poor Joyce's fault." He looked over his shoulder. "That all you want now, sergeant?"

"That's all, thank you, sir."

"Then I'll go." He turned again to George. "I'm going down town. Can I give you a lift?"

They discussed the accident and Burnaby's future for some time, then Marr made a remark which set George's heart beating quickly.

"No," said the doctor, slowly, "I don't think the old fellow will survive this very long. It's been a great shock to him and his heart's not too strong. And there's another person whom I'm afraid won't be with us long. I'm sorry to tell you, Surridge, that your aunt, Miss Pentland, is seriously ill."

George gripped himself. "I'm sorry to hear that, Marr," he said, as steadily as he could, "terribly sorry. But I can't pretend it's much of a surprise. I've noticed how ill she's been looking and I've been going to ask you about her."

"Yes," returned Marr, "I've suspected it for some time and now I'm sure. It's cancer, and we can't operate, even if she could have stood it."

George strove to steady the beating of his heart. He was not wholly callous and he found himself really distressed at the poor old lady's fate. But he was also human, and little surges of an almost painful joy shot through him. His aunt's death would be for her a happy release, and to him—it would mean just everything. This terrible lack of money would cease. The problem of Nancy would be solved. *All* his problems would be solved. His aunt's legacy was all that was needed to alter his life from the half heaven, half hell it now was, and to make it wholly heaven.

But one question was still unanswered: not a vital question exactly, but still a terribly important one.

"There's nothing immediate to be—er—anticipated, I suppose?" he asked, striving to give his manner only the proper interest.

Marr hesitated. "Nothing immediate in the sense of days," he replied. "But I think we may consider it a question of weeks rather than months."

A question of weeks! Then there would be legal delays over the granting of probate: it might be three or four months before the money was paid over—perhaps six months in all. Could he keep going for six months?

Not as things were up to the present. But now they would be different: he could borrow on his prospects. How he wished he knew the exact sum he might expect! He did not see, however, how he could find it out.

As it turned out he learnt it almost at once, and in a way he had never expected. A day or two later he received a note from Miss Pentland, asking him to call. He did so on the same day, and, to do him justice, he was really kind and sympathetic in his manner. He obtained his reward—if it could be considered a reward.

"I asked you to come," his aunt remarked, after he had said his say, "because I wanted to tell you about my affairs. You know that

I'm leaving you the bulk of my money—not that it's very much, I'm afraid. But I thought that as it will be soon now, I should give you an idea of how much I have, so that you shouldn't count on more than you'll get, and so be disappointed."

George felt horribly ashamed as he heard these words, and tried hard to avoid letting her see the intensity of his interest.

She had, it appeared, about £12,000 in all. Of this, £1,000 each was to go to three old servants, and the whole of the remainder, less the death duties taxation, would be George's.

He sat trying outwardly to take the news calmly, but inwardly he was seething with a thrilled delight. Over eight thousand! Why, it was enormously more than he had expected! Suppose the Government took £600, which he imagined would be about their proportion, that would leave him £8,400, or say, deducting solicitors' fees and so on, a round figure of £8,000. And the most he had expected was £5,000! Truly his troubles were over.

He could scarcely refrain from writing the glad tidings to Nancy. However, they had agreed that letters were not safe and he contained himself till the following Wednesday. Then he told her: in general terms only. He had, he said, been a little hard-up and so unable to do all he should have liked for their mutual benefit. Now, he was thankful to say, that bad time was over. He had come in for a legacy and there was money for anything in reason.

He longed desperately to mention the little cottage of his dreams, with the garden and the roses over the porch, but something in her manner warned him not to risk it. Well, there was no hurry. They were getting on very well as it was. Later perhaps that would come.

Just one thing remained to be settled to put him in a really satisfactory position. He must get hold of some ready money.

He didn't want to borrow from the bank. Even if he could, he didn't want any local people to know he was in difficulties. From whom, then, could he borrow?

Frequently he had seen advertisements in the papers from persons who, it appeared, were anxious to lend money to all and sundry on their "mere note of hand alone." Now he looked up some of these advertisements. Three with London addresses seemed suitable and he determined to try his luck.

On the next occasion, therefore, on which he had business in London, he adventured himself down into the narrower streets of the City and made some tentative inquiries. The result was disappointing in the extreme. "Mere note of hand alone" seemed to be an elastic term: indeed, he didn't see what connection it had with the business in hand. At all events, Messrs. Solomon & Goldstein required a great deal more before they would make an advance. He found, in fact, that he would be unable to get one unless he supplied them with proven details about the legacy. This he could not do, having only his aunt's word on the subject. The affair accordingly deadlocked.

So much for Solomon & Goldstein: perhaps Abraham & Co. or Velinski Bros. would be more accommodating? George called on both: with the same result.

He returned to Birmington realising that the matter was not going to be as easy as he had hoped. In fact, he did not see just what else he could do. These moneylenders had been in the nature of a last hope.

Then, through some caprice of fate, he had a run of luck at cards. He not only paid off the more pressing of his smaller debts, but actually finished up with money in hand.

For the time being his situation was eased.

CHAPTER VI
VENOM: IN SOCIETY

AFTER his successes at cards, life for the time being grew easier for George Surridge. With ready money available and assured as to his ultimate security, he now drew more freely from his tiny balance, with the result that he and Nancy were able to go on longer excursions and to carry them out more comfortably. For a time indeed, there was little outwardly to mar his happiness.

Inwardly, however, he remained dissatisfied. Except when actually in Nancy's presence, the knowledge of the double life he was leading was a persistent, though subconscious, load on his mind. There was also the continuous fear of discovery. Both he and Nancy were extremely careful, but he could not hide from himself that up to the present they had had wonderful luck. No one other than themselves, so far as either knew, had the slightest inkling of what was going on.

But had George been aware of some other events which were taking place simultaneously, he would have received a very rude awakening.

Not far from the Zoo lived a tall and angular maiden lady of uncertain age, Harriet Corrin by name. She was clever, entertaining and well-to-do, and was in demand by hostesses who wished to brighten what promised to be dull parties. Her popularity on these occasions came neither from brilliant repartee nor kindliness of heart, but from a malicious wit which gave piquancy to her conversation. People asked her to their houses in the hope that her scandalous remarks would thrill their guests and bring their social efforts into the news, though always with a lurking if rather delicious fear that they themselves should prove the victims. As something of a public character, Miss Corrin knew and was well known to the Surridges.

It happened one soaking Wednesday in late February that Miss Corrin had business in a small village named Bramford, some forty miles to the east of Birmington. It was a mildly picturesque little place. It boasted a sizeable river, a humped three-arched bridge, an inn which gave teas in a surrounding garden, and a church with a squat Norman tower. In fine weather it was not unattractive, but to-day in the streaming down-pour it looked frankly forbidding. Miss Corrin had come to interview a prospective maid, and she wished she had stayed at home.

But these aesthetic drawbacks made Bramford just the kind of retreat which appealed to men who were taking out for the afternoon women other than their wives. On this same afternoon George and Nancy had become so tired of sitting in the car that they determined for once to break their rule and have tea, not from the tea-box, but in some inn. So much granted, where more suitable than the Magpie's Claw in Bramford? Thus it happened that as Miss Corrin sat in the window of her prospective maid's father's house in the main street, which provided an admirable view of the inn, the lovers were approaching the same hostelry as fast as the hired car would bring them.

The fact that the prospective maid had gone to get copies of her testimonials enabled Harriet Corrin to give her undivided attention to the street and its traffic of two consequential ducks and a harassed looking hen. Even this sight palled, however, when a magnificent N.J. Gnat entered her field of vision, drew in regally to the inn, and disgorged its passengers.

With eyes becoming rounder, Miss Corrin witnessed the debarkation. First George Surridge emerged from the driving seat, and, hurrying round, opened with solicitude the opposite door. Miss Corrin was pleased to see his attention to his wife: she had sometimes feared there was less love lost in that *ménage* than was meet. But when, instead of Clarissa's somewhat considerable bulk and dull colouring, there appeared a *petite* and elegant stranger, whose dark hair was surmounted by a coquettish little hat of vivid red, Miss Corrin fairly goggled with amazement and a fierce ecstasy.

She sat staring fixedly across the road even after the unconscious objects of her regard had disappeared into the inn. So full indeed was she of the spectacle, that she engaged the prospective maid at a pound a month more than she need have paid, a thing which in all her experience had never before happened.

Next day Harriet decided to enjoy the treat which Fate had put into her hands. Among her invitations was one to a cocktail party at which she thought Clarissa would be present. She had never liked Clarissa, whom she considered superior, and the prospect of getting one back on her was very sweet.

Her belief proved to be well founded. The first person she saw after greeting her hostess was Clarissa. She formed one of a group of some half-dozen women, all well known to Harriet. Harriet metaphorically preened herself, and moving graciously forward, greeted them with a disarming sweetness.

"I didn't know you'd got a new car," she began, innocently, when a suitable pause occurred in the conversation. "I was so glad to see it."

"I didn't know myself," Clarissa returned, with outward ease but inward trepidation, "but I'm glad about it too."

"Oh, yes," Miss Corrin continued, "you needn't try to be mysterious. I've seen it. A lovely N.J. Gnat. I quite envied you."

"You can't be more pleased than I am," Clarissa parried, now sure that her tormentor meant mischief. "Let's have the particulars."

"Yes; where's the little place? Bram-ley, Bramwick; no, Bramford. Nice little place, Bramford. A backwater: nice and quiet."

"Not many of them left, I'm afraid. I don't know your particular paradise. Where is it?"

Harriet registered surprise. "Didn't Mr. Surridge tell you? Or perhaps," she became adequately confused, "I—I hope I'm not being indiscreet? I know I'll be told to mind my own business some of these days."

Clarissa's heart began to sink. For some time George had been different. He had become more absent in manner, more irritable, with fits of brooding, alternating with a strange expression of exultation. She had noticed it for two or three months and had soon guessed a possible cause. George, she believed, had done at last what he had never done with her: he had fallen in love. When and with whom, she could not imagine, but each day that had passed had strengthened her conviction. Now she felt she was going to learn the truth. She braced herself. This old cat mustn't be allowed her obscene triumph. She smiled indulgently.

"Had you and he an assignation there?" she asked in an amused way.

It was first blood to Clarissa. Two or three of the listening women laughed, and those laughs poured bitterness into Harriet's soul. If the days since anyone would have an assignation with her were past, people at least needn't laugh at the idea. But she smiled back.

"Now, my dear, is that likely?" she returned protestingly.

Clarissa warmed up to it. "Not very perhaps," she admitted cruelly. "But this is getting interesting. I suppose you're leading up to a mysterious charmer? Won't you describe her?"

"Oh, I'm not giving away cabinet secrets." Miss Corrin was arch, though a glint of evil triumph showed in her eye.

"I feared as much," Clarissa sighed. "But don't you see that if you withhold information, the thing won't work? I can see that you're hoping for a broken home and a divorce. But, you know, if you're to succeed, you must play up. How can I get the necessary detectives to work if you don't give me a description? Isn't that only fair?" she looked smilingly round the little assembly.

She did it so well that for a moment doubts swept through Harriet Corrin's mind. Then a certain something in the manner of those two visitors to the Bramford inn recurred to her and she knew she was right. She thought, however, she had said enough. She had emplanted a little poisoned dart and it could be left alone: it would fester all right. She laughingly said she wasn't going to be drawn into any divorce proceedings and attempted to turn the conversation. But Clarissa thought the matter could scarcely be left where it was, and in the friendliest aside, which could be clearly heard by the entire group, she added: "I'm afraid you won't have the chance this time. I hate to spoil a joke, but unfortunately I know all about George's excursions. It's only a prosaic house-hunt and—a frightful blow to me after having my hopes raised—in his cousin's car."

Clarissa couldn't estimate how far her effort had succeeded. That Harriet Corrin had not believed it she was sure, though she didn't know about the others. But she had no doubt whatever as to her own feelings. She accepted every word of the story and it made her a little sick. Though her married life had not been happy, she thought it had been at least outwardly as successful as the average. Now even that success was at an end. From that moment she had begun to live as did so many other unhappy women: on a volcano. At any time it might erupt, and she would find that her pride was crushed and her home was gone. Clarissa longed desperately to get away from this party, to drop this intolerable effort to hide her feelings. But to leave early would be to give herself away. She must endure it for her usual time.

When eventually she did reach home, her whole body ached with weariness. Gradually there was growing up in her mind a deep, resentful anger against her husband. George had never really thought of anyone's happiness except his own, but if this story were true, he was completely outside the pale and need be considered no more.

Along with this deep anger, a feeling that at all costs she must know the truth was taking possession of her. Terrible as was the threatened disaster, uncertainty was worse.

That night at dinner an unexpected opportunity occurred. A visitor happened to mention the fatal Wednesday, saying that on it she had had to give up an excursion on account of the weather. "About the grimmest day I remember," she ended up.

"Yes," Clarissa remarked. "I was to go over to the Fortescues', but I couldn't face the rain." Then on the spur of the moment, she added: "How did you get through the afternoon, George? You couldn't have had any golf?"

The stage had missed an actress in Clarissa. Outwardly she spoke with cool indifference, obviously making polite conversation. Inwardly she awaited George's reaction with an intensity which surprised herself.

Then she learnt that she had been wrong in thinking that uncertainty was the worst thing she could suffer. Now she found that it was infinitely worse when no hope remained. And no hope did remain. George started, glanced at her with a look of dismay, hesitated, then said with a burst of false cheeriness: "Golf? Not a hope! I stayed in the club and had a rubber of bridge."

That he was lying was as clear to her as if she had been present with him at Bramford. What that snake Harriet Corrin had said was true. She had lost her husband, and how long it would be till she lost her home she didn't know.

It was not often that Clarissa Surridge showed signs of weakness. But that night, when at last she reached her room and could relax, she suddenly realised that she was sobbing—long, slow sobs of misery and impotent anger. It was not for George she cried: as far as he was concerned, she didn't care if she never saw him again. What hurt her was the injury to her pride. That she, of all women, hadn't been able to hold her husband! That while she had remained loyal to him, he had thrown her over! What would not all those old cats say about her?

Presently her thoughts turned towards the future. At least she would be all right materially. She had enough to live on, though not much more. The first thing would be to get a divorce—if she could. George was clever and there might be no evidence. On the other hand, he might want it, and then she would get it. Probably she would marry again. This time, she told herself bitterly, she would make a better choice.

She wondered if she should take any immediate steps? That joke of her's about detectives didn't now seem so absurd as when she had made it. What she could not bear would be to have Harriet Corrin and those other women whispering and sniggering behind her back, while she herself didn't even know what was going on. No, she must find out where she stood. If she couldn't learn the truth for herself, she would have to consider outside help.

Wearied out at length, Clarissa fell asleep, and when she awoke things somehow looked less hopeless. As far as she herself was concerned, she need not despair. If she lost her present home, she might make herself a very much better one. The whole affair might be a blessing in disguise.

Meanwhile George also was putting serious questions to himself. He had had a moment of panic when Clarissa asked how he had spent that Wednesday afternoon. At first it had seemed as if only one thing could have dictated the question, but he had watched her carefully and he was sure from her manner that she had meant nothing particular. But the incident had given him a jar.

In his professional capacity George had been worried by another matter: the change in Professor Burnaby. After the death of his daughter the old man had been prostrated for several days. Then one morning he had reappeared at the snake-house. George had been rather shocked at his appearance. He seemed to have aged by twenty years and looked frail and broken down. His conversation showed, moreover, that he had lost his grip.

George grew really uneasy about his having access to the snakes. Milking them for venom was tricky work and if Burnaby allowed a snake to escape it might prove a very serious matter.

So much was George obsessed with his fear that he suggested to his Committee that the permission they had given the old man should be withdrawn. This would not end his research; if he wanted venom he could still get it from Nesbit, the snake-house attendant, who would be authorised to obtain it for him. This decision was conveyed to Burnaby by a letter from the secretary, which George delivered personally, softening the blow as best he could. The old man took it well, agreeing that the

Committee's action was reasonable, and that he was lucky to have the facilities which still remained.

About this time two events took place, both of which had their effect not only on George's immediate actions, but also on his whole future life.

The first was an opinion given by Dr. Marr during a chat at the club. "I'm sorry to tell you, Surridge," he said, gravely, "that Miss Pentland is very seriously ill," and when George once again asked if anything immediate was to be anticipated, he had not denied it. "Nothing immediate, perhaps," he had pronounced, "but soon. I'm afraid the poor lady can't last many more days."

George expressed suitable concern, but his heart leaped. Not many more *days*! In not many more days his aunt would have passed away and his troubles would be over! What an unspeakable ease to his mind that would be!

The second event gave him even more to think about. A couple of mornings later there was a telephone call from Nancy, saying that something unexpected had occurred and that she wanted to see him. She would give no particulars, but having arranged a meeting she rang off. George, feeling he must account for the call, sent Miss Hepworth to inquire if a lady's umbrella had been found in the lion house on the previous day.

When that evening he had hired the car and picked Nancy up at the rendezvous, he realised that her news was going to make a further upheaval in his life. The lady to whom she had been acting as companion had died suddenly; in fact, Nancy herself had found her dead when she brought her her early morning tea. It had been a dreadful shock, but that was the smallest part of it. What really mattered was that her job was gone. As soon as possible after the funeral the furniture would be sold and the house closed. She herself was moving immediately to Hampshire, where a friend had invited her to stay while she was looking round for something else.

This news was a terrible blow to George. Nancy had become a part of his life, and though he had never really faced the question of how the entanglement was to end, he had long since rejected a permanent parting as impossible. Now the issue was forced upon him and he was not prepared for it.

It was at this point that the idea of the little cottage, with roses over the porch, which had been for some time a cherished if unrealisable dream, re-entered his mind and gripped it till it became an obsession. This was due partly to Nancy's news and partly to the fact that on one of their recent excursions they had seen just such a cottage. It was exactly the size, surrounded by what might be made a delightful garden, and if it had not roses on the porch, it had at least a porch over which they might be trained. It was built on heathland, away from both farm workers and tourists, and yet within five-and-twenty miles of the centre of Birmington. Moreover, it was empty and for sale. George had stopped the car on the rough gravel lane and they had walked round it. The more he had seen of it, the more perfectly he believed it would meet his purpose, and Nancy had also greatly admired it. He had not dared to say all that was in his mind, but now he began to wonder if something of the kind might not have been in hers also.

However, out of the question as the idea had then seemed, it had suddenly become one of pressing importance. Of its two tremendous difficulties, one, marvellously, had been overcome. The death of his aunt would find him the necessary money for its purchase. There remained, therefore, only the second— would Nancy agree?

As George considered this it seemed to grow more and more formidable. Nancy in some ways was very conventional. He doubted lest his suggestion might antagonise her.

Not quite certain as to the best way of introducing the subject, he suggested a drive. "We can talk better when the car's going," he declared, starting forthwith.

While giving no apparent attention to their route, he chose that which would take them past the cottage, and when they reached it, he stopped.

"I've taken a tremendous fancy to this little place," he said, as he got out of the car. "Let's have another peep at it. It looks somehow like a haven where one could find shelter and peace if ever one was really up against it."

She shook her head. "No, I couldn't bear to look at it again," she returned. "It would make me simply sick with longing. To settle down in a place like that would be heaven; particularly when I'm looking out for a horrible job, probably with horrible people."

His heart leapt. He hesitated for a moment, then plunged.

"Nancy," he said a little hoarsely, in spite of all his efforts to be calm, "I brought you here to-day with an object. I'm renting this cottage, and if for a little time you'd condescend to use it, I should take it as the greatest privilege and proof of friendship you could give me."

She was obviously surprised and touched, but he did not think she was antagonised. "It's good of you," she answered, taking his hand and pressing it warmly, "very good of you, but—I couldn't."

"Why?" he asked. "I wouldn't bother you more here than in the past. Instead of going for drives, I would come here; that's all. I'm not suggesting a permanent arrangement; only for a time till you can look round and find a job you can tolerate."

Again she declined and he presently changed his petition. "I won't try to persuade you against your own will, even if I could. But grant me at least this. Let's have a proper look over the place. I'll find the agents and borrow the key."

It was clear that she was torn between her better judgment and her reluctance to refuse his request. He left her walking in the garden while he drove a couple of miles to the address given on the notice board, a house agent's in the small town of Cleerby. There, after the agent had glanced at the Gnat, he handed over the keys.

The more he and Nancy investigated, the more desirable the cottage seemed to George, and the more impressed he thought she grew. It was tiny, containing only a sitting-room, a bedroom and a kitchenette; all in quite good repair. The sitting-room had a french window opening into the garden, with as a background a row of fine Scotch firs, the advance guard of the surrounding wood. Water was laid on, but neither gas nor electricity, but, as George pointed out, with oil lamps and stoves anyone could do very well. He said no more about taking it, but he thought Nancy looked at it with more and more longing, and he waited with a slowly-growing hope. Then suddenly, instead of answering one of his remarks, she turned abruptly away and stood looking out of the window.

He was amazed to find she was crying. A moment later she was in his arms and weeping unrestrainedly on his shoulder.

"It's too good," she presently sobbed. "I know I shouldn't, but I just can't help myself. George, if I ruin you, will you forgive me?"

George's heart swelled with unspeakable delight. He did not realise that those words represented a turning-point in his life, and rendered inevitable the tragedy which had even now grown on the horizon to a cloud like a man's hand.

CHAPTER VII

VENOM: THROUGH
SURROUNDINGS

THE price of the little estate was seven hundred pounds, and George told the agents he would buy. A deposit of fifty pounds was required to clinch the bargain, the balance being handed over before occupation. It would take a few days, he was told, to get the legal business through, but he could move in directly the money was paid.

The seven hundred pounds for the house did not represent the total expenditure. There would be at least another hundred for furniture, as well as small sums for legal fees, minor repairs and one or two small alterations. Altogether the amount required would not be much below nine hundred.

The borrowing of a sum of this magnitude from the bank or from friends was simply impossible. George could manage the fifty pounds, but not more. Regretfully, he therefore decided that only this fifty pounds could be paid, and that the completion of the purchase would have to wait till his aunt's death had actually taken place and he was able to raise the balance in a normal way.

He naturally did not wish to appear in the affair, and now bitterly regretted that he had himself called at the agent's for the key. However, he had taken the precaution to give a false name and address, and as, owing to the rain the day was dark and his coat collar was turned up and his hat pulled low over his eyes, he did not think he could be traced. He had let Nancy return the key and now she conducted all the negotiations, also in an assumed name. She called on the agent with the fifty pounds and engaged a local solicitor to act for her. For this purpose she stayed at a neighbouring inn, which incidentally added to George's bill.

Though at last George was achieving a dream which he had scarcely dared to hope would ever materialise, he was not wholly happy. Sometimes he was almost delirious at the prospect of having Nancy permanently within reach, because though he had spoken of her spending only a short time in the cottage, he had really meant that she should make it her home. But at others he felt the weight of living a lie, the discovery of which would mean ruin. Sometimes he asked himself was the pleasure worth the pain, and he did not always answer Yes. For nearly three weeks things went on as usual, George growing daily more impatient at the delay. Then at last took place the event for which he had been so long waiting.

He was dressing one morning when Marr rang him up with the news. He was sorry to tell him that his aunt had just passed away. The end had come suddenly. As Surridge knew, he, Marr, had been expecting it, but on the previous evening there was no more appearance of anything immediate than at any time during the preceding three weeks. Miss Pentland had died in her sleep, and the family must not mourn her, as her death had been for her a happy release.

George smiled grimly at the idea of his mourning the death, but he replied sympathetically to Marr, and said he would go round immediately to see what he could do.

This proved to be little. Marr, of course, was able to give a certificate, so an inquest was unnecessary. The undertaker, once George had given him his instructions, took over all the details of the funeral. The elderly maid was told to look out for another job, though she was retained for a few days to help to clear up the house. George intended to sell both house and furniture, and he was anxious to see his aunt's solicitor, who, he thought, might do this for him.

He was surprised, and by no means pleased, to find that this was none other than Capper, the nephew of old Burnaby, whom he had met at the party to celebrate poor Joyce's engagement. At first he felt inclined to get someone else to act for him, then he thought he could not pass by a relative of Burnaby's in so marked a manner, and decided to employ him.

Slowly the leaden hours crept by till at last there came the funeral, and after it that moment for which George had so long waited, when he, Clarissa, and the maid met in Miss Pentland's sitting-room to hear the reading of the will. He had never questioned his aunt's good faith, but all the same a verbal promise and a binding legal document were different matters. Once he had seen in black-and-white that the inheritance was coming, the little gnawing pain of doubt would be finally removed.

He was astonished on reaching the house to meet a stalwart young stranger, who said he was Patrick Logan, Capper's partner, and that he would read the will. Capper, it appeared, was abroad. He had had to go to America on business, but he would be home in two or three weeks. Meanwhile, Logan was at George's disposal if any legal business should be required.

George found it hard to sit still during the reading of the document. Logan was slow and evidently unaccustomed to the task. He was, indeed, surprisingly young to be a partner. George wanted to get up and scream at him. "Get on, man!" he wanted to shout. "For heaven's sake get on with it! Don't stand there gaping like a boiled haddock!" Clarissa, he could feel, was similarly on edge, though she had far less cause than he. In the maid's mind the same struggle was also in progress: all tense with eagerness, all trying to disguise the fact.

At length Logan got under way, stumbling laboriously through masses of preliminary verbiage: "Last will and testament ... of sound mind ... give and bequeath. ..." Then the words were spoken, the words that for years George had longed to hear: "That ... to my dear friend and maid ... save the said ... and the said ... all that I die possessed of ... to my nephew, George Humphrey Surridge...."

In spite of himself, George heaved a great sigh of relief. Surreptitiously he wiped the beads of sweat from his forehead. Then it was true! There was no longer any doubt! He could now borrow on his expectations, and send that six hundred and fifty pounds to the agent at once. In a day or two Rose Cottage would be his!

In a dream he heard himself talking to Logan. Much obliged for all his trouble. Yes, everything had gone without a hitch. There would be a little business to be done. Could Logan undertake it for him? Good, then he would call him in the course of a day or two. When would suit?

George soon found that the only time he could spare for the meeting was the following morning. He simply could not wait any longer. He had controlled himself admirably; he did not think that any of those present had suspected his eagerness. But it was beyond his powers to continue the strain.

He thought very carefully over what he should say to Logan: how he could get his information unsuspiciously. Then he saw that he only wanted to know what any man in his position would want to know. There would be nothing in the least suspicious in his questions. But there might be in his manner. Finally, to avoid a show of eagerness, he decided to prepare a small questionnaire, hand it to Logan, and ask him to reply to it at his leisure.

Next morning he drove the forty-odd miles to Bursham, the town in which Capper & Logan practised. The name had been freshly lettered on the door, and it was obvious that the junior partner was a recent addition to the firm. The young man was evidently impressed by the call, and assumed a portentously professional air, though he had the good sense to consult his chief clerk on George's questions before attempting replies.

In accordance with his decision, George adopted a leisurely attitude. He sat down and began to talk about the weather. When Logan held out a box of cigarettes he chose one deliberately and was in no hurry to light it. He talked about smoking, about Capper's absence, reaching by easy stages the matter of the deceased Lucy Pentland.

"I'm sorry for seeming to hurry this affair," he went on, "but after this morning I am engaged for several days, and there is no reason why probate and so on should be held up."

Logan expressed cordial agreement.

"I have prepared," George continued, "a few questions, which I thought might get us at once to the heart of things. If I have omitted anything important, I should be obliged if you would add it to the list."

Slowly he searched his pockets and produced a paper. "It seems a little heartless to be going into all this, when my aunt has only just died," he murmured, "but I have explained the reason. Now, these questions are the obvious ones which would occur to anyone in my position. I have known for years that I was to be my aunt's heir, but I have never had the slightest idea of how much she was going to leave me. That's the first thing I want to know; very approximately, of course. Then I should like to know how she held it: whether it is in stocks or property, or otherwise: all those sort of things. Perhaps you could tell me how I stand?"

Logan was anxious to oblige. The actual figures he hadn't had time to get out, but, roughly, he understood that when death duties and legacies to the present and two former maids had been paid, there would be left over for George between eight and nine thousand pounds. This money, it appeared, was in shares, mostly industrials of various kinds, with a sprinkling of corporation and other stocks.

"I have the list here," went on Logan, "and you will see that the choice of investments has been pretty good. Not only are the investments sound, but they are widely distributed both as to situation and type, while the proportion of trustee stock adds security. I think I may be allowed to offer my congratulations, Mr. Surridge."

Up till now, George had striven to hide his eagerness; now he strove to hide his satisfaction. This, certainly, was a magnificent list. He was no authority on finance, but he knew enough to realise that these investments represented a good income with as close an approach to security as was possible in this financially distracted period. Nothing would have been better.

Two of his three fundamental questions had now been answered: he was the heir, and there was plenty of money. One other point only remained to be cleared up.

"That's a fine list, I agree," he said, as coolly as he could. "I admit I'm delighted with it. But I don't suppose I'll see the money for a little time. It'll take—what? Three or four months to get probate and everything straightened up?"

"Less than that, I should think."

George chatted on rather aimlessly about the delays in the law. Then he became slightly more confidential.

"There's just one other matter I'd like to ask you about. It has been in my mind that if this legacy came to over five thousand, I'd like to blue part of it: I'd like to take a holiday with my wife round the world. I don't know whether I shall do so or not. But if I do, I should probably do it soon: I mean in spring, so as to avoid the extremes of summer and winter. Suppose I wanted to get some money before probate was granted, could I do so?"

Logan seemed slightly embarrassed. "I'm afraid not through us, sir," he answered. "We don't do that class of work. There are plenty of firms who do, of course."

George hastened to explain. "I never for a moment expected that you did, Mr. Logan," he said, pleasantly. "What I meant was: have I now sufficient security to borrow in the ordinary way?"

Logan again hesitated. "I do not think you could borrow, say, from your bank at the present moment. I imagine they would require the actual scrip to be deposited first. That Mr. Capper has in his safe deposit, but you will understand that until probate is granted I am not in a position to hand it over; nor, of course, would he, if he were here. But there are lots of firms which would lend on knowing that you were the heir and that we held your securities."

"And how could they know that?"

Logan shrugged. "I don't think you need worry. If you tell them the facts, they'll make their own enquiries."

George nodded. "I may do so: I don't know yet. By the way, when will Mr. Capper be home? I've met him, you know. He's a relative of my neighbour, Professor Burnaby."

The remainder of the interview passed off as normally as even George could have desired, and he left the office profoundly satisfied with what had taken place. His prospects were splendid, and he had not at any point acted in the slightest degree suspiciously.

A couple of days later it happened that he had business in Town, and he took the opportunity to call once again on Messrs. Abraham & Co., the moneylenders. There he was received with the same formal courtesy, but with much more interest.

"We do not usually make loans otherwise than after the securities have actually been deposited with us," Mr. Abraham explained, when George had stated his business. "However, in your case, where there is obviously no doubt as to the security, we might meet you to a certain, I'm afraid very limited, extent. You say that Mr. Capper will be home in a fortnight and that then these scrips will be available?"

"No," George answered, "I didn't say that. I understand the firm won't allow the scrips out of their possession until probate is granted. But, of course, if I were to wait till then, I should have the money myself and should not require a loan. If the facts as I've mentioned them are not enough for you, I'm afraid we can't do business."

Mr. Abraham hummed and hawed. Mr. Surridge, he said hesitatingly, was a man of business himself and would therefore understand business methods. He, Abraham, was personally satisfied, and if it concerned him alone he would willingly advance up to seventy-five per cent of the capital. But the affair involved his partners and therefore must be conducted on business lines. Without further security he could only advance what would be to a man like Mr. Surridge mere pocket money, say up to £250. "I suppose the matter couldn't be dealt with in some other way?" Abraham concluded. "You wouldn't care to say just what you wanted the money for?"

George hesitated in his turn. "It's rather confidential," he said, "but as a matter of fact I want to buy a cottage."

"And the price of the cottage, sir?"

"Seven hundred pounds, of which I have already deposited fifty. That leaves six-fifty, but I shall want a hundred or two for furniture and repairs."

"Eight hundred and fifty," answered the moneylender. Then, after a moment: "Will you excuse me while I consult my partners?"

What this meant George could not imagine. Abraham had suddenly become more eager. However, there wasn't much time to think things over, for in a few minutes the man was back.

"I'm sorry that my partners agree with me that we could not lend the sum you require without the scrip as security, but perhaps we can meet your wishes in another way. Supposing we buy this cottage for you—assuming our inspection satisfies us as to its value? Supposing at the same time we advance you £150 in cash; that is £800 altogether? For this we should have the security of the house as well as your statement about the inheritance. What about that, Mr. Surridge? Would it be of any use to you?"

It was not exactly what George wanted, for it meant a publicity that he would have much preferred to avoid. However, it seemed that he had no option and with some misgivings he agreed. He promised Abraham an authority from Nancy to act on her behalf, explaining that the negotiations to date had been carried on in her name. He was slightly annoyed, as well as a good deal relieved, to see at the mention of a lady a sly and understanding smile hover for a moment round the corners of Abraham's mouth.

"Then, sir," the man went on, "it only remains for me to hand you our cheque for £150. Or perhaps you would prefer notes?"

George stared. "But I thought you had to make enquiries first?" he asked.

Abraham smiled broadly. "We made them after your previous call, sir," he declared. "We know all about you and we know that we can trust you. Notes, you say?"

When George returned that night to Birmington he was in so exalted a frame of mind that he could scarcely refrain from hiring the car and going off there and then to pass on the good tidings to Nancy. However, the fact that he would have to knock up the inn to do so proved sufficient discouragement, and he contented himself with telling her over the telephone next morning.

Abraham was as good as his word. The next day there called on Nancy a smartly dressed young man with oily manners and black hair plastered down till it shone like burnished metal. With her he went to see first the cottage and then the agent. Finally, on obtaining her authority to act for her, he bowed himself off, stating the purchase would be completed in a couple of days.

For Nancy directly and for George at second hand, a period approaching ecstasy ensued. There was first the joy of discussing with the local builder the required alterations and repairs. It was delightful to hear him promise to have the work done by a certain date, and only a little less so to receive later his explanations as to why he had been unable to fulfil his bargain. George would have loved to inspect the progress of the work, but he considered it dangerous to be seen near the cottage, and decided regretfully to wait till the job was finished before satisfying his curiosity.

He did not even accompany Nancy when she was buying the furniture. Indeed, they cut down the number of their meetings, waiting for the glorious time when Nancy would be settled in, when the last of the tradesmen would have gone, and when it would be safe for George to pay his calls.

The most important of the alterations was the provision of a garage. George had decided that as soon as he could provide the money, Nancy must have a car. A Morris Minor, a Baby Austin, or an eight-horse Ford would suit the cottage and be inconspicuous. It would not only be a tremendous advantage and pleasure to Nancy, owing to the un-get-at-able position of the cottage, but she could drive him to and from one of the many surrounding railway stations or bus stops. This would enable him to do without the Gnat and thus avoid one of his chief dangers.

In spite of the builder's procrastination, the work was at last finished. By this time the furniture had been delivered, and one glorious Friday morning Nancy moved in. She could easily have run the establishment herself, but George urged her to have a girl in for a couple of hours each morning. Firstly, he wished to prevent an air of mystery growing up round the place, and the daily visit of a charwoman would enable the entire economy of the household to be discussed in all the surrounding cottages and bars. Then there was the question of illness. If Nancy felt unwell, she would be certain of help within a reasonable time. Lastly there was the mere getting rid of the heavier housework, leaving her more time for reading, gardening, and developing her genuine talent for music.

Then one evening at long last George drove out to see her. He parked in a side road nearly a mile away and walked to Rose Cottage by a woodland path—meeting no one. Oh, the absolute bliss of that first evening! The delight of the cosy sitting-room with drawn blinds and a blazing wood fire on the old brick hearth! Above all, the thrilling joy of each other's company, which this charming haven of refuge made possible!

Their belief that no one had any suspicion of their intimacy gave them a profound sense of satisfaction. They had,

of course, been extremely careful all through, but even with
extreme care accidents do happen. Now the acutely dangerous
time was over. Nothing in reason that Nancy might do could
give them away, and George had only to continue his precautions on the journeys to and from Birmington to ensure continued secrecy.

Had they known of the ideas which Harriet Corrin had
implanted in the minds of half the women of George's circle,
they would have felt very differently. Had they had an inkling that Clarissa was even then considering the pros and cons
of employing a detective to find out where George went on
Wednesday afternoons, their satisfaction would have been cut
off as electric light ceases with the blowing of a fuse. Fortunately
or unfortunately for them, they didn't know, and they hugged
their happiness while they might.

A couple of days after this first visit to Rose Cottage, George was
seated in his office when the telephone rang. "Is that Mr. George
Surridge?" Pause. "Just a moment, please." Then came another voice,
a man's. "This is the office of Capper and Logan. Capper speaking.
How are you, Mr. Surridge?"

The curve of George's interest rose acutely. "How are you,
Mr. Capper? You remember our last meeting? You've got back?"

Capper had got back. Moreover, he was very well and he
recalled their meeting with pleasurable memories. He was now
ringing up Mr. Surridge on business: to suggest an interview for
the discussion of Miss Pentland's legacy. "Unfortunately I have
to be away from the office for a day or two," he went on. "I have
to visit some invalid clients. But I am free at my rooms over the
office in the evenings. Would it be convenient to you to drop
in there? I realise it's rather a lot to ask and I should suggest my
calling on you, except that all the papers are here."

George didn't care if he had to drive a hundred miles instead of forty, provided some more ready money would be the result. Once again he felt he simply could not wait, and he told Capper that that very evening was the only one he could manage for some time to come. Could Capper see him on such short notice?

It appeared that that evening was also the most suitable for Capper. For what he hoped would be the last time, George after dinner hired the N. J. Gnat, and after leaving the city, turned to the right at the Bursham road fork.

It was an unpleasant evening for his expedition. The day had been dark and raw with a gusty wind eddying round the chimneys and the corners of the streets. Now the wind had fallen, but the rain had come down in a deluge. The pavements glistened and reflected the lights of street lamps and approaching cars. Driving was difficult and George was frequently dazzled and had to reduce speed. Altogether instead of completing the journey in a little over the hour, it took him nearer two to reach his destination.

Capper himself opened the door. "I'm sorry to have brought you out on this miserable evening," he greeted him. "I'm afraid you've had an unpleasant drive. You are alone?"

"Yes, I drove myself. It wasn't too bad except that I couldn't make the speed I otherwise should."

"If you're not in a hurry, I'm not. But I'm sorry they won't let you park here. Will you put your car round the corner?"

George did so, though he mentally damned the local pundits who prohibited parking late at night in a semi-residential street which carried no through traffic.

Capper was still standing at the door. "Come up to the fire," he invited. "I'm alone in the house this evening: it's my housekeeper's night out."

He seemed anxious to get George inside and as soon as possible shut the door. He led the way upstairs to a large bare sitting-room on the second floor. It struck George with an air of discomfort. The furniture was old and worn, and the fire was black and gave out but little heat. Capper drew up an arm-chair and took bottles and glasses from a sideboard.

"You'll want a drink after that drive," he went on, picking up a decanter. "Say when."

The whisky warmed George and helped him to play the part he had intended. Capper was obviously a man of very different calibre to Logan. While George felt an instinctive dislike to him, he could not but recognise how wide awake and competent he was. Unless George was extraordinarily careful, this man would read his mind as he would a child's. Now more than ever must George avoid any appearance of eagerness.

"I had no idea," he began easily, sipping his whisky, "that we should meet so soon and over business. I didn't know you acted for my late aunt."

Capper poured out whisky for himself. He seemed nervous and on edge. He drank off the whisky almost neat and poured out a second helping.

"She used to live near Stamworth," he answered, "and as you know, Stamworth is not far from here. My father acted for hers, and when both died, the next generation carried on."

George nodded. "He was a wonderful man, old Pentland, I remember," and he told one or two reminiscences.

They settled down into a rather forced discussion: on the families which were breaking up, the changes in social life, and Capper's journey to America. Increasingly George felt that there was something amiss with his host. He kept jerking about, apparently unable to sit still. Some of his remarks were vague and hesitating, some brusque, and all suggestive of a weight on his mind. At last, however, he turned to business.

"I was sorry to be away at the time of Miss Pentland's death," he said. "Logan's a good fellow, but of course he's young and inexperienced. I hope he carried on satisfactorily?"

"Quite," said George. "I found him very helpful."

"It's good of you to say so. He does his best. I thought, however, we should have a chat over things ourselves. I wanted to tell you one or two things about the legacy."

Capper rose slowly and stirred the fire into a blaze. Then he straightened up and began to fiddle with the objects on the chimneypiece. He picked up something from behind an ornament. To George's amazement it was an automatic pistol.

"Ever go in for pistol practice?" he asked, with slightly twitching face, as he turned round and balanced the weapon in his hand. "No? I do. I'm rather a dab at it, though I say it myself." He replaced the pistol, continuing: "I prefer rifle shooting, but I can't get a range here. However, that's not what you want to hear about. It's your legacy, isn't it?"

"Well," said George, rather surprised by the whole incident, but smiling steadily, "it was you who suggested the meeting, you know. Not that I'm not delighted to have it. But I think Logan has told me all I wanted to know. The amount I am likely to get is between eight and nine thousand, and it will probably be paid within three months or less. Is there anything else?"

George noticed that his host grew increasingly abstracted, indeed he seemed deeply moved. For a moment he kept silence, looking strangely at George.

A disconcerting idea suddenly shot into George's mind. Capper was acting in an extraordinary way. There was his absent manner, his slightly disconnected remarks, his evident apprehension, and the curious episode of the pistol. Had the man gone off his head? They were alone in the house. Had George to deal with an armed madman? Had he, in short, come to one of the major crises of his life?

Once again Capper took up the pistol and began to fiddle with it. He was obviously trying to control deep emotion of some kind. Then suddenly grasping the pistol firmly, he looked George straight in the eyes. In spite of himself, George gripped the arms of the chair.

"I'm afraid there is something more, Surridge," Capper said, hoarsely. "I have to tell you that—that—there's no legacy!"

George felt his heart miss a beat. He stared speechless, unable to move.

"It's gone," went on Capper, in that strange hoarse voice. "I've spent it all!"

CHAPTER VIII

VENOM: THROUGH TEMPTATION

GEORGE sat as if turned to stone. The money was gone! His aunt's money! This money to which he had been looking forward for years, this money which was to get him out of all his troubles, this money which was to buy the cottage for Nancy and give her all those other things she so much wanted: this money—was gone!

Petrified in body, George's mind continued to grapple with the situation. Why, he was now in debt: in debt and with no prospect of being able to pay. He was ruined!

And Nancy! What would happen to Nancy? She would have to leave Rose Cottage and get a job. She would be heartbroken. And suppose she didn't find a job immediately? She had spent her savings while waiting for the cottage to be ready. And he, George, couldn't help her! He couldn't help himself.

At last he looked at Capper. "Is there *none* left?" he heard a voice say, a croaking voice that he didn't recognise.

Capper shook his head. He made an effort to speak, then almost whispered: "Your money—and my own; it's all gone."

A whirl of furious hate flared up in George's mind. This man, this thief! He had stolen *his* money! He had wiped out *his* chance of happiness and doomed *him* to years of misery! And Nancy also! George saw red. His hands clutched the air. He wanted to get them round this man's throat and squeeze and squeeze till the face grew black and the eyes started from their sockets and Capper *died*! He wanted Capper to die! Now! He would get that much back on him!

Involuntarily he started forward, only to find the pistol pointing straight at his head. "Steady, Surridge," came Capper's voice. "You can't do anything that way. My pistol's loaded, and if one of us has to die, it won't be me. When you've got over the shock we'll talk it over!"

"Steady!" roared George, though he sank back into his chair. "Do you know what you're saying? You thief, do you know that you've ruined me? Talk it over!" He thought again of Nancy and words failed him. ...

He became conscious presently of a monotonous sound. Capper was speaking. "I know," he was saying, more earnestly than George had thought possible, "I know that any expression of regret or sorrow would only be adding insult to injury, but I must say it formally just this once. I am more sorry about this than about anything that has ever happened in my life. I loathe myself because of it. I will do anything, *anything*, to minimise its effect or to help. I do say that most earnestly, Surridge, though of course I don't expect you to believe me."

George had sunk into a sort of stupor. What had Capper's sorrow to do with the thing? He did not reply and Capper went on.

"I wish you'd tell me just how this hits you. It's not impertinence or idle curiosity. It really is that I want to help. Things may not be as bad as they seem."

At last George moved. "It hits me, yes," he said, in a tone of concentrated bitterness, "but nothing to the way it's going to hit you. I'll at least have the satisfaction of seeing you in the dock and of thinking of you in your cell in some convict prison."

Capper nodded as if pleased at this outburst. "I'm glad you said that," he declared, "because it helps me to talk to you more normally. We must talk this out, you know." He replaced the pistol on the chimneypiece as if no longer fearful that he might need it, and sank down in the other arm-chair. "You can do what you say," he went on, "If you wish to. I admit that you have only to tell your solicitor or the police what I have done, and I will get the penal servitude you desire. I could put up no defence. I forged your aunt's signature."

"I shall do it," George returned. "Don't make any mistake about that."

"It would certainly," Capper admitted, "give you a temporary satisfaction. But don't forget that that would be all. That would be all, Surridge," he repeated, then added meaningly, "It wouldn't, for instance, get you back your money."

George sat up in his chair. "Can that be done?" he asked, his mouth dry.

"It was to discuss the possibility that I asked you here. I could have seen you in the office, but I thought we could talk better in private."

He was speaking as if he really had some plan. A faint ray of hope flashed into the darkness of George's mind. "Do you mean the money's not all lost?" he queried sharply. Then with suppressed fury, "Damn you, can't you answer a straight question?"

"It's all lost," Capper answered slowly, "but"—he paused significantly—"it might be replaced."

"What do you mean?" George shouted, at the end of his patience. "If you've anything to say, for heaven's sake get on and say it!"

Capper poured more whisky into both glasses. "There's a way in which you can get back every penny," he returned gravely, "provided you agree to help me in a certain matter. I'll tell you everything, but to understand it I must explain just how I'm fixed. Drink up and listen."

He swallowed another stiff tot himself, then went on. "I'm not trying to excuse myself; I admit I've done you a great wrong. You don't want to hear that, of course, but only my suggestion for righting it. I may just say that my madness was speculation. I wanted to marry, but my business is not large and I wasn't making enough to ask any woman to share her life with me. I'm not looking for sympathy, Surridge, but if you've ever loved, you'll know how I felt."

George, who had a weakness for seeing the other fellow's point of view, felt some of his bitterness evaporating. Suppose this man had wanted to marry Nancy and found he hadn't enough money? Yes, George could understand what that might mean.

"I looked about for money, unsuccessfully. Then I remembered how often I had been right about the movement of shares: more correct even than my stockbroker. I felt I had a flair for that sort of thing and I tried some operations with my own tiny capital. The frequent international crises helped me: prices rose and fell quickly. I bought and sold and made. But my capital was so small I didn't make enough to matter. You can understand the temptation which arose. Though I owned but little money, I had control of a good deal. I saw that if I could make the same profit on the money I controlled as I had on my own, I should have enough to marry.

"I won't weary you with the fight I put up. I knew it wasn't honest, but I swear before God I had no intention of stealing— only of borrowing. My clients' capital, I felt, would be safe. I should only buy into stock that I was sure would rise, and if it didn't do so, I should sell before harm was done."

In spite of himself a certain sympathy for the man was creeping into George's mind. The story was uncannily like what might have happened to himself. He wondered whether, had he had access to large sums, he would have acted so much better than had Capper. . . .

"For a time I did quite well, so I suppose I grew bolder. Then disaster came. One of the innumerable international scares took place and stocks fell everywhere. I found myself several hundreds to the bad. The problem, therefore, arose: to hold on or to sell? If I sold, I should find myself just where I started. If I held on, I might still get my profit.

"You can guess what happened. The stock fell further, and in fear of ruin I sold. I was now nearly a thousand to the bad. I tried to carry on and recoup my loss, but either I had reached the end of my luck or my failure had destroyed my nerve, for from then I began to lose. I became faced with utter ruin. Finally I put all the money I could get together on a single throw: if I lost I could scarcely be worse off, if I won I might get all square. I lost."

For some moments there was silence while Capper poured out and tossed off another tot. Then George muttered, "Well?"

"There was a little left, of course, from that, but there were other expenses, and now—" Capper again seemed overwhelmed, "now I may say that there's practically nothing. Your aunt's money's gone, on the top of my own."

George snorted. "Damn your impertinence!" he broke out, savagely. "What do I care about your money? It's the stealing of mine that matters!"

Capper made a deprecating gesture. "I know. I've admitted all that. You don't see what I'm driving at. What I mean is that in this affair we're in the same boat."

"Like hell we are! The burglar and the householder? We'll see about that."

"We're in the same boat," Capper persisted, "in that we're both hard up and we both want money. You can do one of two things,

Surridge. You can prosecute me and whistle for your money, or you can realise the past is past and join with me in getting it back."

"You haven't told me how," George said, sullenly.

"All in good time. I want you to realise first that our interests are identical."

George could scarcely contain himself. "For heaven's sake go on and explain. You said all that before."

"No," Capper returned, "we can't go on till you make up your mind. Are you going to prosecute or are you going to work with me?"

George twisted in his chair. "How the hell can I answer when I don't know your proposal?" he stormed. "Think I'm a thought reader?"

Capper remained silent for a moment, looking strangely at George. Then once more he filled up the glasses. "Drink up," he invited, and as George automatically picked up his glass, he went on in a more confidential tone. "I have twenty-two thousand coming to me," he almost whispered. "If I could get it now, we should both be happy."

George stared. "What's the hitch?" he asked at last.

"The same as yours," Capper answered. "It's a legacy; a very old man in poor health, but still hanging on. If you must know, it's my uncle, Matthew Burnaby."

"Good heavens! Are you his heir?"

"I'm the only one of the family left. When Joyce was alive she was to get it, but when she was killed he made a new will, leaving everything to me."

"You made it?"

"No; don't be a fool. But I've seen it. It's all right. When death duties are paid there'll be about twenty-two thousand. And when

I get it I'll halve it with you. That'll be nearly three thousand interest on my loan."

George turned this over in his mind. "But damn it all, Capper," he said, "what good will that be to me? Burnaby's old and frail, but he may live for years yet. I'll not get it till it's too late to be any use."

Capper looked at him more strangely than ever. "He might, of course, live for years," he said, then paused and added slowly, "but then again, he mightn't."

"What do you mean?" George asked sharply.

"He's very old and very frail," Capper repeated, in that slow voice. "No one could be surprised if he were to die at any time."

George sat up. "Good God, man! What are you saying? Do you know what you're hinting?"

"Only that an accident might happen. Nothing more than that, Surridge."

"An accident? Come on, Capper; say what you mean. Are you hinting that you want me to be party to a murder?"

Capper shook his head. "No one could suggest such a thing. Don't be an utter fool. If there was a murder neither of us would get any money. An accident. I've thought it all out. It would be sudden and practically painless: and most certainly an accident."

Once again George raved angrily. He really was shocked and indignant. "Damn you, Capper, you dirty skunk! You want to murder the old man and you want to drag me in as an accomplice." He got up suddenly. "I'd see you in hell first." He moved towards the door, then turned back. "I've had about all of you I can stand. But I warn you, if anything happens to Burnaby, I'll go straight to the police. I may be bad, but I'm not as bad as that."

Capper rose also. "Right," he said. "Just as you like. I can wait. I can keep going one way or another for a year or two. It's all right."

"It's well you think so," George returned. "I'll tell you something you seem to have forgotten. I'll be paid when Burnaby dies—naturally. But you'll be in jail."

Capper laughed, a cold mocking laugh. "All right," he jeered, "if you feel that way just go ahead. But when you find yourself left, don't blame me."

George flung himself out, slamming the door. He ran downstairs, and jumping into the car, drove off at top speed. He was furious with this lying scoundrel. Capper would see the inside of a prison for this. The very next day he would lodge an information. He would see the Chief Constable, whom he knew. And he would give him a hint about the man's hideous suggestion.

Next day George had cooled down considerably. He decided that the information he had scarcely justified him in reporting to the Chief Constable. Instead he spent the day thinking over the situation. And the more he thought, the less he liked it.

In his indignation against Capper, he had rather lost sight of his own position. Now he saw it more clearly with every minute that passed. If he could not get money his life would be spoilt. He began to count up his debts. He owed small sums amounting to perhaps £150. Next, there was Abraham's advance, which he had spent on furnishing Rose Cottage. That was another £150. Lastly there was the cottage itself. Abraham might not be able to get what he gave for it. Suppose he dropped £100 on the sale: another £100. Altogether, as far as George could estimate, he would require anything up to £400 to clear his debt. And if Nancy were to continue in Rose Cottage, he would want a lot more.

As George pondered over the threat to his own happiness, the importance of punishing Capper grew less vital. What mattered was the raising of the money, not the satisfaction of his revengeful feelings.

That afternoon he happened to be passing the snake-house when Professor Burnaby came out. George was shocked by the old man's appearance. He was certainly going rapidly down the hill. What, George wondered irritably, was he doing in the snake-house? Since the permission to work with the snakes had been withdrawn, there was no reason why he should be there; yet he seemed to spend as much time as ever hanging about the place. It wasn't good enough. If he began meddling, there might easily be an accident.

Suddenly Capper's suggestion struck him in a new light. He had not realised Burnaby's condition. Really the old man had one foot in the grave. He could not be enjoying his life and he was a danger to his fellow men. If a painless accident were to happen. ...

George pulled himself together. What was this he had been thinking? Thank heaven, whatever he might be, he was not a murderer.

But it was true that the man's death would be nothing but a blessing for himself and everyone about him. He could say that with truth and yet detest and oppose Capper's scheme.

What, he wondered, *was* Capper's scheme? An accident, practically instantaneous and practically painless. Was that so very bad? The old fellow might die of some terrible long drawn out disease, or what might be even worse, his mind might give way. How many poor people in this unhappy world would give all they had to end up practically instantaneously and painlessly?

And then if what seemed best for Burnaby meant George's own escape from ruin? If it meant Nancy? If it meant, in fact, everything that made life worth living?...

The sweat formed on George's forehead as he considered these alternatives. It was not, he told himself, a question of doing right or wrong; whatever he did would be wrong. It was a choice of two evils. Which was the lesser? Which—was—the—lesser?

By the time he had passed a second sleepless night, George had moved a good deal further. Of course, under no circumstances could he have anything to do with murder. But he now remembered that Capper had said that he would arrange the "accident" and that he, George, actually *would* have nothing to do with it. He thought it would be no harm to find out just what Capper's scheme was. If it were true that he himself should know nothing of any accident. ... Well, he might ask about it at all events. Asking would commit him to nothing.

That night George went to a secluded street booth to make an appointment with Capper. But when he put out his hand to lift the receiver he had a curious and upsetting experience. He seemed to see placed before him a choice: of good and evil. He told himself his action was only exploratory: to learn Capper's plan. But deep down in his mind George knew that he was faced with one of the major decisions of his life. What he did now he would never be able to undo.

He had had a religious upbringing, and some of the lessons he had been taught as a child recurred with extraordinary vividness to his memory. Of course, he had long ceased to believe in that sort of thing, and yet these memories seemed insistently to be urging him back, away from this deed which he contemplated.

For a moment, he felt completely unnerved. Then he called back his common sense. This was pure funk. It could do no harm to find out what Capper proposed. If it was really bad, of course he would have nothing to do with it.

Presently his hesitation passed away and he rang up Capper and fixed an appointment for the following evening.

All next day George felt uneasy, but he banished the thoughts as mere weakness. After dinner he hired the Gnat and drove over to Bursham, parking as before down the side street. He had determined to take a strong line with Capper, agreeing to nothing which he felt would be morally indefensible.

The solicitor welcomed him unemotionally. "I'm glad you came," he said, as he took George's coat. "You may not like my plan. You may even turn it down. But in our very unpleasant position I think it should at least be discussed."

"This commits me to nothing," George declared, as stoutly as he was able.

"Of course not," Capper agreed smoothly. "The idea may appeal to you and it may not. Come upstairs."

When they were seated with whiskys and sodas, Capper gave his visitor an exceedingly searching glance from his shrewd eyes. Then, after a moment's thought, he said the very thing which had already occurred to George.

"Of course, you realise that we are faced with a choice of evils? It is not a question of choosing right or wrong, but of selecting the lesser of two wrongs."

These words and the earnest manner in which they were spoken influenced George as the solicitor had intended. He appreciated Capper's moderation and apparent desire to do right, and much of his antagonism evaporated.

"You needn't harp on that," he returned. "I realise it perfectly well. Go on, let's hear the plan."

"Right," Capper answered, "if you want directness I'll be direct. I won't tell you the plan because I've let you in for this, and if there's going to be trouble, I'll face it alone."

"I'll have to know more than that," George declared.

"Of course. And you'll have to be in it to a very small extent. I'm being straight with you, Surridge, and you will see that's necessary for my own safety. I'm not suggesting you'd give me away: I trust you completely; but this is business, and as a matter of business you must be in it enough to ensure your loyalty. After all, I'm taking ninety-nine per cent. of the risk."

George nodded. "Go ahead."

"You," continued Capper, "would have to do four things, and four things only. First, lose and re-find your keys as I describe; second, obtain some snake venom, preferably from a small snake; third, take a snake of the same kind from the snake-house and drown it; and fourth, post the venom and the dead snake to me. That is everything."

"And what would you do?"

"That, for your own safety, you mustn't know. What would happen would be that on the following evening my uncle would be bitten and die."

George moved impatiently. "But, you ass, he couldn't be bitten. The snake would be dead."

Capper nodded. "Quite. You would therefore feel innocent about what you had done."

George hesitated. The whole thing sounded horrible to him. Snake-bite was certainly quick, but it was sometimes very painful also. Under no circumstances could he agree to anything of the kind.

"I don't like it," he said. "In fact, whatever your idea is, I loathe it and I won't have anything to say to it."

"No suspicion can arise," Capper pointed out. "It will be clear to everyone that my uncle, disappointed at being refused facilities at the snake-house, took a snake home to experiment. It escaped and bit him."

George shook his head. "Suspicion might always arise," he said, gloomily.

"Very well, suppose it does? It won't settle on you, for two reasons. First, though you could have stolen the snake, you could not have got it to bite Burnaby. I will arrange an absolute alibi for you during the whole period. Secondly, there would be no reason to suspect you, because you could have had no motive. Nothing about my sale of your securities will come out. It will be understood that, till probate is granted, you can't expect to handle your legacy. Probate for my uncle's money will be granted just as soon, so that I can pay you at the very time you should be getting your own money."

"I must have some before that."

"Directly my uncle dies I shall be able to raise three or four thousand on my expectations. I can hand you a couple of thousand at once."

"But suppose you are suspected and our association comes out?"

"I won't be suspected, because, though I would have an obvious motive, I couldn't get either the venom or the snake."

"I'd like to know your plan," George persisted.

Capper smiled a little grimly. "Ignorance is always more convincing if it's genuine," he retorted, and from this position George could not move him.

George felt terribly upset. Capper's scheme seemed safe—for him. If the theft of the securities did not come out—and there was absolutely no reason why it should—no suspicion could possibly attach to him. And he would not commit the murder: in fact, he would know nothing about it. His part would be limited to a quite harmless action. True, he would be taking a snake which did not belong to him, but surely in all these years he had put in enough extra work for the Zoo to balance that?

And if he declined? Once again George pictured the ruin which must follow. The loss of Nancy, the misery of Nancy, the probable eventual loss of his own job. ...

Two evils indeed: both hateful, both utterly ghastly. Which—was—the—lesser?

George still tried to temporise. "You spoke of involving me sufficiently to safeguard yourself. What about the reverse? Why, if it suited you, should you not give me away—speaking from a business point of view, of course?"

Capper, seeing he had conquered, smiled. "That's not difficult," he said, in a pleasanter tone. "As I see it, there are four points to be considered. First, you cannot give me away, because you will have provided me with the venom and the snake. Second, I cannot give you away, because I shall have used what you have sent me to kill Burnaby. If either of us talked, we should involve ourselves. Third, I cannot refuse to pay my debt to you, because, if I did, you would proceed against me for theft; and fourth, you cannot get more from me than you're entitled to, as the papers held by both of us give the amount. Therefore, each of us is completely safeguarded against the other. It's true, of course, that you've no check about the extra two thousand five hundred I've promised you, but I'll pay it all the same."

"I'm not worrying about that," George admitted.

Capper poured out some more whisky and then leant forward. "That's all right then; let's go into details about your part of it. Your keys first. Now there's a small gate," and their heads went closer together.

When, after midnight, George left the house, he found himself definitely committed to the scheme.

CHAPTER IX
VENOM: IN ACTION

GEORGE reached home with his mind in a whirl. Now that the die was cast he was already bitterly regretting his decision. Rather, perhaps, he oscillated between two views, at one time dreading and loathing what lay before him, at another thankful that he was avoiding the much worse alternative.

He felt he must begin to act, partly to finish the burning of his boats, and partly to get the hideous affair over as quickly as possible.

The first thing to be attended to was the matter of the keys, of which Capper had given him full details. This should be carried out immediately. Capper wanted as much time as possible to elapse between it and Burnaby's accident, so that a connection between the two should not be too obvious.

On his ring, George had, besides the keys of his private house, office, safe and desk, keys for various locks about the Zoo. One fitted the main gate and one the side door near Burnaby's house, and three master keys opened between them the entire range of animal houses. George carried these—they were all small—so that he could at any time of the day or night enter or leave the grounds, or, should occasion arise, visit any animal or enclosure. Before explaining his plan, Capper had asked what keys he carried, and had seemed well pleased with George's reply.

George began by thinking out an excuse to use the side door. This door, as has been explained, was a small one for foot passengers only, and led from near the snake-house out on to the road close to Burnaby's. It was not used by the public, but was reserved for business purposes, and was kept locked. Burnaby had been given a key when he began his researches, so as to save him the walk round by the main entrance, and in order to spare his feelings this key had not been withdrawn from him with the permission to handle the snakes.

George found his excuse in the illness of his artist friend, Richard Mornington, the man with whom he often walked to lunch. Mornington lived close to Burnaby, and the nearest way from the Zoo to his house was through the side door. George had not been to inquire about him and in the normal condition of affairs might never have gone, but now he felt that friendship demanded a visit.

That afternoon he paid his call, sitting with the artist for half an hour, much to the latter's surprise. He walked back to the Zoo, opened the side door with his key, passed through and drew it shut. But he left his bunch dangling from the keyhole.

Half an hour after reaching his office he decided it was time to open his safe. He put his hand in his pocket for his keys, when lo! they weren't there. More or less noisily he searched the room, then, having no success, he rang for his secretary.

"Have you seen my keys, Miss Hepworth?" he asked. "I seem to have mislaid them somewhere."

She looked at him with but slightly-veiled disapproval as she replied that she had not. "When did you have them last?" she went on, in an accusing tone.

"Well, if I knew that, you know." He smiled. "I had them just before lunch, because I had the safe open then. I remember locking it before going out."

"Yes, I saw it open before lunch," she admitted, unhelpfully.

"Then after lunch I went round to see Mr. Mornington. He's ill, you know. I used the side door and I had them then. I must have brought them back with me, but I don't remember using them since I came in."

"You've dropped them somewhere," she suggested, as if administering a reproof to a naughty child.

"I suppose I must," he answered meekly, "seeing that they're not here now. Let's have a look round the office."

He stood feeling in the pockets of his clothes, while with quick efficient fingers and sharp eyes she searched the room and furniture. Presently both had to admit defeat.

"If I dropped them in the grounds, ten to one someone has found them. Better have Taylor in."

She withdrew silently, and he heard her voice at the telephone. Presently a reliable-looking man in a blue uniform appeared. This was the head ranger or grounds caretaker. His duty was to see that the public did as little damage as possible to the flowers, shrubs and various other outdoor objects which the Zoo provided for their delectation.

"I've done a stupid thing, Taylor," George explained. "I've mislaid my keys. There are about eight on the ring, mostly small and of the Yale type."

"Yes, sir. Any idea where you lost them?"

George smiled. "That would be telling, you know. I let myself in through the side door about half an hour ago, so I must have had them then. I walked straight here, but when I looked for them just now they were gone. See if I've dropped them in the grounds, will you, and make inquiries if anyone has found them."

The man saluted and disappeared, while George sat thinking over the affair. He wasn't quite clear as to Capper's motive in requiring all this. It couldn't be that he intended someone to steal the keys or take impressions, for no time had been arranged for the affair to take place. Yet his direction that they were to be left in the *outside* keyhole of the door did suggest something of the kind. It was certainly connected with the access of some unauthorised person to the snake-house, as he had insisted that a key of this house must be on the bunch.

George continued working, though with indifferent success. Miss Hepworth must not be allowed to suspect. He felt that to hoodwink Miss Hepworth was going to be one of his greatest difficulties. She was extraordinarily efficient, and her very excellences were now his danger.

Presently Taylor was announced, the keys dangling from his finger.

"Found 'em in the door, sir; the side door."

George looked suitably shocked. "Good lord!" he exclaimed. "I must be getting senile decay. Were they in the lock?"

"Hanging in the lock, sir, outside."

George shook his head. "Goodness only knows how I did that! Well, fortunately, no harm seems to have been done. Thank you, Taylor; I'm glad you got them."

Though George at times was consumed with fear lest Capper's plans should prove faulty, he was pleased with the way he had carried out this first step. Nothing he had so far done could possibly be used against him. He had his story ready to explain how he came to overlook the key: Capper had sketched its outlines and it was reasonably convincing. If he did as well with his next step he would certainly be all right.

This next step involved the stealing and drowning of the snake, the collecting of the venom, and the sending of both to Capper. It was really also the last, because all these matters must be dealt with at the same time.

For some incomprehensible reason Capper had insisted that this must be done on a Tuesday night. Moreover, it could only be on the night of a day on which Burnaby had been in the snake-house late in the afternoon. It was therefore necessary for George to keep an eye on the snake-house on each Tuesday afternoon, the understanding being that he should act on the first one on which Burnaby was there.

This was Thursday, so that he had five days before the great effort became possible. Meanwhile, certain preparatory matters must be seen to, and on the following Saturday he took advantage of a visit to London to deal with them.

His business was at the London Zoo, and when it was completed he went down to the East End and bought a pair of black sand shoes, rubber gloves and other small items, as well as thirty feet of light rope, to the end of which he got the shopman to attach a small hook. The rope he knotted at intervals of about a foot, and when he had finished he had a light and portable ladder which would easily reach from his bedroom window to the ground. The staircase creaked so much that he dare not use it. He took the rope upstairs in a suitcase, leaving the case locked in his room.

On the Tuesday afternoon he saw that business took him, not to the snake-house, but to areas from which he could see it. To his mixed relief and disappointment Burnaby did not put in an appearance, which gave him a week's respite, as well as an extra week's suspense.

The next Tuesday he was again on the look-out, and this time he saw Burnaby going to the snake-house. He busied himself in the neighbourhood, and about a quarter of an hour before closing time saw Burnaby leave, as usual by the side door.

To-night, then, was to be the night of his great effort, perhaps the most momentous in George's life. After to-night there would be no drawing back: he would be irrevocably committed.

He did not, as a matter of fact, wish to draw back. Familiarity with Capper's plan had largely removed its horror, while the fear of financial ruin had grown more insistent.

That evening George's dominating aim was to be natural. He must do the things he was accustomed to do, he must speak as he usually spoke, he must not betray the anxiety which was consuming him; he must not, in short, do anything which would enable Clarissa or Miss Hepworth or any other person to say afterwards: "Well, he *was* in an excited condition that night."

When at long last he was able to go to bed, he believed he had succeeded. Conversation at dinner had been normal. After the meal he had read the evening paper for his usual time in the sitting-room, then going, as he so often did, to his study. Later he returned to the sitting-room for a drink, making a few quite ordinary remarks to Clarissa.

But after reaching his room his actions no longer continued normal. First he softly locked his door. Then he changed into the clothes which he had prepared: a black suit, black socks and sand shoes, while he left aside to be assumed later, thin black rubber gloves and a black cap with a hanging mask all round. Then he disarranged his bed, got out an electric torch, and sat down to wait till it was his normal time to turn out the light.

This moment having arrived, he switched on his torch, put out the mains light, and got out his knotted rope. Inch by inch he pulled his window curtains back, opening two adjoining sashes. The window was fitted with lead lights and dividing mullions, and this left a mullion standing clear. Round the mullion George wrapped a cloth, and on the cloth he hooked his rope, satisfied that, thus protected, his weight on the rope would not mark the paint. Then once again he settled down to wait.

As he sat there in the dark, he learnt something about the passage of time which he had never known before. He simply could not have conceived that it could drag so slowly. He would look at his luminous watch, decide he would not do so again for half an hour, and when he did look, find that only four or five minutes had passed. He had read of time passing like that in the case of prisoners: how dreadful for them! He had also read about that converse phenomenon: how for those awaiting execution there was added to these dragging minutes the terribly swift and inexorable approach of the final day. This thought, which had come unbidden to his mind, filled him with a sudden panic. For a few moments he felt physically sick, while a cold sweat broke out all over him. With trembling hands he took out the flask which he had put in his pocket for use in this very emergency, and swallowed a small quantity of the spirit. There was danger here also: he could so easily take too much.

The whisky steadied him and he grew more normal. As he looked out of the open windows he congratulated himself that the weather at least was aiding him. A better night indeed he could scarcely have had. It was dark, but not absolutely black. There was no moon, but the sky was clear and the stars gave just the right amount of light. No rain had fallen for some days and the ground was too hard to show footmarks. Finally, there was just enough wind in the trees to cover up any slight sounds he might make, but not enough to flap his curtains and prevent him leaving his window open.

Over and over again he reviewed what he proposed to do, so that he would forget nothing. It would be easy, he felt sure. He had only to keep his head and all would be well.

Except for a telephone call on the previous Tuesday, saying in an innocuous code that he was unable to despatch the snake, George had not communicated with Capper since the vital interview at which the affair had been agreed on. That call, he told himself, would be the last. To-night would finish his part in the affair.

At long last the hands of his watch drew on to half-past one, zero hour for his operations. With a look round he crept noiselessly to the window, climbed out, and lowered himself to the ground.

His immediate danger was now the night watchman, though as he knew the man's rounds, he felt he should be able to avoid him. Without incident he reached his office, let himself in, and took from his safe certain articles which he had prepared: a tiny phial, a Pravaz syringe, a special tongs consisting of a leathern loop at the end of the stick for picking up a snake by the neck, and a screw clamp of a novel kind. Carrying these under his coat, he let himself out of the office and crept silently towards the snake-house.

His nerves were on edge and twice suspicious sounds sent him crouching behind shrubs. But these proved to be false alarms and he reached his goal unobserved. Safely he entered, locking the door behind him.

He had already solved one of his major problems: which snake to select. It must be small enough to go into a package which could be posted in a letter box, and its venom must be deadly and act quickly. He had decided on the smallest of the Russell vipers. As well as meeting Capper's requirements, these snakes were rather sluggish and comparatively easy to handle. Moreover, there were four of them in the cage, and as they frequently lay coiled together, it was unlikely the keeper would immediately miss the absentee.

Now that he was actually at the critical stage of his operations, George's nerves steadied. From the service passage at the back of the cages he unlocked and slid open the metal door of the vipers' cage, put in his tongs, skilfully slipped the noose over the selected snake's head and drew it out, twisting and wriggling, but held securely by its neck. Then, with the Pravaz syringe, he collected the drops of venom which in its rage and fear oozed from the ends of its poisonous fangs. Having transferred several drops to the phial, his work in the snake-house was done. He looked carefully round to see that everything was in place, then slipped stealthily out and drew the door behind him.

Carrying the writhing snake at the end of the tongs, he crept silently back towards the office. He had been quicker than he expected, the whole operations in the snake-house having taken less than ten minutes. The worst of the affair was now over. He had only to drown the snake and despatch it to Capper and his part of the ghastly job would be done.

Suddenly he received a shock which made his heart miss a beat and brought him up rigid in his tracks.

On the path some fifty yards before him a light was dancing. The watchman was approaching.

The path was edged with herbaceous borders, backed by shrubs. Like a shadow George tiptoed across one of the borders and crouched behind a thick evergreen. He stood in a sweat of fear, scarcely daring to breathe, while the heavy steps came slowly nearer. The snake was hissing angrily and George was panic-stricken lest the man should hear it. However, the steps passed and slowly began to recede, finally dying away in the distance. To George's intense relief that danger was over.

Without further incident he reached his objective, a water barrel at the back of his office. Placing his torch in position, he fastened the clamp to the edge of the barrel, and into its other end he screwed the handle of the tongs, thus fixing the viper's head beneath the water. Snakes were hard to drown and he would have to leave it there for a considerable time.

He was doubtful as to how long. He had assumed it might take an hour, and decided to allow two. In a way it did not very much matter whether or not the creature revived. It could not escape from the box in which he would send it, and he had warned Capper to look out for himself when opening the package.

When at the end of the time he retrieved it, the snake, however, seemed dead. It hung limp and motionless from the tongs. George dried it and carried it to his office. There he packed it in an old tobacco tin, which he knew would pass into a large postal receiver. In the centre of the coils, steadied by cotton wool, he placed the phial of venom. He also made a second parcel of his tongs and clamp.

Now came another dangerous part of the affair. To reach a box with a large enough opening George had to carry his parcel about half a mile towards the City centre, and he mustn't be seen doing it.

In fear and trembling he crossed the gardens, let himself out of the side gate, and hurried noiselessly along the deserted streets. It was by this time after four and some early workers would soon be afoot. However, he was lucky and posted his package unobserved. Once he heard the slow regulation tread of an approaching constable, and made a small detour. When crossing the river he dropped from the bridge his parcel of appliances. As they sank into deep water it seemed to him that with them the last chance of discovery disappeared.

With a feeling of overwhelming relief he got back to the gardens unseen. It took him only a few minutes to reach his house, climb the rope, draw it up after him, and repack it with his clothes in the suitcase. Then closing the windows and drawing the curtains, he slipped silently into bed, well satisfied with the competent way in which he had carried out his part of the scheme.

At the same time, in the background of his mind a feeling of unease gnawed uncomfortably.

CHAPTER X

VENOM: THROUGH FALSEHOOD

GEORGE slept brokenly and with disturbed dreams, waking with a feeling of depression which he could not understand. For a moment he lay puzzling over the matter, then memory flooded back and he shivered.

To-day would be a terrible day: yes! It could not be long before the absence of the snake was discovered, and then would come his testing time. Earnestly, almost desperately, he hoped he would be equal to it. He turned his programme over in his mind, realising that to act his part convincingly would be no easy matter.

His most difficult period would probably be that he was now entering on: from the time he went downstairs until he received the report from the snake-house. Throughout this period he must be absolutely normal. The news of the disappearance of the snake would naturally tend to upset him, so that after receiving it he need not be so careful. Then, indeed, he should show a certain anxiety.

Another danger would be the fact that he knew too much. If in an unguarded moment he were to mention something that he should not have known, it might mean the end for both himself and Capper. Suspicion was so terribly easy to arouse. The very slightest hint would be sufficient, and suspicion once aroused, investigation would follow as inevitably as day follows night.

Panic began to mount in George's mind. Then resolutely he pulled himself together. No investigation could possibly bring to light his part in the affair. He had been too careful. Even if suspicion were aroused, there could be no proof of his actions. The one thing he still had to do was to get rid of his knotted rope, and that afternoon he hoped to drive out into the country and throw it into a gulley of the Orlop Hills. If it were ever found, it would be assumed that it had been dropped by a climbing party.

He believed his manner was normal when he met Clarissa at breakfast. Fortunately they were in the habit of reading their papers during the meal, he the *Telegraph* and Clarissa the *Mail*. As soon as he could without appearing to hurry, George propped up the *Telegraph* and buried himself in its columns. Though he forced himself to eat and make his occasional remarks with his usual deliberation, he was inwardly in a ferment. When would the alarm be raised? Nesbit, the keeper at the snake-house, would now have been on duty for some time. At any moment the summons might come.

As a matter of fact, George had finished his bacon and was wondering how on earth he was going to swallow anything more, when he realised that the moment had arrived; there was a ring at the hall door bell. He could follow the entire little drama: Jane's footsteps crossing the hall, the sound of the weatherboard dragging over the step, the murmur of voices (heavens! would they never stop talking), then at last Jane's approaching steps and the opening of the room door; her voice: "Keeper Nesbit would like to see you, sir."

"Let him wait," said Clarissa, sharply. "Aren't you going straight over to your office after breakfast?"

"No, no; I'd better see him," George answered. "It must be something in a hurry or he wouldn't have come here."

The maid withdrew and George, with a great effort, finished in a leisurely way his toast and coffee. Then still without hurrying, he rose and left the room. Nesbit was standing, cap in hand, in the hall.

"Sorry to trouble you, sir," he said, urgently, before George could wish him good morning, "but there's a snake missing."

George stared. "A snake missing?" he repeated. "What do you mean, Nesbit?"

"It's gospel truth, sir," the man returned. "One of the Russell's vipers. We have four, as you know, and there were four yesterday. There are only three this morning."

George allowed himself to look impressed. "Good God! A Russell viper! How did it get out? Was the cage open?"

Nesbit shook his head vigorously. "No, sir, everything was closed up just as usual. The house locked up and the cage padlocked, all just as usual."

George tried to appear sceptical. "But, damn it all, man, that's impossible! You've made some mistake."

"I'm certain sure it's gone, sir," the man declared, doggedly. "Come and see for yourself."

"I'll go this moment. What have you done? Have you taken any steps?"

"I locked the snake-house door, so as it couldn't get out into the grounds. Then I went round to the office, but I couldn't see anyone about. I thought you ought to know at once, so I came on here."

George became more serious and two minutes later they were walking across the gardens.

"I can't understand this at all," George said, in puzzled tones, as they paced along. "Tell me, are you sure it didn't escape from the house when you went in?"

"I don't think so, sir. Of course, I wasn't looking for it, but I'm sure I'd have seen it if it had."

George nodded. Enough had come out to allow him the luxury of looking anxious.

"Look here," he said suddenly, "we'll have some nets in case the chap's loose in the house. Come round to the office. There's Milliken," he went on pointing to the figure of the head keeper which suddenly appeared from behind the lion house. "Tell him what's happened and let him get one or two more to give us a hand."

Nesbit rejoined him at the snake-house door. "Now see that the chap doesn't escape while we're going in," George went on. He was finding a strange pleasure in playing his part. He tried hard to forget what had taken place and to believe that a Russell viper was really loose in the house. Already he had found that this was the best way of getting his stuff across.

Looking sharply about him, George stepped up to the cage and glanced in through the glass. "You're certainly correct about the number there," he said presently. "There are only three. Now let's find how the fourth got out."

The two men passed round from the public window to the service passage behind.

Though George spoke in this way he knew, and he knew that Nesbit knew, that escape was absolutely impossible. The cages were built of reinforced concrete—monoliths, in fact—with embedded in the concrete a double sheet of plate glass to the front or public side. At the back or service passage side there was an opening about six inches above the cage floor, some nine inches by a foot in size. This was closed by a sliding steel door, rigorously kept padlocked. Some distance above the door there was a service inspection window, sealed with glass. The roof consisted of a lid, normally kept shut.

The vipers could raise themselves only a short distance above the floor. Escape for them was possible in two ways only. Had the sliding door been left open or had both sheets of plate glass been broken, they could have got out, but in no other way. They could not possibly have reached up either to the service window or to the lid.

"The door must have been open," George said, shortly. He tried it. "It's fastened now all right. Did you close it when you came in this morning?"

"I tried it to see that it was fast, and then I opened it and closed it again to see that it was working," Nesbit answered earnestly. "Everything was exactly as you see it. I'll swear it."

"I'm not doubting you, Nesbit." George straightened himself up and spoke gravely. "But if you didn't open it, someone else did."

The keeper made a gesture of bewilderment. "I know, sir. That's what gets me. I don't understand it at all."

Knocking came suddenly at the door and Milliken and another keeper, Moon, were admitted. They also carried nets.

"We want to find this blessed snake and get it back in its cage before someone's bitten," George told them. "It may be somewhere about the house."

Half an hour later the four men ceased their labours, all looking exasperated and puzzled.

"It's not in the building, sir," Milliken voiced the general opinion.

"No," George agreed, "I'm afraid we must admit that. And so the question arises, Where is it?"

"Well, if it's not here," began Milliken and stopped.

"Yes, Milliken?"

"I was going to say it must have got outside, sir, only it seemed a fool remark."

"Perhaps," admitted George, "but pertinent all the same. I'm afraid, Nesbit, the chap must have slipped out when you opened the door. It wouldn't be easy to see."

"I'm sure I'm very sorry, sir," Nesbit apologised, "but I hadn't an idea that it might be loose."

"Of course not," George returned pleasantly. "You've nothing to reproach yourself with. All the same, the affair opens up some nasty questions. How did it get out of a perfectly constructed and properly fastened cage? Where is it now? What are we to do? I think we may drop the first two questions and concentrate on the third. Has it occurred to you that if this snake is at large in the grounds, the gardens are not safe?"

"I've been thinking that, sir," said Milliken. "The staff should be warned."

"Quite. Nesbit and Moon, will you go and do it now. Better tell everyone to come to the office and we'll organise a proper search. Let's see," George continued, as they trooped out and Nesbit locked the door after them, "it's now nine-thirty and the gates open at ten. We've got to decide whether we hadn't better close down for the day."

"I was thinking that too, sir."

George already knew what he was going to do, but he thought it better to advance his ideas gradually, as if they were just then occurring to him. He knew perfectly well that if a dangerous snake really had escaped, the public could not be admitted. He also thought that the public should be told the reason, though this would be a good point on which to consult his chairman, Colonel Kirkman, and thus bring him early into the affair. Accordingly on reaching the office he rang him up.

The colonel was aghast at the news. "But, good heavens, Surridge," he declared, "this is incomprehensible. If the cage was as you describe, the snake *couldn't* have escaped."

"I agree with what you're suggesting," George answered. "But we must leave that for the moment and concentrate on trying to recapture the snake. I'm organising a search of the grounds and I've decided, with your approval, to exclude the public till it's found. Question is, shall we tell the public the reason?"

For a moment there was no reply. Then the colonel said he would come round immediately and they could discuss the point.

Keepers and groundsmen of various kinds began to troop in, and George divided them into squads and apportioned areas of search. One by one they left to begin work, and George turned to Miss Hepworth and told her to type notices for the gates, stating that the Committee much regretted that owing to the unfortunate escape of a snake, the Zoo would, as a precautionary measure, be closed till its recapture was effected.

George was immensely relieved to find that all this activity had removed his sense of panic. By now he almost felt that the snake really had escaped, and he made every effort to carry on as if this were the truth.

Colonel Kirkman, the Chairman of the Corporation Zoo Committee, arrived at five minutes to ten and approved George's notices. These were at once put up and instructions were issued for the gates to be kept shut. Then, with Nesbit and Milliken, George led the Colonel to the snake-house and they again examined the vipers' cage.

Only one conclusion was possible, and as George and the Colonel returned to the office, they no longer avoided the issue.

Kirkman opened the ball by asking George if he didn't agree that someone had deliberately let the snake out.

"I may as well admit," George answered gravely, "that my preliminary examination convinced me of that. As a matter of fact, that's why I rang you up, and I'm only waiting your approval to call in the police."

Kirkman looked at him. "You take it as seriously as that?" he asked. "Well, I think you're right. Will you ring up?"

George did so and the Colonel went on: "Sit down and let's discuss this for a moment. Someone has either stolen the snake or let it loose. Why? What possible motive could there be?"

George shook his head. "I don't think there could be any motive," he declared. "I should say it was the act of a madman."

"A madman who was able to get into the snake-house: in other words, who had the keys. Who could have had the keys, Surridge?"

George had some slight belief in thought transference, and now he concentrated his mind on Professor Burnaby. At the same time he declared that, so far as he knew, no unauthorised person could have had access to the snakes.

Kirkman did not reply and George again fixed his mind on Burnaby.

This time it actually worked. Kirkman leant forward and spoke more confidentially. "What about the old professor?" he asked, meaningly. "He had keys, hadn't he?"

"Yes," said George, "but he gave them up when his permission was rescinded. He retained only a key of the door to Calshort Road."

The Colonel lowered his voice still further. "He could have had them copied before returning them?" he suggested.

George shook his head. "Physically possible, perhaps," he admitted, "but I can't see the old man doing it. He was a man with a code, and I'm perfectly convinced it wouldn't have allowed him to steal keys."

"That's my own idea," Kirkman agreed, then after a pause: "What about Nesbit? Suppose it were made worth his while? Do you know anything about the man?"

"Nothing except from his work. But I haven't the slightest reason to suspect him; in fact, quite the contrary. I believe him to be an honest man who wouldn't do such a thing."

"Every man has his price," remarked the Colonel darkly.

"Oh, quite," George agreed. "Even you or I could be suspected. But not on the probabilities, and neither could Nesbit."

"Any other possibles?"

George hesitated. He mustn't answer too quickly. The interview was going well, and it must continue to do so. As he had intended, Kirkman had made all the desired suggestions, while he himself had been against suspecting anyone. His conduct had been that of an innocent and high-principled man, and he felt sure this would afterwards be remembered in his favour.

"There are possibles, of course," he replied, doubtfully. "Most of the men about the Zoo could have obtained impressions of the keys. Milliken, for instance, possesses a set of his own. Someone might have got hold of his or of Nesbit's. But I don't suspect anyone."

"Milliken himself?"

"No, I'm sure he's innocent. He's far too good a type."

A few minutes later two well set up young men arrived and introduced themselves respectively as Detective Inspector Rankin and Sergeant Risbridger of the Birmington City Police. They were competent looking men, dressed in plain clothes and with pleasant straightforward manners. George met them, introduced them to Colonel Kirkman, and calling Nesbit, led the way to the snake-house. As they walked he explained briefly what had taken place.

George was impressed with the way in which they took hold of the affair. They listened carefully, asked one or two pertinent questions, and said they thought they should begin with an examination of the cage.

"I hope the snake is not concealed anywhere about it?" the inspector asked, with a rather wry laugh. "We're not proposing to take on the job of keeper, you know."

"If you can find it, you'll lift a weight off our shoulders," George returned. "But I don't think you need worry. We made a very careful search."

George was further impressed with the officers' devotion to duty. They were clearly terrified that at any moment a death-dealing speckled band should flash from some unsuspected hiding place. But they never hesitated. While obviously hating the job, they pushed on with it steadily.

For the third time that morning the cage of the Russell vipers was subjected to a careful inspection. The door and padlock Rankin tested for fingerprints and was disgusted when he found that Nesbit had handled them that morning.

"Destroyed a chance of getting the thief's prints, you have," he said, reproachfully. "I suppose those *are* yours? We'll get yours in a moment and check up."

The investigation passed on to the house generally. The entrance door was powdered and the resulting prints were photographed, as well as those on certain handrails, wall surfaces and other places on which an unwary thief might have laid a hand.

"I shall want now to check up these prints with those of your staff," the inspector went on to George. "Perhaps, sir, less objection might be raised if you would set the example. May I have yours to start with?"

George agreed with readiness, remembering thankfully his rubber gloves, and the others followed suit.

"Next I want statements from all concerned," continued the inspector. "Perhaps we might begin here with Keeper Nesbit's. Will you, Mr. Nesbit, tell me all you can about this affair?"

Nesbit repeated his story. The first thing he did on coming on duty was to inspect the snakes to see that all were in order. He had as usual started at the door and worked along from cage to cage. Everything was normal till he reached the Russell vipers and there he saw that the snakes seemed disturbed. They were moving restlessly about, instead of being coiled up motionless, as he expected to find them. He saw at once that one was missing. It was then that he had made the investigations which had so aroused the inspector's ire. He had not delayed to make any further search, but had at once gone to inform Mr. Surridge.

"And what, sir, did you do when you obtained Keeper Nesbit's report?" Rankin asked George, and when George had detailed his activities, he went on: "I think that's all we want in the snake-house for the present. Perhaps, sir, you could let us have a room with a table?"

"Come to my office," George invited.

"I think if you, sir, and Colonel Kirkman would come in, the others could wait outside," the inspector went on, when George had installed him at his own desk. This sounded ominous and George braced himself to meet the bad time which might be coming. He had just the one thing to guard against: not to know too much.

"Now, gentlemen," Rankin went on, while the sergeant at the end of the desk prepared to write, "the Zoo and what takes place in it is a sealed book to me. I'm therefore depending on the help of your special knowledge. But before we go on to details I want to put one question. I want to know if you think this snake escaped?"

George looked at his chairman.

"You'd better answer," the latter suggested. "You know more about it than I do."

George shrugged. "Well, inspector," he answered, "I put it to you. Do you think we should have applied to the Criminal Investigation Department of the City Police if we had?"

"That's what occurred to me," Rankin admitted, "though," he smiled pleasantly, "if you'll excuse my saying it, I'd rather have the direct form of reply. What exactly did you suspect?"

George still answered for his chairman. "It was obvious to both of us that the snake could not have got out of its cage unaided, and therefore that it was assisted by human agency. Beyond that we did not go."

"But you must have thought of something?"

George shook his head. The inspector looked disappointed.

"Oh, come now, sir," he protested, "I hope you'll do better than that. Any suggestion would be helpful and I shouldn't abuse your confidence."

"I suppose," George answered, with a show of unwillingness, "it's possible that through some carelessness the cage was not properly closed after its last opening, and this morning Nesbit realised it and did what was then possible to repair the error. But I want to say distinctly that I don't believe this to be true. Nesbit is a reliable man of excellent character."

"Supposing your suggestion correct, how would the snake have escaped from the snake-house?"

"That's a different matter. They're very quick-moving creatures, and if it were anywhere near the door when it was opened, it could easily have shot out unseen."

"I should like Nesbit's record."

This was obtained from the file and supplemented with George's impressions. Then Rankin passed to another subject.

"I should like a list of all those who had access to the snake-house and were in a position to open the cage, apart from any question of motive."

"Practically the whole staff, beginning with myself," answered George. "Three of us have keys of the building, myself, Milliken, the head keeper, and Nesbit. But I dare say anyone could get one of these men's bunches and take impressions of the keys."

"The keys we'll come to later. Now, supposing this affair was neither carelessness nor accident, can you suggest a motive for, firstly, letting the snake escape, or, secondly, stealing it?"

George glanced at the Colonel, then shook his head.

Kirkman moved uneasily. "Well," he said, and then stopped.

Rankin turned to him. "Yes, sir?" he said, invitingly.

"Hang it all, Surridge," went on Kirkman, "we'll have to tell the inspector about Burnaby."

"Yes, of course," George returned, with an expression of mild surprise, "I propose to tell him everything. But I don't think his question led to Burnaby."

"I'm not suggesting anyone's guilty," Rankin pointed out. "I'm only trying to get the facts."

Without any attempt to hide or colour, George told him what was relevant about the professor. While Rankin did not seem impressed, he was careful to get down all the details.

"And just what was your theory, sir?" he went on, turning to Kirkman.

"Theory? I've no theory," the latter returned, unhappily. "But you can see the suggestion of the facts for yourself. Here is this old man, anxious to get venom for his experiments. Owing to his breakdown in health, mental as well as physical, the permission for him to work with the snakes is withdrawn. Well, does anything occur to you?"

"You mean he may have stolen the snake to get the venom?" the inspector suggested, imperturbably.

"He wouldn't need to," George put in. "He could get all the venom he wanted for the asking. Besides, the old man has a strict moral code and I don't believe he would do such a thing."

"That may well be," Rankin admitted. "All the same, I'm obliged for the hint. Has any other motive occurred to you?"

George and his chairman shook their heads.

"Well, one occurs to me," Rankin went on, a little grimly. "A parcel through the post." For a moment a hand seemed to clutch George's heart, then it relaxed as the man continued evenly: "The recipient opens it and——" He shrugged. "If this snake isn't found soon, I'm afraid we'll have to consider whether anyone in the Zoo wished an enemy out of the way."

Again the hand closed on George's heart.

It was beginning.

CHAPTER XI

VENOM: THROUGH MURDER

NEITHER George nor Kirkman replied to Rankin's disquieting suggestion and the inspector, after a short pause, continued: "Do you think that's impossible?"

George, with a confused idea that attack is the best defence, answered at once. "I may admit, since you ask me, that the same idea had occurred to me. But I have no reason whatever to believe it."

"I'm not saying it's true myself," Rankin agreed, "but we mustn't overlook the possibility. One thing, however, is certain: until we know more about it we must treat the matter as serious."

"Your presence shows that we have done so," George reminded him.

"Quite so, sir, and it must excuse my questions. Now one or two points: I'll start with the keys. You and Keepers Milliken and Nesbit have keys of the snake-house. Beginning with yourself, will you please tell me how you ensure that no one gets access to them?"

George absently took a cigarette from his case, as an afterthought handing it to Kirkman and the officers. Kirkman took one, but the inspector declined on the ground that policemen did not smoke on duty. The little incident seemed to George a pointer to the fact, real for all its concealment, that he and this civil-spoken man were deadly enemies; that unless he, George, could lie sufficiently convincingly to deceive him, he literally would have George's life. George crushed back the thought as he answered.

"I need scarcely tell you that I realise the potentialities of these keys and am correspondingly careful. I carry them in my hip pocket and change them into whatever suit I am wearing. At night I leave them at the head of my bed."

"Do you ever lend them? I mean, it's easy to say to someone, 'Here are my keys. Get me such a thing from such a drawer.'"

"I never do that and I'm careful never to leave them about. But since we're on the subject, something did happen which I'm rather ashamed of. On," George took his diary from his pocket and slowly turned the pages. "I'm not sure of the exact day," he went on, "but it was between ten days and a fortnight ago. I went over to see my friend, Mr. Mornington, who's been ill. He lives in Calshort Road, and my direct way was through the Zoo side door. I don't know if you noticed it, not far from the back of the snake-house?"

"I noticed it, sir."

"On my way back I very stupidly left my keys in the side door. I don't remember anything about it, and this explanation is not what I know happened, but what I afterwards thought must have. I had opened the door to enter, when a car drew up at the footpath, and the driver asked me if that was the road to Bursham. I went over and explained the route, then returning to the office. Presently I wanted to open the safe, and when I felt for my keys, they weren't in my pocket. They were found where I told you, hanging in the lock of the side door. I presume I had left them in the door when I was called to the car, and simply forgotten about them. This is the only case of mislaying them I remember."

"How long were they left hanging in the lock?"

"Oh, quite a short time: little more than half an hour."

Inspector Rankin rubbed his nose. "I'm glad you mentioned it, though speaking offhand, I don't think it's likely to help us.

If this thing is not an accident, it was carefully thought out beforehand. But no one knew that you were going to leave your keys in the door, and no one could have been prepared with material to take impressions. Now another point. What about the relations of the staff? Any feuds or hatreds raging?"

"Obviously," George returned, "I can't answer that exhaustively, but so far as I know, there are none. We all get on amicably, and I think the men are as pleasant to each other as they are to me."

"Any grievances?"

"I'm sure there are, but none of importance that I know of."

"Anyone dismissed recently?"

George hesitated. An appalling thought had suddenly shot into his mind. He had been so skilful that he knew he himself could never be suspected. But suppose someone else was? Suppose the police fixed the crime on Cochrane? What would he do then? He couldn't allow an innocent man...

He quickly pulled himself together. Cochrane was innocent and no one could therefore prove him guilty. To cover up the slight pause, George took out and slowly used his handkerchief. "One dismissal a few weeks ago," he answered. "That could have nothing to do with it."

"Probably not, sir, but I'd like particulars all the same."

George gave them. He admitted that Cochrane seemed to consider his treatment unfair, and also that in his capacity as night watchman he might have been able to obtain impressions of the keys, both of which statements were strictly accurate.

"Now, sir, can you tell me anything else that might help me? Any theory you may have, even if you can't prove it?"

George really didn't think he could. He was very anxious to help, as for his own sake and the Zoo's he wanted the affair cleared up as quickly as possible, but the circumstances seemed to him inexplicable.

"And you, sir?" Rankin turned to the chairman.

Colonel Kirkman was unhappily no more accommodating, and the inspector went on to ask for the evidence of members of the staff.

When George had arranged this, he and Kirkman went out to see how the search was progressing.

In accordance with George's instructions, the men had begun by throwing a cordon round the grounds. These were bounded everywhere by roads, and a few watchers were sufficient to see that the snake did not cross these plain surfaces. The others then formed a line across the gardens, and starting at one side, were pushing gradually through to the other.

"It seems to me," said George, to his chairman, "that it's going to take the whole day. The little beggar might be anywhere. The one blessing is that it's not a tree climber. But it doesn't follow we'll get it on the ground. It might have gone down any of the drains, for instance."

"Your cordon ensures that it's in the gardens at all events."

"No, it doesn't really," George returned. "It might have crossed the road before the cordon was set there. It might be *anywhere* now. And there is the chance, of course, that Rankin is right and that it was stolen to murder someone."

"I don't like to think of that," said Kirkman, with a shudder.

George shook his head. "The whole thing is damnable," he declared. "There's the danger: half a dozen people may be bitten before the brute's caught. There's the drop in our prestige for letting a dangerous reptile escape into a crowded neighbourhood. And there's the loss of revenue: we can't do without our daily gate. It's the worst thing that's happened since I've been in charge. I don't pretend it hasn't worried me greatly."

"I don't see that you could do any more than you're doing," put in Kirkman.

"I'm grateful to you for saying so. However, things may not be so bad as we fear. They may find the chap at any moment. Of course, that wouldn't end it. There'll be a nervousness among the public which will be reflected in our receipts for many a day to come. Can't blame them. I'm going to clear my wife out till the beggar's found."

As soon as they had seen the workers, Colonel Kirkman left the gardens and George went home to carry out his threat. "You must be out of the house in half an hour's time," he told Clarissa. "These chaps are dangerous. It'll be frightened and it'll go for anyone it sees. Take rooms at the Midland, or somewhere, and I'll join you later."

George wondered what he should do at lunch-time. If he went down town his walk would constitute a gap in his alibi. Besides, would it not look better to remain in the gardens during the search? On the plea, therefore, of maintaining a line which the snake could not cross, he arranged with a firm of caterers to serve a plain meal at the "front." He himself stayed with the men, thus safeguarding his alibi and strengthening his reputation as a good employer.

All the afternoon the work progressed, until just as it was growing dusk the entire gardens had been covered. George exhibited a growing dismay as the unexamined area grew smaller, and as soon as it was finished he rang up Kirkman, asking him to come round for a further consultation. The Colonel was out, but he appeared about seven.

"We've done our level best," George told him, in the presence of Milliken. "We've searched everywhere. We've even torn up drains and pulled away brickwork from narrow corners. Could we have done more than we have, Milliken?"

Milliken agreed that no search could have been carried out more thoroughly.

"And that means?" queried Kirkman.

"One of two things, as far as I can see," George answered. "Either the chap got across one of the roads before we put our men out, or else the inspector's suggestion is the truth."

"If the inspector's right, we'll hear about it before long," Kirkman said, gloomily.

George nodded. "That's unhappily true, and of course if we hear, all our problems are solved. But I'd like to discuss what we should do if we don't hear. Shall we, for instance, open to-morrow?"

"What do you feel about it yourself?" Kirkman asked.

"I shouldn't do so," George answered decisively.

"While I don't believe the snake is in the gardens, we can't be *absolutely* sure. If a visitor was bitten, we'd be ruined for years to come. No, I should wait for another day or two."

"I think you're right."

"And to-morrow I shall repeat the search."

"I think you're right again."

"Very well," said George, "that's settled. Will you tell everybody, Milliken? And without making much of it, you may hint there'll be extra money for a dangerous job."

The head keeper saluted and went out, and George turned to his chairman.

"I don't know what to do myself to-night," he said wearily. "I don't altogether like to leave the place, and yet there's nothing

I can do here. I moved my wife down to the Midland. That house of ours is too much in the danger zone."

"Quite right. I don't see any point in either of us staying. If you like to join your people, my car's at the gate and I'll run you down on my way home."

George smiled. "That would be a really friendly act," he declared. "Thank you, I'll go."

George was truly grateful. This was the thing of all others he had wanted, company from the gardens to the hotel, a continuation of his alibi. And not he, but Kirkman, had suggested it. Splendid!

"Why not stay and have a bit of dinner with us now you're here?" he went on as they reached the Midland. "I know Mrs. Surridge would be delighted."

The Colonel looked at him. "As a matter of fact, I should be glad to," he answered. "Mrs. Kirkman's in London and I'm all alone."

It was nearly eight when they sat down and getting on for nine when they returned to the lounge for coffee. But before it arrived George was called to the telephone. He hurried off, and when he heard the message his heart seemed to lose a beat.

"Good God!" he ejaculated. "Dead!" He paused, fighting his emotions, then went on, "Colonel Kirkman's here. We'll go round at once."

George had no need to screw his features into an expression of surprise and horror as he beckoned Kirkman out of the lounge. He felt both, more intensely than he could have believed possible.

"That was Marr," he said in a low, strained voice. "He has bad news. He rings up to say Professor Burnaby is dead—from snake-bite! I told him we'd go round at once."

The two men looked at each other in an awed silence. Then Kirkman made a sudden gesture. "Burnaby!" he ejaculated. "So it was Burnaby after all! Though I suggested it to Nesbit, I didn't really believe it myself."

George looked—and was—deeply moved. "Nor did I," he answered slowly. "I didn't think he had it in him." He paused and shook his head. "But it shows how far gone the poor old fellow was. A year ago such a thing wouldn't have happened."

"It justifies our withdrawal of the permission."

"I never had any doubt about that."

Kirkman shook his head. "Where did it happen?" he asked.

"At Marr's apparently. Marr rang up from his own house."

"Well, I'm at least glad it wasn't in the Zoo."

"Yes, that would have been even worse," George admitted, with some impatience. "But shouldn't we go over? I told Marr we would."

Dr. Marr's little place, "Rylands," was at the other side of Liverham Avenue from the Zoo, and some hundred yards to the left of the main entrance, just opposite where Calshort Road ran off at right-angles. As they approached the gate a car swung in.

"The police," said Kirkman. "I saw Rankin and that sergeant of his as that street lamp shone on them."

Since the news of the tragedy fear had once again filled George's mind: a greater fear even than before. For the first time he was up against the unknown. He had no idea what Capper had done. Capper seemed to be efficient, but no man is infallible. If he made a mistake, it would not be his own neck only that would be in danger. If Capper had made a slip—the thing seemed to hit George like a physical blow—he, George, might be hanged! A cold sweat of terror came out over his body as he realised that this was not a mere theoretic contingency, but a very real and pressing danger. Fighting to control himself, he stepped out of the car.

"Rylands" was a long, low, old-fashioned house, which had been built years before the city had swept into its maw what had then been woodland country. At one time the house had been the centre of a little estate of some dozen acres, but various encroachments had taken place, and Marr was now well satisfied to have retained a tenth of the original area. The door lay open and a bright light streamed out from the hall on to the two cars and the shrubs behind. George, who was no stranger, entered without knocking. Marr's voice came from a room to the right. As George hesitated, Marr himself moved across the doorway and saw him.

"Come in, Surridge," he invited. "Come in, Colonel. You know Inspector Rankin, I suppose?"

"This is a terrible affair," George said, as he followed his chairman into the doctor's waiting-room. "Is he really—dead?"

"Oh, yes. I could do nothing. He was unconscious when I saw him and died shortly after."

"Where did you find him, Dr. Marr?" Kirkman put in, a little testily. "Perhaps you would tell us something about it? We have heard no details."

"I was just telling the inspector," Marr rejoined. "I may tell that little bit again, inspector?" He turned towards the new arrivals. "It was cook who found him. It's her evening out and she was starting off when she found him lying on the drive. At least, she saw a figure; she didn't then know who it was. She rushed back, screaming for me, and I hurried down to where he was lying: just inside the gate. He was stretched on his face with his head pointing towards the house. I could see him clearly in the light of a street lamp. I turned him over and realised at once it was Burnaby. As I said, he was unconscious."

"And then, sir?" queried Rankin.

"Then," said Marr, "I carried him in and laid him on the couch in my consulting-room. I examined him, and I saw his right hand was swollen. Further inspection showed in the palm what I took to be the marks of a small snake's fangs. I had heard, of course, of all this fuss at the Zoo over an escaped snake, and it seemed to me that there might be a connection. I treated him as best I could for snake-bite, but unhappily he was too far gone, and he died in a few minutes. I immediately rang up, first, Burnaby's nephew, a man called Capper, and then yourself, inspector. I had heard you, Surridge, had moved to the Midland, so I 'phoned you there, thinking you might be an interested party. We are fortunate in having Colonel Kirkman also."

"Very fortunate, sir," Rankin returned, politely. "Do I understand you to say that the death was caused by snake-bite?"

Marr seemed suddenly to awake to his duties as host. The five men had been standing in the middle of the room, but now the doctor indicated chairs. "Won't you sit down," he invited. "Take the side table, inspector, if you want to write. I'll get you drinks presently. I expect we could all do with them."

They absently seated themselves and Marr went on. "You were asking if it was death from snake-bite? Officially, I'm not satisfied. Privately, I haven't the slightest doubt, but officially I must wait for a post mortem."

Rankin nodded understandingly. "You were in some danger when you lifted the deceased, were you not?" he went on. "You didn't see the snake?"

"No, I didn't, and I didn't suspect its existence till I had carried the body in."

"We'd better have a look at the body. Perhaps Mr. Surridge can tell us whether the fang marks might belong to the escaped snake. I understand they vary considerably, Mr. Surridge?"

Though he knew that this was coming, George felt a horrible spasm of fear. Then it passed and he heard himself speaking in his customary tones.

"Fang marks naturally vary according to the size of the snake. The Russell's viper which escaped was a small snake, less than three feet long. The marks would be fairly close together."

"How close, sir? Could you form an opinion?"

George shook his head. "I don't think I could say exactly. Less than half an inch, I should think."

"Well, let's see what they're like at all events."

They trooped next door into the consulting-room. On the couch lay the body. To his relief, George found he could look at it with reasonable calm. The eyes were closed: the doctor had probably seen to that; and the face was peaceful enough. If the old man had suffered, no traces remained in his expression. The right hand was swollen, and when Dr. Marr turned it over, they could see the two little wounds in the palm. They were less than half an inch apart.

"Do you think those might have been caused by the snake which escaped?" Rankin asked, and George, when he replied that he believed so, was able to show just the right amount of feeling.

Then suddenly George saw that he was on the verge of making a terrible mistake. As head of the Zoo, one idea, and one only, should be paramount in his mind. The recapture of the snake! And he had forgotten it! He hastened to amend his error.

"Excuse me, inspector, but there's one matter that can scarcely wait for your investigation. I mean the recapture of the snake.

This affair shows it's alive and not far away from where we're sitting."

"I was coming to that, sir," Rankin returned, civilly, "but a few moments' discussion won't make much difference now, and may save time later." He turned to Marr. "Can you give us any help, doctor, as to when the accident might have occurred?"

Marr shook his head. "I should have to look up authorities," he returned. "The professor died about twenty minutes to nine. Probably, though this is rather a guess, he was bitten about half an hour earlier."

"Say a few minutes past eight?"

"Yes, subject to correction."

"Good enough for the present. Now another question. Where do you think the accident might have taken place? I take it, not necessarily on your drive?"

"You mean the professor might have walked to where he was found after being bitten?"

"Yes; is that possible?"

"I think so. But as to how far he might have walked: well, that's more difficult. What do you say, Surridge?"

"I couldn't tell," George returned, "except that Russell's vipers are very deadly and the poison acts quickly."

"Again speaking subject to correction, I imagine he could scarcely walk for more than about five minutes after being bitten."

"And he certainly couldn't do more than seventy or eighty yards a minute. That means he must have been bitten not more than a quarter of a mile from here?"

"Less, surely," suggested George.

"Less, I fancy," Marr agreed, "but we cannot say to a yard."

Rankin nodded. "I appreciate that, sir. Now another question. Were you expecting the deceased to call?"

Marr lit a cigarette. "No. It would have been a most unusual thing for him to have done."

"Then can you account for his being found on the drive?"

"I imagined he had been struck somewhere nearby and was coming to me for professional help."

The inspector looked at George. "You knew the deceased, Mr. Surridge. Would that appeal to you as likely?"

George thought it must be what had taken place.

"Now," went on Rankin, whose methods seemed to George slow, if unpleasantly sure, "perhaps we could go a step farther. Where, within a quarter of a mile or less, might he have come from?"

George calculated mentally. "It's about two hundred and fifty yards to his own gate and, say, three hundred to his hall door. And it's a little under two hundred yards to the side door of the Zoo."

"That's helpful, sir. He might have come either from his home or the Zoo. And on the probabilities I should say from his home. Does anyone know his usual movements at home?"

Beyond the fact that Burnaby usually spent the evenings reading in his study, no one did.

"Then it seems to me I must start work at his home," Rankin concluded, closing his note-book. "Now, doctor, what about a post mortem?"

"There's something more urgent than that," George reminded him. "What about a search for the snake?"

"I suggest, sir, that you're the best man to undertake that. If we can help you, we shall be glad to do so."

"I'm afraid we can't do very much in the dark," George pointed out. "I might get a cordon round the place, though even that won't be easy. Let's see, just what would we have to include?"

Rankin looked from one to the other. "I don't know the place very well," he was beginning, when Marr cut him short.

"To be any use, you'd have to surround that whole lot of houses from this road up to Mornington's. How many are there, Surridge? Mornington's is the last. Beyond it there's a lane running from the road to the river and connecting with the path along the bank."

"Eight or nine certainly," said George. "The frontage must be nearly four hundred yards."

"Yes, I should say about that," Marr agreed.

George rose. "I'll fix it up," he promised.

A few moments later the little gathering broke up, George leaving to get out his search party, the inspector and his sergeant to continue their inquiries at "Riverview," and Marr to start his detailed examination of the body.

CHAPTER XII

VENOM: THROUGH DECEIT

HEAD KEEPER Milliken lived some half mile from the Zoo, and thither George took his way. He was feeling shaken from the strain of the interview which had just taken place. But though his limbs ached with weariness and he was slightly tottery about the knees, he had at the same time a feeling of immense relief. The learning of Burnaby's death was by far the worst ordeal he would have to face. Now that was over, and well over. Looking back on all he had said and done, he thought his conduct had been beyond praise. At no single point could the slightest suspicion have been aroused.

In one way it had been unexpectedly easy. It had not been hard to show surprise, because he had been surprised. He had no difficulty in exhibiting horror, because he felt horror. He could ask for details with an appearance of ignorance, because he was ignorant. He was, in fact, completely puzzled by the whole affair. What *had* Capper done? The snake was dead and could not have bitten Burnaby. Capper must therefore have had a second snake, a live one. Why had he wanted the dead one?

As George paced along, gradually the answer occurred to him. Capper had not wanted a dead snake or a phial of venom. What Capper had wanted was a hold over George which would prevent him from ever giving away what had been done.

Well, he had certainly got it. Whatever part the sending of the snake had played in the affair, George had sent it and he could never shuffle out of his responsibility. With all his relief at the way things were going, he felt that responsibility like a physical weight on his shoulders.

But he must not, he felt, think of that. To do so would be to unnerve him, and he wanted all his nerve for what was coming. Banishing, therefore, all thoughts save those of the immediate present, he reached Milliken's and told him the story. Once again he was delighted by the natural and unsuspicious manner he achieved.

"I'm sorry to hear it, sir," the head keeper answered. "I've known Professor Burnaby now for the most of five years and I always thought him a fine old gentleman. Very civil and pleasant spoken he always was, and generous too. I'm sorry about it and I'm sorry for the way he went. But, of course," he added, after a pause, "he didn't ought to have taken the snake."

George started. So absorbed had he been in his own part in the affair that he had actually overlooked this point of view. Why of course! What a fool he had been! Capper's plans had been better than he had realised. If Burnaby had stolen the snake, the affair would naturally be dismissed as an accident. No hint of any second person being involved would arise. As Capper had said, the thing was *safe*, absolutely safe!

But he must not unduly support this theory. "We can't say that definitely," he answered, judicially, "though I admit it looks like it. But the police will soon clear it up. In the meantime what we're concerned with is the snake. It must have been within quarter of a mile of Dr. Marr's gate at eight o'clock. Now I'm not on for searching in the dark, but I think we should cordon the roads."

"Right, sir," Milliken returned. "You say the word and I'll get the men out."

Some half-hour later the Burnaby-Mornington block was surrounded by keepers with flares placed where they considered the street lighting insufficient. George thought it right to warn the householders to keep their doors shut and not to go out in the dark without a torch, and this he did personally.

It was getting on to eleven when he had finished and he felt ready to turn in. But more powerful than his fatigue was his anxiety to know what Rankin had discovered. For once discretion and desire pointed in the same direction. He walked over to "Riverview" in the hope that the man might still be there.

Rankin appeared to expect him. "I thought you'd be round," he said, in a friendly way which George found very comforting. "We haven't cleared up everything, but I don't think there's much doubt on the broad issue. I'm afraid the poor old gentleman had only himself to thank for what's happened."

"Then you think he took the snake?" asked George.

"I think so. Mind you, I can't prove it as yet. But it looks that way."

George strove hard to suppress his rising feeling of jubilation. "If it's a fair question," he went on, "what have you found out?"

"Nothing that won't come out at the inquest," the inspector returned. "When we got here we found the house empty. Sergeant Risbridger happened to know the maid, Lily Cochrane by name, and went to find her. She explained that she was only a day maid and left every evening at six. But she put him on to where he would find Mrs. Pertwee, the housekeeper, and he brought her back. Wednesday's her evening out and she had carried on this evening as usual.

"She said the professor had dined this evening at his ordinary time of seven, and had been quite normal in manner. He always went on Wednesday evenings to his friend, Mr. Leet, to play chess, coming home about ten. She went out herself as soon as the dinner things were washed up, which was about eight, and she wasn't expecting to return till half-past ten, by which time the deceased was usually on his way to bed."

"He was always an early man," George put in.

"Is that so? Well, that's what she said. When she left he was still in the house, but she supposed he was going out. I may say that she was very much upset about the old man and a bit incoherent, though—" Rankin's eyes twinkled as he continued—"it wasn't till she understood the snake might be loose in the house that she woke up properly. Her employer's death became pretty small beer to her then. She had her skirts up round her knees and was making for the door before I had finished my sentence, and it was only by telling her that it would be more dangerous outside that I got her to finish her story. Then I went with her while she packed a few things and Sergeant Risbridger saw her to an hotel."

"Then the professor didn't go to Mr. Leet's?"

"While Risbridger was out with Mrs. Pertwee I went round to inquire. Mr. Leet lives, as you probably know, in the next house to Mr. Mornington, the first beyond the lane to the river. Leet was properly horrified at the news; said he'd been expecting the deceased for their game of chess, but he hadn't turned up. Leet said he half thought of going round to 'Riverview' to find out if anything was wrong, but the professor didn't always go for his game: only if he felt like it. Leet didn't suppose it was more than that."

"And what do you think happened?" George asked, as the inspector came to an end.

"We can't say in detail yet, but I expect a search of the house will tell us. I'm assuming the deceased had been looking at the snake before going out, and had somehow let it escape from its cage, and got bitten. Then see the fix he'd be in.

He was alone in the house and I suppose he couldn't treat himself, and he evidently thought his best plan was to get over to Dr. Marr's as quick as he could. Quite natural, too, I should say."

"Couldn't he have telephoned?"

"No, he couldn't. That was the first thing I asked. It appears he had answered the telephone at the time of his daughter's accident and some fool had blurted out without any preparation that she was dead. That had put him off telephones, and he had had his removed."

"A bit drastic, surely," George commented.

"He was old," Rankin pointed out, in the tone of a man making generous allowance for his fellow's frailty.

George pondered the story. "Was the house door open or closed?" he asked presently.

"Closed."

"Do you think, under the circumstances, he would have closed it? Wouldn't he have just hurried off without bothering about it?"

"A good point," the inspector approved. "I thought of that. But I don't agree with you. He was an unselfish man, I understand, and his thought, even in the emergency, would be for others. The snake, I assume, was loose in the house. He would close the door to keep it in."

"You may be right," George agreed. "And you haven't searched the house?"

Rankin shook his head. "There hasn't been time," he pointed out. "All the same, I think it would be safer to wait till daylight. And I was going to suggest," again the suspicion of a smile appeared in his eyes, "that your men would do it more skilfully. It really isn't our dirty work, you know."

"I expected that," George answered. "As a matter of fact, I've already arranged for this entire block to be done as soon as it gets light. But I thought that this house should be taken first, and I was going to speak to you about it."

"Right, sir. That's fine. Now, I expect you're tired. My car's outside. Can I run you wherever you want to go?"

Half an hour later, George, having consumed a comforting double whisky, was stepping into bed in the Midland Hotel.

His relief at what had taken place was little short of overwhelming. Poor old Burnaby was dead, and his death, as Capper had promised, had been rapid and almost without pain. His money was already virtually Capper's. Capper, at least, could raise a comfortable sum on his expectations. And part of that sum would come to him, George. Within a few days at least George's financial worries would be over.

Still more important, all this had happened without arousing the slightest suspicion. It was clear that Rankin had made up his mind on the case. He believed Burnaby had stolen the snake and had an accident with it. How clever, George thought again, had been Capper's plan! How amazingly clever that all the false suggestions required should have been made, not by Capper nor himself, but by the police!

But, George reminded himself, he was not yet out of the wood. It was still true that one unguarded word, one indication that he knew more than he had been told, might give away the whole affair. Profoundly satisfied though he was, he saw that he could not for one moment relax.

Next morning he was out early with his men. Those who had been on duty all night, he sent home with orders to turn out again in a couple of hours. All the rest who could be spared from the closed Zoo he set to work in Burnaby's house. The search was to be absolutely exhaustive, and if no find was made, the party was to move on to the grounds.

He stayed with the men for some time, then went for breakfast, and from that to the office. Though this business of the snake must be treated as of vital importance, the Zoo itself could not be entirely neglected. Two days' correspondence made a sizeable pile, and though Miss Hepworth had done her best, a great many matters required George's personal attention.

About eleven he went back to help the searchers. He found them working next door to Burnaby's. They had completed the house without result, and then, going to the lane, had started a drive through Mornington's ground. In another half-hour they would be through the hedge and on Burnaby's half acre.

George worked with the others, his presence encouraging them, and the fact that he was willing to share this dangerous job adding to his prestige. He kept on reminding himself that he must show eagerness, though, as he knew they would find nothing, this grew harder and harder. Then he received another surprise.

They had worked through into "Riverview," and all instinctively redoubled their efforts. Every inch of the ground was covered, every pile of rotting leaves turned over, the base of every shrub and plank examined. Then suddenly one of the keepers gave a cry.

George hurried over. The man was gazing down into a water barrel which stood against the side wall of the house, close to the french window of Burnaby's study. He had run most of the water off, and on the bottom, almost invisible against the dark wood, lay the snake.

"At last!" cried George, trying to exhibit satisfaction instead of the astonishment he felt. "Thank goodness we've got the brute! Milliken!" he shouted. "We've found it! You may call off the search."

The keepers, ceasing work, moved across and crowded round the barrel.

"It looks to be dead, sir," Milliken exclaimed, as he peered in.

"It certainly does," George agreed. "But we'll run no risks. Someone get a tool and lift it out."

A rake was speedily forthcoming and the snake was hoisted from the water. It hung limp from the crossbar, and when it was dropped on the grass it remained motionless.

"That's it all right," said George. "What do you say, Nesbit?"

"That's it, sir," the keeper pronounced. "Thank heavens, the place is safe again."

"Better get it secured in case it revives," George advised. "You brought a cage, didn't you?"

A box had been provided for emergencies, and the snake was fastened up. "Bring it along to my office, Milliken," George went on. "You other men get off home and be back at your jobs by two o'clock. We'll reopen after lunch."

George was absolutely delighted as he considered this last factor of Capper's scheme—however the man had arranged it. The finding of the snake's body at Burnaby's house was the one thing needed to clinch the accident theory. No one could now doubt that the professor was the thief. The discovery would be hailed by Rankin as proof of the theory he already held, and because it was his theory he would hold it more tenaciously than ever. The objections of others he would brush aside. In fact, further inquiry would be eliminated and the case would be closed. George felt he need be anxious no longer. The wretched business was as good as over.

There ensued a somewhat hectic half-hour. George telephoned the news to Rankin and Kirkman. He asked the various newspapers to exhibit it on posters at their offices, as well as prominently in their next issues. He arranged for the whole cumbersome machinery of Zoo service to be put once more in motion. Lastly, he rang up Clarissa at the Midland and told her she might return home.

He would have given almost anything to be in similar touch with Nancy. Nancy would certainly have read of the disappearance of the snake, and would no doubt be anxious about him. How he longed to reassure her! How desperately he desired to see her! But he realised that any communication with her was out of the question. The slightest deviation from the normal would be dangerous. The police were apparently satisfied, but one could never be sure of them. They might talk the friendliest platitudes and yet be watching his every move. Not for a long time could he risk another expedition to Rose Cottage.

Nor, what was worrying him even more, could he get out to the Orlop Hills to dispose of his rope. As long as that was in his suitcase he would be in danger. He wondered, could he not destroy it in some other way? He thought it would burn, though probably it would take a very hot fire. But Rankin might come in when he was burning it, and that would be worse than ever. Perhaps he could weight it and drop it into the river, but there again, if he were seen, a grab would bring it up, and once again he would be for it.

Rankin, in reply to his message, had asked him to attend an informal inquiry at "Riverview," taking with him the snake, and at three o'clock he went across. Besides the inspector and Sergeant Risbridger, he found Marr and Professor Blaney-Heaton, of the local university, whom he knew as a real authority on snakes.

"I congratulate you on your find, sir," Rankin greeted him. "It has ended a very difficult situation for all concerned."

"For everyone, whether concerned or not," George retorted, thinking he might now exhibit better spirits. "The poor old viper mightn't have confined its attentions to those working on the affair."

For a few moments they chatted, and then Rankin proceeded to business. After an inspection of the snake, he continued: "I wanted everyone to see just where it was found, in case we might get something from the position. Also if we can learn how it was killed."

This was by no means reassuring. If a detailed inquiry were intended, it didn't look as if Rankin was so satisfied as George had supposed.

George led the way to the barrel. "It was in here," he pointed.

"Then was it drowned?"

"I presumed so," George answered, "as I could see no other cause of death. But I couldn't, of course, be sure from casual inspection. They're not easy to drown, you know. They swim and it takes a long time."

"That's one of the things I wanted to ask. How long, would you say?"

George shook his head and looked at the specialist: "I should scarcely like to say. Perhaps Professor Blaney-Heaton could tell you."

Blaney-Heaton awoke from a reverie in which he seemed sunk. "Couldn't say either," he declared. "As Mr. Surridge says, they swim, but they do drown eventually."

"I'm speaking only very approximately. Might it be one hour or six or twelve?"

"I don't know. I should guess six, but I won't stand over that. Would you agree, Mr. Surridge?" Blaney-Heaton blandly returned George's compliment.

George shook his head with a faint smile. "We don't experiment on those lines at the Zoo," he explained.

"I suppose not," Rankin agreed drily. "What I wanted to get was the approximate time at which the creature fell into the pool. I presume that's the time it would take to drown plus the time it was dead before it was found. I hope you gentlemen can tell me that."

"We haven't made a proper examination yet," Blaney-Heaton pointed out, not unreasonably.

"When you do, sir, will you keep the point in mind? Next, I take it, it couldn't have got in itself? It must have been put in deliberately?"

Blaney-Heaton shook his head. "That depends on what you mean by deliberately. Suppose the snake attacked you and you managed to catch it by the neck. How would you get rid of it? You might throw it away in a moment of unreasoning terror. It might fall into the barrel."

"That's interesting, sir. If it was thrown in unhurt, could it have got out?"

George realised how very critical was the question, and decided to answer it. "I should say not possibly," he declared, and was delighted when Blaney-Heaton emphatically agreed.

After some further discussion, Rankin closed the session. "That's very helpful, gentlemen," he approved. "Now, what the police would like to know is, first, what caused the snake's death?

and, second, when did it get into the barrel? I think that's all, unless you find something unexpected when you make your examination. I'm much obliged for your attendance."

Feeling like a schoolboy dismissed at the end of lessons, George returned to his office.

CHAPTER XIII

VENOM: THROUGH THE LAW

THE inquest was to be held at ten next morning in a hall not far from the Zoo, and a few minutes before the hour George left his office to walk across. No formal subpoena had been served on him, but he had promised Rankin to be present. He had heard nothing more about the affair since the interview at "Riverview," which he took to be a good omen. Further, he felt sure he was not being shadowed or watched. He banished morbid thoughts and held his head high as he reached the hall, looking forward to what was coming with confidence.

The affair had aroused a good deal of popular interest, and the hall was full. Rankin and Risbridger were already there, and Marr and Blaney-Heaton came in almost at once. Milliken and Nesbit had been summoned and were in their places, while Mrs. Pertwee and Lily Cochrane, the "Riverview" staff, were seated close by. Capper was there also, and George, in the hearing of Rankin, offered him formal condolences on his loss. Behind were members of the general public, persons unconnected with the case, but who exercised their rights as British subjects to be present and enjoy a morning's free entertainment.

George took his place beside Marr. "I suppose," he said, "there's nothing fresh since our meeting yesterday?"

Marr thought there was nothing that George didn't know. He was beginning a discussion on Burnaby's state of health when the coroner entered and he broke it off.

Mr. Herbert Finlater, coroner for the City of Birmington, was a tall, lanky individual, whose side view, presenting his bent head, narrow chest, and protruding abdomen, inevitably suggested a query mark. His face was drawn and dyspeptic-looking, apparently mirroring a sombre outlook on life, but George had heard that he was an able lawyer and highly competent at his coroner's job. He nodded gloomily to Marr and Rankin, bowed to the company generally, and took his seat.

Certain preliminaries followed. Finlater announced that he had decided to sit with a jury, and six men and one woman were empanelled. They were asked whether they wished to see the body, and said they did, whereupon they trooped off, returning apparently impressed, if not enlightened. Finlater made a dry little speech deploring the tragedy and reminding the jury of their duties, then got down to business.

"Call Marjorie Harper," he directed.

The order was obeyed with hearty thoroughness by his officer and a policeman, the latter seemingly to have the job of master of ceremonies. Marjorie Harper George recognised as Marr's cook. She came forward, slightly flustered by all the shouted repetitions of her name, and, having been sworn, was motioned to a chair facing the jury.

She had not a great deal to tell, and nothing which George had not already heard. Wednesday was her evening out, and on leaving the house she saw the body on the drive. She ran back and told the doctor. She was able to fix the time at exactly 8.21. She had looked at the clock in the hall as she started, as she was hurrying to catch a bus which passed the Choole Bridge at 8.25, a distance from the house of some three minutes' walk.

Marr was the next witness. He also had glanced at the clock in the hall as he ran out, and it was just twenty-three minutes past eight. He described his recognition of Burnaby, his carrying him to the couch in his consulting-room, and the efforts he made to save his life. These, unhappily, were unavailing, and the old man passed away about twenty minutes to nine. In reply to a question, he admitted he was not an expert in the treatment of snake-bite, as that was a contingency which had seldom to be met by English practitioners. He had not, however, believed that any of the other local men were in a better position than himself, so he had not called in a second opinion. Indeed, there had scarcely been time. He was glad, however, to be able to say that Professor Blaney-Heaton had expressed himself as satisfied with everything he had done.

"We're not questioning your treatment, Dr. Marr, which, I'm sure, was all that could be desired," the coroner assured him mournfully. "I only want to get the facts. What happened after that?"

Marr explained that when once he was satisfied that he could do no more for Burnaby, he had rung up the dead man's only relative and the police. As he had known a snake was missing from the Zoo, he had assumed that it was this snake which had caused the tragedy, and had also rung up Mr. Surridge. Inspector Rankin, Mr. Surridge, and Colonel Kirkman, who happened to be with Mr. Surridge, quickly arrived, and the inspector took charge of the case.

"Quite so," said the coroner. "We'll get that later. Now, Dr. Marr, can you tell us the cause of death?"

"Shock following poisoning through being bitten by a venomous snake."

"How did you reach that conclusion?"

"Firstly, the symptoms were those of snake poisoning. Secondly, external inspection showed the marks of a snake's fangs in the right palm near the base of the first and second fingers. The hand also was swollen and discoloured, as might be expected. Thirdly, a post mortem confirmed the diagnosis on every point, and also revealed that, while the deceased was in a poor state of health, there was nothing functional to account for his death. I may say that Dr. Hawthorn assisted me and expressed agreement with my conclusions on every point."

"Did you actually find snake poison in the body?"

"Yes, we did."

"Now, Dr. Marr, you say that the deceased passed away at about eight-forty. Can you tell us at about what hour the snake must have struck him?"

"Not, I am afraid, with any degree of exactitude. The results of a bite vary enormously. If a healthy person is treated immediately, death need not necessarily ensue at all; whereas in the case of a victim elderly and in poor health, it would probably follow quickly. Again, a great deal depends on the bite itself: if much or little venom is passed, or just where the fangs penetrate. If, for instance, venom were introduced into an artery, the effect would be more rapid."

"In the case of the deceased, can you go nearer than that?"

"The deceased was elderly and in poor health. Also, the post mortem showed he had received a large quantity of venom. My opinion, therefore, is that death would have taken place quickly, though exactly how quickly, I'm not prepared to say."

"Would you consider it possible that it should have taken in as little as half an hour?"

"Yes, I should say that was possible."

"Quite." The coroner turned to another point. "Were you this old gentleman's medical attendant?"

"I was."

"Will you tell the jury something of his condition of health, both physical and mental?"

Marr hesitated, as if to collect his thoughts. "I'm afraid it wasn't very good," he began, going on to give a detailed reply. Up till a few months previously Burnaby had been physically very fit for a man of his years, and of course his intellect was outstanding. Lately, however, this condition had much deteriorated. He, Marr, attributed this to a shock he had had when his daughter had been killed in a motor accident. He would not say the mental deterioration amounted to what was commonly called softening of the brain, but he did mean that the old gentleman was no longer able to meet the small problems and crises of everyday life in a normal manner.

"Then in your opinion he might recently have acted in ways which some months ago he would have avoided?"

Marr thought so.

"Do you consider this applied to moral standards also?"

Marr said that was a more difficult question, but finally admitted that he believed there had been a moral weakening corresponding to the physical and mental change.

Professor Blaney-Heaton followed. He went more learnedly into the matter of the snake and the effects of snake-bite, but except on one point his statement was merely a confirmation of what Marr had said.

"Did you see a manuscript on the treatment of a certain disease with snake venom?" the coroner went on.

The professor inclined his head. "Yes," he admitted, "such a manuscript was shown to me by a police officer."

"This police officer?" persisted the literally-minded coroner, pointing to Rankin.

Blaney-Heaton inspected Rankin coldly and admitted his identity.

"Were you able to discover the aim of the deceased in his work?"

"Yes, he was apparently trying to cure cancer by injections of venom."

"Can you tell me whether a person carrying out such work would have required to perform experiments with snakes?"

The professor could not express an opinion. The experiments would naturally involve the use of snake venom, and he thought it was possible that in special cases the actual use of snakes themselves might be required.

George could scarcely contain his satisfaction as he listened to this interrogation. The line the coroner was going to take was now clear. An admirable case was being built up for the theory that Burnaby stole the snake and was afterwards bitten. George could have wished nothing better.

The coroner then turned to the snake itself. "Have you examined the body of a snake which was found in a barrel close to the deceased's study door?"

"Yes, I made a post mortem of it."

"And what can you tell us about it?"

"It is that of a female Russell's viper, three feet one inch long, and was in a good state of health. It had died as a result of drowning. Its neck was somewhat bruised and swollen, presumably from being held in a snake tongs."

"Do you consider the snake was alive when it fell or was put into the barrel?"

The professor shrugged. "The reptile was found dead in a barrel of water, the cause of death being drowning," he pointed out. "I think, sir, the jury are as capable as I to form a conclusion."

"Now, professor, in your opinion could the snake have got into that barrel accidentally?"

"I don't think it could have got in by itself, if that's what you mean. But"—and Blaney-Heaton outlined the suggestion which he had put up to Rankin on the previous afternoon.

"Are you satisfied that once in the barrel, the snake couldn't have got out?" went on the coroner.

"Quite satisfied. These are not climbing reptiles and it would necessarily have been drowned."

"From all that, then, professor, is it your theory that the deceased was threatened by this snake, caught it in his hands, was bitten, and either accidentally or intentionally threw it into the barrel?"

Blaney-Heaton made a gesture of slightly horrified dissent. "No," he answered, with scientific caution, "I have only said that in my opinion that might have happened. What did happen I don't know."

When the professor left the witness chair, Mrs. Pertwee took his place. She introduced a human interest into the proceedings which up to now had been markedly absent. Her sorrow for her employer was obvious, as also her desire to defend his memory against all attacks.

Briefly she told of her own connection with the household. She had been engaged as cook when the family moved to "Riverview" some five years before, and on Miss Burnaby's death had been promoted housekeeper. The professor had been one of the best and kindest of men, and while he had his health, was extremely good-humoured and able. The loss of his daughter had unfortunately broken him up and recently he had not been himself. He had become absent-minded and forgetful and the smallest things had become a burden to him. She had lately been afraid of his experimenting, fearing he might set himself on fire or hurt himself in some other way.

She then told of his Wednesday evening visit to Leet. On the evening of his death he was in a perfectly normal state of mind and mentioned that he intended going as usual for his game of chess. It was her evening off, and after she had washed up the dinner things she had gone out. She had actually left the house at five minutes past eight, and as she did so she had seen the professor in the hall. She could not say that he was getting ready to go out himself, but she had thought so at the time. Her help, Lily Cochrane, came during the day only, and as she had gone home, there was no one except the professor himself in the house.

"Now tell me, Mrs. Pertwee," went on the coroner, "did you ever know the deceased to keep snakes in the house?"

Mrs. Pertwee exhibited horror at the very idea. The professor had never done any such thing.

"What makes you so sure of that?"

The witness bridled. "A gentleman like him would never have brought one of those horrible creatures into a civilised house," she explained, with indignation.

"No doubt you are correct," the coroner admitted, with unexpected tact, "but if you have any actual proof of the statement I should like to hear it."

She had none. She had never seen a snake, but she had to admit that there were boxes in the professor's study into which she had never penetrated and which, she eventually agreed, "might have contained anything." Certainly the professor had all kinds of queer instruments and bottles and little pipes of glass, and worked a lot with his chemicals and what not. Mice he had, too: three large cages of them, and a few guinea-pigs. But these latter were kept outside.

Leet then gave his evidence. He explained that he was a novelist and had known the deceased for many years. He had an extraordinarily high opinion of him, not only as a brilliant investigator and scientist, but as a man of integrity and great kindness of heart. He had, however, to agree with the evidence which had already been given about his decline of health.

Leet then went on to tell of the evening in question, repeating his statement to Rankin about expecting the professor for chess, his not turning up, and Leet's considering whether or not he should walk over to "Riverview" to learn the cause.

Inspector Rankin was then called. He was very efficient and professional, giving his evidence concisely, and answering just the questions he was asked and no others.

He described his call to the case and summarised his discoveries. Every sentence he uttered delighted George. Though he didn't say it in so many words, he made his own opinion clear. Burnaby, he obviously thought, had stolen the snake and been bitten by it, and as the easiest way of getting rid of it, had dropped it into the barrel. Hope that this terrible episode in his life was over and might be forgotten, was rapidly giving place to conviction in George's mind.

To those present Rankin's evidence conveyed little which they had not already known or guessed, and George's was the next name called. As he moved forward to the witness chair he reminded himself that he was now in deadly danger, and that if he allowed his growing optimism to make him careless, he might find himself trapped.

The coroner, however, handled him with gentleness and consideration. Under his suave questioning George explained that he had been director of the Zoo for eleven years. Under the Corporation Committee he was in supreme command of all departments and head of the entire staff.

He went on to give the history of the late professor's negotiations with the Committee, leading to the very unusual facilities which had been granted him in connection with his research. The Committee had acceded to the deceased's request, as they appreciated the value to mankind of the discovery which he believed was all but within his grasp. For five years the professor had worked with the snakes, during which time he had shown such care and skill as completely to justify the confidence placed in him. Then his health had deteriorated and he had lost his nerve. He, George, had therefore, with regret, recommended his Committee to withdraw their permission, and this was done. The deceased still spent some time in the snake-house, but never again, so far as George knew, had he personally interfered with the snakes.

Questioned further, George said that in his opinion the escape of the snake was utterly impossible, and that the reptile must have been deliberately withdrawn by someone who had both the keys and the necessary technical knowledge. This led to questions about keys, and with contrition George confessed his own lapse in the matter of the side door.

"What keys had the deceased?" went on the coroner.

"When enjoying his full facilities, he had keys of the side door of the Zoo leading to Calshort Road, of the snake-house and of certain cages, including that of the Russell's vipers. When the facilities were withdrawn, he gave up the keys of the house and cages, but out of regard for his feelings he was allowed to retain that of the side door."

"Do you happen to know whether the snake which we are to-day discussing was of a type with which the deceased was experimenting?"

George stiffened suddenly as he sensed danger. This was a point he had entirely overlooked. To have made his case water-tight he should have chosen such a variety. For a split second he hesitated, then he hedged.

"I'm afraid," he said, "I can't answer that question, except in the general way that he was trying all kinds of venom. Whether he was working on that particular variety at the time of his death, I don't know."

It seemed all right. At all events the coroner did not press the matter, but turned to the question of what other persons might have obtained keys.

This point George had foreseen and replied that it was unlikely in his opinion that anyone outside the staff could have done so, while all of the staff who could were beyond suspicion.

To George's intense relief, this ended his interrogation. After him Milliken was called, and then Nesbit. Both were asked whether other persons could have obtained their keys long enough to take impressions and both strenuously denied the possibility.

Nesbit was the last witness, and when he stood down the coroner shuffled his notes and addressed the jury. Again, as George listened, relief and satisfaction swelled up in his mind. If he himself had been making the speech, it could not have been more to his liking.

"You have, members of the jury," Finlater said, after a few preliminary remarks, "four distinct questions to answer. First, you must declare, if you can, the identity of the deceased; second, what was the cause of his death; third, was that death due to accident, suicide or murder; and fourth and lastly, was any person to blame, and if so, who?

"With the first and second of these questions I do not think you will have much difficulty. A number of witnesses have identified the remains as those of Professor Matthew Burnaby, and nothing has come out in evidence to throw the slightest doubt on their statements. Secondly, you have had direct medical evidence that death was due to the bite of a snake and to nothing else, and here again no alternative has been suggested. So far the case seems straightforward.

"When, however, you come to the third and fourth points, you are on less firm ground. Let us for a moment consider the issues raised.

"A snake disappeared from the snake-house in the Zoo. The first thing I think you will have to decide is, did that snake escape, or was it deliberately removed? Here you have heard the evidence of three experts, all of whom have told you that escape was impossible. If, then, it was deliberately removed, the further question arises, Who took it out? Now upon this point you may either give your opinion, or you may decide that you have received insufficient evidence to reach one.

"In this connection I think you should consider what motive might exist for removing the snake. You might, for example, think that the deceased himself took it out for experimental purposes in connection with his researches. This would be an act of theft, and you would have to balance the probabilities as to whether a man of the deceased's character would have performed such an act. Here you would take into account what you have heard about the deterioration in the deceased, due to shock and ill-health. You might also consider an alternative:

whether, in view of the extremely beneficial results to humanity resulting from a solution of the deceased's problem, he might not have considered that so large an end justified a slight deviation from the path of perfect probity." The coroner looked faintly pleased with himself as he delivered this alliterative gem. "Further, you have to consider whether a man in the professor's state of health would have been physically able for the deed. You would, of course, bear in mind that if you accept this theory, the difficulty about the keys vanishes, as the deceased could have kept duplicates.

"But before you could accept this theory, you would have to satisfy yourselves that it is in accordance with the remainder of the evidence. If the deceased took the snake, what did he do with it? Did he put it in one of the boxes we have heard of? If so, what happened? Did it escape? Did he grip it and drop it into the barrel outside his study?

"If you reject this hypothesis, you must consider who else might have abstracted the snake, and for what purpose? And, of course, again you must explain how the deceased came to be bitten and the snake to be drowned.

"All this will lead you to the third question you have to answer. Was the death due to accident, suicide or murder?

"Of these, I think you will probably dismiss suicide. If the deceased had wished for death he would surely have committed the deed in the snake-house. Why should he go to the trouble of carrying off the snake, when all he had to do was to put his hand into the cage? Further, the evidence of Mrs. Pertwee as to the deceased's frame of mind and of his intention to go to Mr. Leet's, you will probably consider tells strongly against suicide.

"The possibility of murder you will weigh carefully. Could anyone have stolen the snake and so arranged matters that it would have bitten the deceased as he left, or was about to leave his house? This person, you will remember, must not only have had keys of the Zoo, but also of the deceased's house, and he must have known intimately the internal arrangements of both. What person or persons in this case had all that knowledge?

"Further, if you support the theory of murder, you must find someone who had a motive for the deceased's death. I do not think evidence of that kind was put before you.

"You will probably then come to the conclusion that there is no evidence for murder, and if so, it leaves accident as the only possibility. You must settle, then, in your own minds whether the theory of accident harmonises with all the other facts that you have learnt.

"Lastly, if you were satisfied that anyone was to blame for the accident or suicide or murder, you should say so. You must understand that you need not go out of your way to find a culprit. You need only mention any person if he or she seems to you obviously guilty.

"Now, if there is no question you wish to put to me, you will please retire and consider your verdict."

The jury were not long in reaching a decision. Fifteen minutes after they had trooped out, they trooped in again, and they gave the verdict which after the coroner's address had seemed inevitable. They found that Professor Matthew Burnaby had met his death accidentally while handling a dangerous snake, and that no blame attached to any other person.

CHAPTER XIV

VENOM: IN THE MIND

GEORGE found his relief and satisfaction almost overwhelming as he walked back to his office after the inquest. The knowledge that the affair was over and done with, and that no terrible consequences would follow, intoxicated him. He wanted to dance and sing and treat everyone he met to drinks. But sternly he took himself to task. Though the danger was apparently over, it remained latent, ready to spring into vigorous life on the slightest inadvertance on his part. Never again could he completely relax.

At the same time he should show a certain pleasure at the rehabilitation of the Zoo management in the public mind. The fact that Burnaby had stolen the snake—for so the man in the street interpreted the finding—showed not only that the Zoo was not responsible for the affair, but that the danger of a repetition was non-existant. George allowed himself a distinctly cheery bearing as he congratulated his staff.

A couple of days of his ordinary routine convinced him, if further proof were needed, that he personally was not under suspicion. Everyone spoke to him normally and he was sure that no unhealthy interest was being taken in his movements.

On the evening of that second day he hired, he hoped for the last time, the N.J. Gnat, and drove with his rope up to the Orlop Hill. It was a fine night, lighter indeed than he could have wished. Anyone could have seen him, had anyone been there to look, but few people were about at such a time and he felt reasonably secure. From another point of view the light was an advantage, as the rocks in the craggy canyon in which he wanted to hide his embarrassing trophy were dangerous for climbers.

He carried out his plan without difficulty, dropping the rope into a practically inaccessible gully. He had been careful to undo all the knots, and after a couple of wettings there would be nothing to suggest the rope had been used for any purpose but rock climbing. Nor if by some miracle it were found, would there be anything to connect it with himself.

Greatly eased in mind at having destroyed the one remaining piece of compromising evidence, George returned home with the intention of settling down to a normal and blameless life.

He was completely puzzled by the whole affair: quite as much, he thought with a grim smile, as the police. What, he asked himself again and again, had Capper done? Obviously he must have had a second snake, because both Marr and Blaney-Heaton were satisfied Burnaby had died from its bite. Where could he have got it? Such creatures were pretty difficult to obtain, even by the authorised representative of a Zoo, and for a solicitor in the Midlands to buy one through the ordinary channels would be approaching the impossible. He must, George supposed, have had some oriental friend who had managed the matter for him, and this fact doubtless suggested the entire scheme.

George's curiosity grew more and more overpowering, till at last he could bear it no longer. A couple of days later he rang up Capper from a call-box, asking for a meeting. Capper was against it, but finally said he was going to Bath on the following Saturday, and if George would be at a certain country road crossing at three o'clock, he could drive with him for part of the way.

George went by train to the nearest station, walked to the rendezvous, and was duly picked up. Capper at once turned on him for forcing the meeting. "Why on earth," he asked bitterly, "couldn't you let well alone? If anyone sees us together it may start a train of thought. The thing's been all right so far: why try and spoil it now?"

Somewhat taken aback, George explained his curiosity. It made Capper absolutely foam at the mouth.

"Of course you don't know how it was done!" he repeated, angrily. "You complete fool, isn't that what you want? I told you before that ignorance was more convincing if it was genuine. Be thankful you don't know, and stay that way."

George was annoyed also, but he could not but recognise that the man was right. "You're not suspected?" he asked, weakly.

This completed Capper's exasperation. "How the hell do I know?" he asked furiously. "Weren't you at the inquest? Don't you know as much about it as I? For heaven's sake, don't lose your wits."

George retorted in somewhat similar vein, then went on to a question of immense, though secondary importance. "When am I going to get any money?"

He expected this would have produced a further outburst, but it had quite the opposite effect. Capper quieted down and replied in his normal tones. "I've been thinking about that. I've already raised a couple of thousand on my expectations, and I want to hand over a thousand to you. But I'm hanged if I know how to do it."

George had also been considering the problem and hadn't discovered any great difficulty. "I was hoping that with your legal knowledge you would have seen a way," he returned, with sarcasm.

Capper made a gesture of impatience. "I see a way all right, but I'm not satisfied that it would be safe. I can't give you a cheque, you know."

"What about notes?"

"If I could get a thousand singles I would hand them to you. But how in hades could I get them without rousing suspicion?"

"Why not tenners?"

"No good. They're traceable."

"I didn't know that."

"Well, it's the fact. The bank records the number of every fiver or over they give out, and who they give it to."

"Then what's your plan?"

Capper shrugged. "I admit I don't like it, but I think the only way is to do the thing openly. You write to me saying you would like to raise some money on your expectations, and asking can I arrange anything. I'll say I can advance up to a thousand and you'll close with my offer."

George didn't like it either. He had hoped to have received notes which no one but he or Capper would have known anything about. So far *nothing* had connected him with the affair, but this would go a long way towards supplying the missing link if there was at any time a recovery of documents. No, he didn't like it at all.

"What's the biggest sum you could give me in singles?" he asked after a pause.

Capper considered. "Not enough to be any good to you," he said at last. "Forty or fifty pounds, I dare say."

This time it was George who did the considering. "A week?" he said at last.

Capper looked startled. "A week?" he repeated, doubtfully.

"Fifty pounds a week in singles," George answered firmly. "It isn't much, but I can make it do. Perhaps fifty this week and forty after that."

For the first time a faint look of admiration showed in Capper's eyes. But he swore he couldn't do it. To increase his expenditure so greatly would make the bank people suspicious.

"Nonsense," said George, who was slowly regaining his confidence. "With all that legacy coming in it would be stranger still if you didn't spend more."

"Yes," Capper grumbled, "if I spent it on anything visible. If I bought a new house or a new car it would be all right, because anyone could see where the money was going. But that's very different from spending money and living in the same way."

"Well," retorted George, "you can draw fifty extra a week and send me forty and make a splash with the other ten. Don't tell me you can't find a way, Capper: you're no fool, you know. And I must have the money."

In the end they compromised. On the following Monday Capper would send to George through the post fifty single notes, and every subsequent week twenty-five more.

George felt extremely disappointed as he tramped to another railway station on his way back to Birmington. Twenty-five pounds a week was a totally different thing from the lump sum of a thousand to which he had been looking forward. He could not now pay off his debts as he had hoped. He could not get the cars for Clarissa and Nancy. He could not buy the title deeds of "Rose Cottage" and get clear of those wretched moneylenders.

Then he saw that he was wrong to grumble. This hitch was entirely for the best. Until probate was granted on his aunt's money no one would expect him to be flush of cash. It was just as well to wait to pay off his larger creditors. The small debts, which really worried him more, could gradually be settled. This would be satisfactory enough and would avoid giving any cause for suspicion.

Things certainly were working out admirably. And yet nothing surprised George so much as the realisation which gradually forced itself into his mind, that, in spite of it all, he was not happy. Beneath the satisfaction of having overcome his immediate difficulties, he was conscious of a fundamental unrest and disquietude of spirit. He was obtaining the material advantage he had sought, but he had got with it an intangible load which seemed to bear him down like an actual weight. He did not realise what this was till a small incident revealed it to him.

One day after lunch he met Burnaby's solicitor, Horace Hamilton, at the club. They began to chat, and their talk presently turned on the deceased professor.

"He was an amazingly kind old chap," Hamilton declared. "I always knew he was liberal, but till I began to go through his papers I had no idea how many people he was helping. He had a good deal of money, of course, and he was using it to boost lame dogs over stiles. There'll be a lot of pretty genuine sorrow for his death."

George murmured something non-committal.

"One fellow in particular I have in mind," Hamilton continued reminiscently. "He'd been a chauffeur and he'd made a break which had lost him his job and a testimonial. Burnaby got in touch with him somehow when he was absolutely down and out, and he was going to set him up with a small van so that he could go round and clean cars and do running repairs at people's own homes. He thought he could build up a little trade that way and make enough to live on. You should just hear that fellow now when his hopes have gone west. And that's only one case of many."

"Perhaps Burnaby's heir may carry out the professor's intentions."

Hamilton shrugged. "He may," he said drily.

It was when George was lying awake that night that he suddenly got a vision from a new angle of what he had done. This harmless, kindly old man was the man that he, George, had killed! These people whom Burnaby was helping were losing their help and their hope through what he, George, had done. And he had done what he had done, not because he was faced with ruin and despair like them—he had no real material needs at all—but because he wanted to amuse himself with a mistress. That, he now saw in its uncompromising nakedness, was the real reason why Burnaby had lost his life, for Capper could scarcely have carried out his plan without George's help. It was for this, George knew, that he had become a murderer. It was for this that he had lost his peace of mind and taken on his shoulders a load from which he never could be rid.

George at last realised the nature of the weight which was pressing him down. It was this knowledge of what he had done, and of why he had done it. He wondered whether he had gained or lost over the venture. He had obtained money, but had he lost the power to enjoy it? He could still meet Nancy, but had he forfeited the joy of her presence? He had arranged the cottage, but had he jeopardised his home? In short, he saw that he had exchanged financial worry for a moral burden. He felt that to all he did there would now be this gnawing background of distress.

Then his mood changed. He told himself that these thoughts of conscience were only unreasoning fear: old wives' tales, nonsense retained in the mind from the false teaching of childhood. In this world, if you wanted anything you had to take it. He needn't be regretful about what he had done. He had only to banish these morbid imaginings from his mind, and he would be once again sane and happy.

But though George sought to convince himself, all the time he knew that the load was there and would be till the day of his death. ...

He was worried, too, about Clarissa. He could not make her out during these last weeks. Her manner towards him had changed. She was colder than before; indeed, she had become icily aloof. She made no pretence of interest in his comings or goings, treating him as a stranger whose unwelcome presence had perforce to be endured. At times he feared that she must somehow have learnt about Nancy; then he felt sure that if she had she would have spoken about it, and he breathed more freely again.

As a matter of fact, Clarissa knew no more than she had gathered from Harriet Corrin's malicious hints. She had dropped the idea of the detective, deciding that unless some new development took place she would let matters take their course without interference. George, she knew, was only doing what thousands of other husbands did, and so long as there was no public scandal she thought she might as well keep her home and outward position. No doubt he would tire of his infatuation, and though her marriage could now never be more to her than a mere business association, she could probably rub along as well as did so many others in a like unhappy state.

George's material outlook, however, now began to improve. On the Tuesday morning after his interview with Capper, an envelope marked "Personal" was lying on his desk. From it he transferred fifty one-pound notes to his wallet. This first fruits of his adventure filled him with satisfaction. Fifty pounds wasn't much; still, it would let him settle one or two of his most pressing accounts, and—splendid thought—there would be more to follow!

The longing to see Nancy had returned, and he wondered whether it would be yet safe to call at "Rose Cottage." He would not, he decided, hire the car any more; that could be too easily traced. His expedition with Capper had given him an idea. There were railway stations within one, two and three miles, respectively, of the cottage. He would use these in turn, walking the rest of the way. From a call office he rang up Nancy and said he would go out the next afternoon.

But this meeting proved less satisfactory than any previously. In fact, Nancy unwittingly gave him a very unpleasant shock.

He had been explaining that his neglect had been due to the extra work at the Zoo resulting from the loss of the snake and the death of Burnaby. Before the true facts had come out, the police had formed a theory of murder. He had believed they were shadowing all connected with the Zoo, himself included, and till he was sure their suspicions had been dropped, he had feared to lead them to "Rose Cottage." It was Nancy's reply which so much upset him.

"The idea!" she said scornfully. "As if anyone would murder that poor old man, and particularly in so horrible a way! Oh, if anyone had done such a thing, I think I'd take pleasure in seeing him hanged."

George pulled himself together. "Don't let's talk about it," he begged. "It's a miserable business. Let's think of something else," and he turned to the breaking-in of the garden, which had grown entirely out of hand.

They dropped the subject, but that evening as George sat in his study Nancy's words returned to him. Nancy, the one person in the world whom he really loved, or thought he did: that one person, if she knew the truth, would take pleasure in seeing him hanged! He had done all this for her—or again, so he thought. He had lost his wife, his self-respect, his peace of mind, for her—and if she were to find out what he actually was like, she would wish to see him hanged!

George felt more alone than ever before in his life. If the truth came out, not only Nancy but everyone, *everyone*, would be glad to see him dead. Clarissa, whom he had once loved and who had once loved him, would be an exception. She would be sorry. But it wouldn't be sorrow for him. It would be for herself, because of the shame and ruin he had brought on her. Him she would curse.

As George sat alone, the thought which had worried him some nights earlier returned. He seemed to see as in a vision, Burnaby, old and feeble, struggling vainly with the snake. There was fear and horror in the old man's eyes; fear and horror that he, George, had put there. Those eyes followed him. Wherever he looked, they were gazing at him—reproachfully. They peered down from the pictures on the walls, they were in the red coals of the fire, they gazed up from the pages of his book. What reproach they held as they stared at their false friend. What sorrowful surprise as they realised what he was.

With an oath George got up suddenly, poured himself out a couple of fingers of whisky, and with only a drop or two of soda, tossed it off. It quickly produced its effect. His mind cleared. The vision of Burnaby and his reproachful eyes faded and his outlook on life grew more normal. He needn't worry, he now saw, over what was past. This old world wasn't such a bad place, after all. Let him enjoy it while he could. And now that he had money coming to him, he could enjoy it as never before.

Absently he poured out a second couple of fingers, added soda, and returned to his chair before the fire. Good stuff, whisky, he thought, as he began to sip it. If you got a bit morbid, it pulled you together. Yes, as long as one had whisky, there was always a way of producing a satisfied body and a contented mind. Wonderful stuff!

Then another thought flashed into his mind and he set the glass down on the table beside his chair. Fool! Fool that he was to think such thoughts! There was no salvation for him in whisky. Fearfully he recalled another effect of alcohol. It loosened men's tongues. God! if he took too much, what might he not say? Better all the morbid and desperate thought that could flood his mind than the risk of babbling out his secret. A word too much and—— He grew cold as what would follow presented itself to his excited imagination in a series of too vivid pictures. The arrest (he had heard they were extremely polite and kindly about arrests, though somehow that would only add to the horror); the waiting; the trial; the waiting again, this time with two warders always there; and then...

George shivered once again and picked up his glass. Then with an oath he flung it into the fire. The glass shivered and the flame fizzed and spluttered. Hell! he couldn't stand this. He would go down to the club and find someone to speak to.

He glanced at the clock. It was too late to go to the club. It was, indeed, past his normal bedtime. But in his present mood he couldn't face bed. He shouldn't sleep and he was better up.

Gradually his mind quieted down. He must, he thought, get off drink altogether. It would be a pretty tough job, but he would have to face it. The first few days would be the trouble, then it would be easy enough.

Then a further thought darted into his mind. Capper! Suppose Capper were feeling as he was: would Capper avoid drink? Would Capper one day take too much and say something he ought not?

All George's fears swept back as he realised that from henceforth his safety, his avoidance of *that*, depended on Capper's abstemiousness. *Was* Capper abstemious? He didn't know.

Something not far from panic gripped George as he realised that his safety was not in his own hands. He must see Capper. At all costs he must see him and get his promise to give up liquor. But what would such a promise be worth?

George once more grew cold as he thought of it. Was this another hideously-contrived trap? If Capper's existence was dangerous to him, only one thing would make him safe.

God, how ghastly! George looked longingly at the decanter, and swore again. He hadn't realised things were going to be like this. If it were to go on, he couldn't stand it. Better to be dead himself. . . .

Once again he sharply rallied himself. All this was just nerves. He was physically upset from the strain. He wanted a holiday. He would soon have this money and then he would take one. He would go off somewhere: to South America or the Cape or—somewhere. And he would take Nancy with him. He would send Clarissa to California, where she had always wanted to visit relatives, and he himself would go with Nancy. He would have a good time and forget all these nightmares.

But though he thought these brave thoughts, in his heart of hearts George knew that never as long as life lasted would he forget—what had happened.

CHAPTER XV
VENOM: IN THE PRESS

WHILE George was struggling with his difficulties in Birmington, events were taking place in London which were destined to have a decisive effect on his life and the lives of a great many others associated with him.

It happened that on the second week-end after the inquest, that on which George had his financial interview with Capper, Chief Inspector Joseph French, of New Scotland Yard, was busily engaged in entertaining a guest. This does not, perhaps, give an entirely accurate picture of the situation, for two reasons. First, it was the guest who was really entertaining French, for Arthur Milliken was an intelligent and well-informed man, with interesting views on people and things and an interesting way of putting them; and, secondly, he was not French's guest at all, but his wife's.

Arthur Milliken was Mrs. French's brother-in-law; he had married her younger and favourite sister. Some years later the sister had died, causing one of Mrs. French's greatest griefs. But by that time both she and French had become fond of Arthur, and when he came to town, as he did every few months, he usually spent a week-end with them.

He was a clerk, was Arthur Milliken, but of a superior type. He was, in fact, chief clerk in the head office of the Winslow and Waterton Insurance Company, of Birmington. He had two brothers, both also living in the city: Peter, our old friend the head keeper at the Zoo, and Charles, who ran a small garage.

They had been chatting for a little time, and Arthur, who had done most of the talking, decided it was time to hear French's news.

"Been busy lately?" he asked, as they reached a pause in the conversation.

"I've just got back from Cornwall," French answered, as he refilled his pipe with the mixture he preferred to all other forms of tobacco. "Been down there for a fortnight. Glad to be back, too."

"A State secret?"

"Not at all. A man was found lying dead on his drive, without a scratch on his body. A post mortem revealed arsenic in his stomach. Problem: how did he come to take it?"

"And did you find out?"

"Suicide, I think. He was elderly and had a pretty young wife, and there was another man, so some of the local boneheads plumped for murder. But I don't think it was. Certainly there was no evidence to convict anyone."

Milliken, in his turn, knocked out his pipe and French pushed over his tin of tobacco.

"A bit of a coincidence your man should have been found dead on a drive," the former remarked, as he helped himself. "It reminds me of a curious case we've just had in Birmington. Rather excited us all really, because my brother Peter was in it up to the neck. I expect you've read about it: the death of an old professor who was working with a snake?"

"I didn't see about it. What was the case?"

French spoke with a polite appearance of interest, though he was feeling a little bored. He wished people would talk to him about anything rather than crime. It was not an extraordinarily cheerful subject at the best, and he got all of it he wanted during working hours. But people seemed to think it was the proper subject to discuss with him, though he was sure that if they only knew how much ignorance they were exhibiting, they wouldn't do it. However, guests, at least, must be humoured.

"He was found on a drive, too," Milliken answered, warming to his task. "That's what put me in mind of the thing. Only it wasn't on his own drive, but on his doctor's. The old boy was experimenting with snake poison," and he went on to give an adequate and slightly humorous summary of the affair.

"An interesting case," French admitted, still conscious of his duties as host.

"Isn't it?" Milliken was gratified at the reception of his tale. "And you know it's a bit of a mystery, too, in spite of the coroner's verdict and all that. A case after your own heart, I should call it."

"Oh?" said French. "How's that?"

"Well, it's only what Peter said, you know. He says he doesn't believe the old josser ever stole the snake. He wouldn't have had the nerve; not recently."

"Then how does he account for it?"

"He doesn't account for it; that's just it. He says the facts that have come out don't explain it and that there must be more to it than we've heard."

"The coroner's jury apparently don't think so."

"That's what I told Peter. But he said the coroner's jury didn't know the old man as he did. He said to steal a dangerous snake would take quite a lot of nerve and old Burnaby just hadn't it. And Peter's a pretty sound man, though I say it as oughtn't."

In spite of himself, French's thoughts slipped back to more than one occasion in the past when he had heard this argument put up by people as a reason for rejecting otherwise obvious deductions. Not so long before he had sat in the police station at Henley and listened to Major Marsh, the local Chief Constable,

declaring that he did not believe the millionaire, Andrew Harrison, had committed suicide, because he knew him personally
and he just wasn't that kind of man. That was the case in which
the millionaire was found dead in the cabin of his houseboat after
suggestive jugglings on the Stock Exchange. On that occasion
the Chief Constable's hunch—or knowledge of psychology—
had been justified and had led to the discovery of a particularly
ingenious murder. It was paralleled, moreover, by several similar
instances. The psychological argument could never be disre-
garded. In fact, the older French grew and the more varied his
experience became, the more weighty he found it.

In this case, of course, it was unlikely to have any significance. The opinion of a chief constable, a man used all his life
to weighing character and its resultant action, was one thing;
that of a head keeper in a zoo was quite another. Peter Milliken
might be all his brother claimed—French had met him and
thought highly of him—but he couldn't have the judgment of a
trained man. Besides, neither the coroner nor police of a great
city like Birmington were fools. If there had been anything
in this argument of Peter's they would have recognised it and
acted accordingly.

"I expect the police went into that side of it," he said easily.
"And they had a doctor, I presume? He would have gone into
it, too."

Arthur agreed. "I don't myself suppose there's anything in it,"
he went on. "It's just that Peter was so sure."

"How on earth would you steal a snake?" French queried.
"It's not a job I should care to tackle myself."

"It seems there's a sort of tongs for catching them: a leather
loop on the end of a stick. You open the cage and slip the loop

over the head of the one you want. Then you lift it out by the neck."

"Not easy, I imagine."

"No, specially if the snake is threshing about, as it would if it didn't want to be caught. I'd rather Peter did it than me."

The more French thought over it, the more heartily he found himself in agreement. It would be a difficult and dangerous job: particularly as presumably the snake must not be hurt. Both nerve and skill would be required.

But if so, was Peter Milliken's belief so very absurd? Could the broken-down old scientist really have accomplished it? French grew slightly more interested.

"What evidence of old Burnaby's condition was given at the inquest?" he asked.

Arthur paused in thought. "A number could have given it," he said presently, "but I don't know exactly who did. There was the doctor, Dr. Marr, and the director of the Zoo, Mr. Surridge, and Nesbit, one of the keepers in the snake-house, as well as Peter. It mightn't exactly be Nesbit's or Peter's place to say anything, but it would be Marr's. If he had thought the old boy couldn't have done it, he'd have said so."

French was not so sure. It would depend on the personalities of the coroner and doctor. If the latter had been throwing his weight about and had been snubbed for it, he might close up on points of opinion and answer only what he was asked.

"What sort of man is Marr?"

"One of the best," Arthur answered, with enthusiasm. "Straight and decent and always out to do anyone a good turn. And very successful in his cases. People like him and trust him and he does them good."

Then he wouldn't be likely to get on his high horse and hold back information on the ground that it hadn't been asked for. It would be interesting to know just what he had said.

"Was the case well reported?"

Arthur smiled triumphantly. "I thought it would interest you," he returned, "and I brought up the *Birmington Times* in case you'd like to see it. The report is pretty full because everyone was interested. There was the scare, you see, that the snake was loose in the town, and if you ask me, most people were really frightened about it."

French nodded. "Very good of you, I'm sure. Yes, I'd be interested to look over it. You don't happen to know if the police have accepted the inquest verdict?"

"I don't. I thought they would do so automatically."

"Not necessarily. But, of course, it's usual."

"Is that so? Well, I can't tell you. I'm not in their inner councils."

Later that evening French read the report. The case appeared to have been well handled by the coroner and the police evidence was just what might have been expected. There was no question of glossing over the deceased's poor state of health: in fact, this was stressed. The point that the old man might not have been able to commit the theft had been made by the coroner himself, and the jury could not have failed to appreciate it. Yet it hadn't weighed with them in bringing in their verdict. Peter Milliken was entitled to his opinion, but in this case he must have been wrong.

French presently dismissed the matter from his mind and turned to his usual Saturday evening pursuits. But that night as he lay awake the affair recurred to him. An unusual case, he thought, and dramatic too. For many people snakes had a kind of morbid fascination, and the idea of this poor old man meeting so horrible a fate alone and in darkness would set the average person shuddering.

French wondered what exactly had happened during that fatal period. Apparently just as Burnaby left, or was about to leave, his house, he was struck. Probably he had been looking if the snake was all right, and in some way had allowed it to escape. Probably again he had caught it by the neck, and the easiest way to get rid of so embarrassing a burden would be to drop it into the barrel. Being alone, he would think his best chance would be to hurry to the doctor's. Yes, this seemed reasonable and was doubtless the view held by the coroner.

French was rather annoyed to find that the affair had taken hold of his mind just as if it were one of his own cases. He could neither sleep nor could he banish it from his thoughts. In spite of himself he continued turning over the facts and weighing their bearing one upon another.

Suddenly a point occurred to him which up till then he had missed, and a faint excitement stirred in his mind as he considered its implications. He switched on his light, and creeping softly downstairs, found Arthur's paper and took it back to bed. Once again he read the evidence. Then after some more thought he put the paper aside, switched off the light, and composed himself to sleep.

On Monday when he had dealt with his letters and reckoned that the Assistant Commissioner, Sir Mortimer Ellison, had done the same, he rang him up and asked for an interview.

"Well, French, what's the trouble?" he was greeted, on reaching his superior's room.

French laid his newspaper on the other's desk. "Have you read that case, sir?" he asked, quietly.

Sir Mortimer looked at him searchingly as he took the paper. "Not in any detail," he answered. "What of it?"

"May I outline the case to you, sir?"

The Assistant Commissioner made a gesture of dismay. "If it's absolutely unavoidable," he breathed gently.

French knew his chief. He grinned appreciatively. "I don't know that it is," he returned, "but I should like to put up a point, if you don't mind."

"I do mind, but a lot you care about that. However, I see you won't be happy till you get it off your chest. Go ahead."

French, well satisfied, went ahead. Long practice had enabled him to condense his stories into the minimum of words. Sir Mortimer sat motionless during the recital, his heavy lids lowered over his eyes as if he were half asleep. But French knew he was anything but asleep. He was aware that he was listening keenly, and that his alert brain was checking up and docketing the facts as he heard them.

"Well?" he said, as French came to an end.

"Just one point struck me, sir. There were no snake tongs found at 'Riverview.'"

Sir Mortimer gave him another exceedingly keen glance and once more dropped to his languishing position. "How do you know?" he asked, presently.

"I don't, of course, know absolutely," French admitted, "but it seems to follow from the facts given. The house was obviously searched by Inspector Rankin, and if he had found a pair of tongs I can't believe he wouldn't have mentioned it. It would have been highly material evidence and of great use in supporting his case."

"There might have been something else."

"You mean some other tool in which the snake could have been carried?"

"Yes: a bag or box or net."

"I should think the same argument would apply. If there had been anything which would have done the job Rankin would have brought it forward."

For some seconds silence reigned. Then Sir Mortimer again looked up. "'Pon my soul, French, I believe you're right. However, don't let's have any misunderstandings. Just put what you mean into words."

"I looked at it like this, sir. To convey the snake from the Zoo to 'Riverview' some apparatus was necessary. I imagine, though of course I can't be sure, that this must have been a tongs, because some way of handling the snake at 'Riverview' would probably have been necessary. Remember also that the snake's neck was bruised from tongs having been used. If I'm right and there was a tongs, and it wasn't found, someone must have taken it away. Who was this? Obviously not the deceased. Therefore someone else was present who did remove it."

"It's not certain."

"No, sir, I admit it's not certain. But I put it to you that it's sufficiently suggestive to warrant investigation."

Again Sir Mortimer remained silent for a moment. "Have you worked out a theory on those lines?"

"To a certain extent, sir; of course, quite tentatively. I suggest someone wanted the old man out of the way, and knowing of his researches, decided he could use a snake with a good chance of avoiding suspicion. This person, I suggest, stole the snake, and——"

"Incidentally you're meeting the difficulty that the deceased hadn't the nerve to do so."

"Quite so, sir. I suggest X stole the snake, and knowing of the old man's chess-playing habits, was waiting for him to set out on that Wednesday night, when, mind you, the house was empty. I suggest he carried the snake in the tongs and held it out towards the deceased, and that it was while the deceased was trying to ward it off that he got bitten."

"It's not a nice idea, French."

"So nasty, sir, that if anyone has done it, he shouldn't get off with it."

"Agreed. Very well: carry on."

"Now think of X's position. He has committed his murder in safety because the old man hasn't seen him in the dark, and in any case will almost certainly become unconscious before meeting anyone. But X has the snake and the tongs on his hands. What is he to do with them?"

"He has already thought of the barrel?"

"I assume so, sir. But that covers the snake only. He will have to decide whether to throw the tongs in too, or remove them. I believe he finds himself forced to remove them. His whole object is to suggest that the deceased allowed the snake to escape from whatever receptacle he was keeping it in, and leaving the tongs in the pool would give this idea away. If he could leave the tongs in the house beside the snake's receptacle it might help him all right. But he probably is unable to get into the house or perhaps doesn't know where the snake has been kept."

"And motive?"

"We don't know it. But my informant tells me the deceased was well to do and someone must have stood to gain by his death."

"It's all very hypothetical."

"I know, sir, and what I wanted this interview for was to ask if you thought that on such hypothetical evidence any action should be taken?"

Sir Mortimer's eyes flickered again. "Now, I confess you've got me puzzled. You know very well we can't interfere."

"I wondered, sir, if you thought the point should be put up to the Birmington force?"

Once again there was a pause, this time longer than before. "It's difficult to imagine them overlooking it," Sir Mortimer said at last, "though, I agree, it's possible. Your suggestion is to ask if a tongs or other apparatus was found?"

French shook his head. "Hardly, sir, I think. To interfere like that would probably annoy them. I wondered if you would consider writing that the point was raised by one of your people and that you pass the idea on for what it's worth."

"Pure altruism?"

French grinned again. "As a matter of fact the case was put up to me by my wife's brother-in-law, who is a brother of the head keeper at the Zoo. That's how I became interested."

The Assistant Commissioner rubbed his chin. "I can see them in Birmington frightfully hurt in their little feelings," he murmured. "I should be myself, you know, if the positions were reversed."

"No, sir, I don't believe that," French returned firmly, though with a twinkling eye. "You'd be glad of anything that helped you to the truth."

"If threats don't work, try flattery? Well, I never was proof against that. I'll write the C.C. a private note."

French returned to his room with rather mixed feelings. He was by no means sure he had not simply made a fool of himself. It was not his business to interfere where his opinion had not been asked, and now that his urge was satisfied, he wondered why he had done so. Of course, it was true that no one who had carried out a ghastly murder should get off with it, but then he was not a keeper of the country's morals. However, since Sir Mortimer had accepted his suggestion there couldn't be so much wrong with it, and in any case the matter was now out of his hands and he need waste no more time over it.

In spite of these admirable sentiments the case did remain a good deal in his thoughts. He wondered what reception the A.C.'s letter had received, and if the officer who had been in charge was fuming with malice and hatred against the Yard. He didn't expect to hear anything more about the affair, which would probably be closed by a polite but noncommittal acknowledgement.

However, to his surprise, next afternoon his forebodings were agreeably dispelled. Just before leaving for home he received a summons to the A. C.'s room.

He found him in conversation with an alert looking young police officer. "This is Inspector Rankin of the Birmington City Police," Sir Mortimer explained. "He's all het up over the brick you've thrown, so I rang for you to come and cool him down."

The startled inspector seemed about to offer a shocked protest, but catching sight of the twinkle in French's eye, he caught himself up in time.

"It's just about knocked the whole of our case into a cocked hat, sir," he smiled, in his turn, doing his best to play up to this novel method of conducting business. "Our C.C. sent me up to talk the thing over with you."

"We only put up the idea," French pointed out, tactfully.

"The fact is, sir," the newcomer looked from one to the other, "that I thought of murder at first, but afterwards it seemed so certain that it was accident that I dropped the murder idea. Having done that, you can understand that I stopped looking for suspicious circumstances."

"Very natural: I should have done the same myself," Sir Mortimer agreed, easily. "But the chief inspector here is the very devil. You can't get anything past him. Better take Rankin to your room, French, and have your talk."

French took an instantaneous liking to the young inspector. Instead of showing resentment, he seemed grateful for French's idea and was clearly out to get any help he could with his case. Moreover, he was efficient also: eager about his work and with the details of what had happened at his finger ends.

"There were no tongs in the case at all, sir," he explained. "None were found at 'Riverview' and none were missing from the Zoo. We found no bag or net which could have been used to carry the snake. There were three boxes in the deceased's study which would have held it, but we could get no evidence that they had."

"There would have been enough air in them?"

"The expert thought so. We assumed the snake had been in one of them, because there was nowhere else it could have been kept."

"Were they fastened?"

"One was locked. The other two were unfastened, though the lids were closed."

"Could the snake have pushed up the lid and got out?"

"The expert thought so, but he wouldn't say for sure."

"And you concluded?"

"We concluded that the snake had done what you suggest: that through a mistake the box hadn't been locked, and that it pushed itself out under the lid. The deceased had found it as he was about to start for his chess, and had been bitten."

"It certainly sounds reasonable."

"But I think, sir, your argument about the tongs upsets it."

"What, then, do you propose? Will you reopen the case or let it go?"

"About that, sir, the Chief Constable wondered if you would be good enough to come down and have a look round and then talk it over with us? That's really what he sent me up to ask. If by any chance the thing was murder, he's very set on getting the man."

Though French made no immediate reply, he was really delighted. The case had taken hold of him and he felt he should be interested to see it through. From a more humanitarian point of view he also would be set on getting the man, even if there were no interesting features in the problem. Yes, he would like to go, and he was sure Sir Mortimer would raise no objection.

In this he was correct. The A.C. agreed at once to the proposal, and it was decided that he should accompany Rankin on the evening train back to Birmington, the formal application then following in punctilious accord with official procedure.

CHAPTER XVI

VENOM: IN THE CONFERENCE

NEXT morning French was early at police headquarters, where a conference on the Burnaby case was to be held. Rankin was waiting for him and took him to his room.

"You can't meet the super, sir, as he's in hospital for an operation," he explained, "but the Chief Constable, Mr. Stone, will take his place. He said he'd be ready about ten."

"That'll suit me," said French. "It'll give me time to read over the inquest depositions."

"I've got everything here, sir. Perhaps you'd care to use the super's room?"

"No," French returned, "I'm all right where I am. You get along with your work and don't mind me; then if I want to ask you anything, I'll have you within reach."

The favourable impression Rankin had made on French was still further strengthened when he came to examine the dossier. The reports were clear, concise, and neatly put together, and what was much rarer, were admirably indexed. The photographs, though few, were illuminating, and when French had finished the file he felt he knew fairly accurately what had taken place.

Chief Constable Stone, who presently received them, was a complete contrast to Sir Mortimer Ellison. He was a tall, powerfully built man with a heavy face and rather sombre expression. His manner was official, and though he was polite to French, he was not in the least cordial. With the briefest of introductions he settled down in a cold impersonal way to the business of the meeting.

"I understand from your letter, Chief Inspector, that you have made certain deductions from the fact that no snake tongs was found on the deceased's premises. I should like to hear you discuss this point, as if I became convinced that there was any indication of murder, I should have no hesitation in re-opening the case. Perhaps you would give us your ideas."

French had expected a question of this kind and was prepared for it. "Certainly, sir," he answered, "but you must please bear in mind that my conclusion was reached from a newspaper report only, and that in making it I recognised that further information might modify it considerably."

The chief constable nodded shortly.

"I'll put what I have to say in the form of questions. First, did the deceased require tongs or other instruments to steal the snake and use it for his experiments at his home? If so, and as none such were found, someone got rid of them. Was this person the deceased? If not, someone else was present and the idea of murder is introduced.

"Now, with regard to the first question—" and French went on to state his views in detail.

The Chief Constable seemed impressed. "I admit you've made a strong case," he said, "but I don't know that it's entirely convincing. I agree with you that the stealing of the snake and conveying it to 'Riverview' would have required tongs or other apparatus. I'm not convinced that the experiments the deceased was carrying out would have done so, because we don't know exactly what these were. It seems possible, for instance, that the deceased might merely have lowered a guinea pig into the cage and lifted it out again when it was bitten, which could have been done with a basket and cord. Upon this point I think we must therefore reserve judgment."

"I agree, sir," French admitted.

"Then I'm with you that if there was a tongs at 'Riverview,' someone other than the deceased removed it, but I'm not with you when you say that murder necessarily follows. I think another person can be introduced into the affair without involving murder. And here I would ask the question: did the deceased steal the snake?"

"The balance of evidence seems to be against it."

"Quite: then why shouldn't he have employed someone to do it for him? Look at it this way. Suppose he bribed one of the attendants to take the snake from the Zoo to his house. This man would probably use a tongs, but on putting the snake in Burnaby's cage—probably one of those boxes—he would return the tongs. If not, the suggestion evidently intended—that the snake escaped—would have been negatived."

French had not thought of this, but he was not going to say so. "I admit that's perfectly possible, sir, but personally I think it unlikely. Some objection was taken to the theory that the deceased had stolen the snake on the grounds of character: that he was too upright to do it. But it would certainly be much more strongly against his code to bribe a servant to steal from his employer, than to steal himself. Frankly, sir, from the evidence, I don't believe he did it."

"Very well. Leave that for the moment and assume that your theory involves murder. Who do you think might have committed the crime?"

"I had no evidence on that point, sir, but I knew that the deceased was well off and assumed he had an heir."

The Chief Constable turned to Rankin. "Tell him about that, Inspector."

"We thought of that as a motive for murder too, sir," the young man answered. "The deceased was worth between twenty and twenty-five thousand pounds, so his heir had a strong motive for doing him in. We found the heir. He's a nephew named Capper, a solicitor. He practises at Bursham, a town about forty miles from here. His practice is small and he lives in a rather poor way. So he had a doubly strong motive. But he was innocent. I went into his movements and he was in his house at the time of the death."

Here was a reversal of all French's theories.

"You're sure of that, I suppose?" he asked, rather weakly.

"Absolutely. The doctor rang him up as soon as the deceased died, which, as you remember, was not more than half an hour after he was bitten, and he answered from his home. He then went to a nearby garage for his car, which was there, waiting some repairs. All that was substantiated by various witnesses. No sir, there's no doubt of his innocence."

"And you heard of no other suspect?"

"None, sir."

This certainly was a blow to French. It was beginning to look as if his fear that he had made a fool of himself would be realised. How often, he thought, when he had suspected someone else of error, it had turned out that he himself was the one in fault. Poetic justice, he supposed, but unpleasant.

He had been surprised at the uncanny readiness with which Stone had invited him down and heard his views. Now he began to wonder if the motive had been less admirable than he had supposed. Had Stone, for some reason jealous of the Yard and anxious to give it a snub, seized what he believed would prove an opportunity for doing so? It wasn't very likely, perhaps, but it certainly was possible.

But though French realised he might be wrong, he was not going to give way without a struggle. He considered the matter for a few moments, then with some misgivings embarked on a reply.

"I appreciate what you say, sir, and you have thought of a good deal which hadn't occurred to me. All the same, I still feel doubtful on the matter. Let me put it as I now see it."

Stone nodded and French went on with gradually increasing assurance. "My first point, modified by your remarks, now stands like this: If Burnaby *alone* had been concerned in the matter, he would have had a tongs or other apparatus. This would have been necessary to capture the snake and convey it to his house, as a man of his years could scarcely have carried one of the boxes all that distance. Once arrived at his house, it is surely unlikely that he would have gone back to replace the tongs, as that would involve a capability for plotting and deceit not in accordance with his character. If I'm right so far, the disappearance of the tongs seems to prove the presence of some other person."

"I don't think you can say it proves it, though I admit the probability. But I point out that this other person need not have been a murderer."

"Very well, sir, suppose another person was involved. Who was that person? Either he was employed by the deceased to steal the snake, or else he *was* a murderer. If he had been a casual or innocent acquaintance, he would have come forward."

Stone nodded again.

"From the point of view of character once more," went on French, "it is unlikely that the deceased employed anyone for such a purpose. Therefore the balance of probability—I put it no higher—suggests the murderer."

"I agree with that so long as you keep it as a probability. But to my mind the probability is over-ruled by the fact that no possible suspect had a motive."

"I suggest, sir, we're scarcely in a position to say that. However, we can easily test the point. If the deceased employed anyone to act for him, it should be easy to find it out. I don't want to push the view, as it's your case, not mine, but I think this is important. If someone stole the snake for him and replaced the tongs, I'd drop the case; if no one did, I should suspect murder and carry on."

It was now Stone's turn to hesitate. "I have felt all along," he said at last, "that the entire theory we are holding is inadequate. I am not satisfied that the deceased ever stole a snake or got anyone else to do it for him. I know it can be argued that for the sake of the greater good which success with his experiments would involve, he might have winked at the smaller evil, but even that does not accord with his character. This is why I asked you to come down, and if I could see that murder was possible, I should concentrate on it."

The man's honesty was patent, and with a slight feeling of shame French mentally withdrew his former suspicions.

"Your idea of finding out who stole the snake seems good to me," went on Stone. "I'm inclined to agree that if we knew that, it would solve the major problem."

French was delighted. Certainly no snub either to himself or to the Yard was intended. He expressed his approval of the other's views.

"What about approaching it from the opposite angle?" he went on. "I mean, considering all those connected with the Zoo, who could have committed the theft?"

"We've done so," Stone returned, "though possibly not sufficiently completely. We took them in order, beginning with Surridge, the director, and going right down to the various labourers. But none of them had any motive that we could discover." Stone paused for a moment, but as French did not speak, he went on: "Very well; the next question is, can you stay and look into it for us? Rankin has unavoidably got behind in his routine work and it would be a convenience if you could spare the time. Of course, Rankin would help you."

This was better and better. It was what French had been hoping for. "You would have to consult Sir Mortimer, I'm afraid, sir," he pointed out. "But it would only be a matter of form. We're rather slack at present and he's certain to agree."

So it happened that through the accident of his wife's brother-in-law trying to make himself agreeable, French became involved in one of the strangest cases he had ever known in the entire course of his career.

He spent the remainder of that day in reading all that had been written on the affair, visiting the Zoo and "Riverview," getting a detailed knowledge of the locality, interviewing Dr. Marr, and making up a programme of future work.

Fortified next morning by the arrival from the Yard of his "first aid" suitcase containing lenses, forceps, bottles, envelopes, note-books, camera, and similar aids to detection, he set to work on the first item of his programme. This was to compile a list of all those who might have been bribed by Burnaby to steal and hand over to him the snake and then to interview all on the list and form his own opinion of their personalities. For this he enlisted the aid of Peter Milliken, to whom Arthur introduced him. He would, as a matter of fact, have applied to George in the first instance, had not George gone that morning to London.

"I don't want it known that enquiries are being made, Milliken," he explained. "I should just like to walk round with you while you speak to the various men; just to see what they're like, you know."

"I understand, French. But you won't get anywhere that way. Not one of these fellows would have done the job."

Milliken proved a useful ally. Under his guidance French talked to all the possible suspects, with entirely negative results.

He was impressed with Milliken's certainty that Burnaby could not himself have obtained the snake. The head keeper argued not from the moral view, but from the physical. To pick out one of four venomous snakes from a cage was a job requiring more skill than the broken old man possessed. This, reinforced so strongly his own and Stone's view reached from other premises, that French felt he might definitely accept it.

If he were right so far, it certainly strengthened the murder theory. But French was always afraid of too rapid work: it generally meant that he overlooked something. At this juncture, therefore, instead of reporting to Stone, he once more concentrated on the list of persons whom Burnaby might have bribed, wondering if by chance he had missed anyone.

Presently he felt glad he had done so. In reading the dossier again he saw that there was another possible suspect. Cochrane! Had Cochrane been Burnaby's tool?

A search of the reports showed that Cochrane had been employed at the Zoo as a night watchman, had been dismissed for inattention to duty, and had evidently taken his discharge hard. His bitter frame of mind would make him a willing agent, as he would feel he would be getting some of his own back. So far satisfactory, French thought. But when he went on to read that Cochrane's daughter was a day maid at "Riverview," and that since his dismissal the man himself had worked there intermittently as a gardener and handyman, he grew very much more interested.

He saw Rankin and put the matter to him. The Inspector was obviously impressed.

"He's started in business for himself," Rankin explained. "I happened to notice him yesterday riding a cycle combination with 'John Cochrane. Window Cleaner' on it."

French looked at him. "Where did he get the money for that, do you suppose?" he asked.

"Just what occurred to me, sir, when you spoke."

"Might be no harm to make a few enquiries," French considered.

"Yes, sir. Will you have Cochrane here and question him?"

"Not for the moment, I think. Let's trace the purchase of the combination. Can you put a man on to it?"

"Certainly, sir. I'll see to it at once."

Either police efficiency or good luck produced an early result. In less than two hours the information had been obtained.

The combination consisted of a three-wheeled push cycle cart, carrying a long light sectional ladder and a box for cloths, etc. Cochrane had bought it, appearing alone in the transaction. He had paid cash—twenty-two one pound notes.

"It's not a big sum, sir," Rankin pointed out. "He might have had it in the bank."

"He can say so if he had," French answered shortly. "I think now we'd better have him in."

At nine o'clock that night French arrived at headquarters for the interview. Cochrane had just come, and after letting him wait for a little to induce the proper frame of mind, he was called into Rankin's room.

French was not greatly taken with either his manner or appearance. The man was strongly on the defensive and appeared to consider his summons a grievance. He was obviously unwilling to give information and suspicious of every question asked. All the same, French had to admit that he exhibited no actual signs of guilt.

"It's just a question or two," Rankin began, French having left the interrogation to him. "You don't have to answer unless you want to, but," he smiled, "it's always wise to help the police when you can."

"You ain't got nothing on me at all," Cochrane returned. "I ain't done nothing and I don't know w'y I should 'ave been brought 'ere like this."

"We're not accusing you of anything. All we want to know is where you got the money you paid to Humphries for your cycle combination."

Cochrane looked surprised, but not specially uneasy. "Think I sneaked it, do you? Well, you've got it wrong this time. I got it puffectly reg'lar, so there."

"That's all right," Rankin returned easily. "I never suggested you sneaked it. But we'd be glad to know where you got it all the same."

"And if I don't tell you? You said I didn't 'ave to."

"If you don't tell us we'll begin to suspect something's wrong. You can surely see that for yourself?"

Cochrane didn't reply. Rankin's quiet manner was having its effect and he seemed to be slowly growing reassured.

"I got it from the old professor, if you must know," he said at last. "'E give it to me the week before 'e died."

"That's all right: I'm not doubting you. Now if you will answer one more question, it'll be all we'll want. What did he give you the money for?"

"To buy me blooming outfit," the man answered, more promptly.

"I didn't mean that. I mean, why did he give it to you? Was he paying you for a service or what?"

Again Cochrane grew aggressive. "No, 'e weren't paying me for no service. W'en I worked for 'im 'e paid me me wages. But this weren't for no blooming work."

"Then why did he give it?"

"W'y did 'e give it?" Cochrane's voice took on a truculent note. "W'y, just because 'e were a gent. 'E saw me threw out of a job there at the Zoo through 'ardly any fault of me own, an' 'e saw I couldn't get another job, an' 'e just give it to me to get a start. An' wot's more, I didn't ask 'im for it. 'E suggested it 'imself, 'e did."

"You mean he simply wanted to help you out of a hole?"

"Isn't that wot I say? 'E said I was to consider it a loan an' I was to pay it back, if an' w'en I could. An' so I meant to, an' would 'ave if 'e'd lived. But I'll not pay it now, not to no one."

"Anyone else know about the gift?"

"Not a blessed soul except me son an' me wife an' daughter, if they're any good."

This seemed all that Cochrane could tell and he was got rid of with a word of thanks for his trouble.

"I've been making inquiries about him since, sir," Rankin went on when they were alone, "and he seems a quiet decent sort of man. He was dismissed for leaving his job as night watchman to go home and give medicine to his sick wife. I'm not excusing him, but it was different from leaving to get drink or something of that kind. Since then he's really been trying to pick up a job, and there's never been any hint of dishonesty against him."

"My impression was that he was speaking the truth," French returned. He spoke a little absently. It had suddenly occurred to him that he had been to some extent putting the cart before the horse. He should have gone on at once to Item 2 on his programme, which ran: "Blaney-Heaton on what Burnaby was working at." The professor's evidence, he now saw, might give the test they required. It might, in fact, not only settle this matter of Cochrane's part in the affair, but also the major question of whether or not Burnaby was experimenting with the snake.

"I'll go round and have a word with Professor Blaney-Heaton," he told Rankin. "He examined those notes of the deceased's, didn't he?"

"Yes, sir, he went through them carefully."

"Where does he live?"

" 'Cortina,' Bloomfield Park. No. 17 bus passes the door."

"Just ring him up, will you, and make an appointment. I'll go now if he can see me."

Twenty minutes later French was ushered into the scientist's library.

"It's all right, Chief Inspector," Blaney-Heaton replied to his apologies for the hour of his call, "I'm a late bird myself. What can I do for you?"

"What I wanted to know, sir, was the exact line of research upon which the deceased was working at the time of his death. I understand you looked over his papers, and I wondered whether you could answer the question?"

Blaney-Heaton passed across a box of cigarettes, and when both men had lit up, he replied: "Yes, I think I can, but I'm afraid," he added, with a slight smile, "it's rather technical. Are you up in organic chemistry?"

"No," French admitted. "I know very little about it. But I don't want technicalities. Really what I'm after is whether experiments with that particular snake were germane to what he was doing?"

Blaney-Heaton favoured him with a keen glance.

"Now that question interests me quite a lot. I should have thought it vital from your people's point of view, but until now no one has asked it. I confess I've been puzzled myself. From the papers I found, the late professor was working on kraits at the time of his death."

"That would be quite a different family or species, however you divide them?"

"A different species, and a different venom." The scientist's voice was dry.

French bent forward and became more confidential. "Clearly, sir, you follow what's in my mind. I want to know whether the deceased really had obtained the snake for experimental purposes?"

"You doubt it?"

French shrugged. "I see I must confide in you fully, sir, but I ask you to respect my confidence. It's important that no hint of this leaks out."

"That's all right."

"Then I may say," French went on, "that there's a suggestion of murder, sufficiently strong to warrant investigation. That's what I'm doing now."

Blaney-Heaton expressed a dignified surprise.

"You astonish me," he declared. "I can't see anyone doing old Burnaby in. I should have said he hadn't an enemy in the world."

"You may prove to be right, sir; at present we don't know. But you see now the purport of my question?"

"I do indeed, and I think I can answer it. Whatever the late professor was in everyday matters, in his research he was precise, accurate and systematic. His whole scheme of work was laid down in his notes. Following the discovery that small injections of venom will coagulate blood without other deleterious effects, it's being tried for every disease under the sun. Burnaby had been testing whether it would destroy cancer cells. He was working on the various venoms in rotation and he completed each before going on to the next. As I said, he was engaged on kraits at the time of his death and on nothing else. That's one answer to your question. But the next I consider even more conclusive. He had some four months earlier dealt in a complete way with Russell's vipers. Their venom proved useless."

All this interested French profoundly. If it were true, as of course it must be, it practically proved that Burnaby had neither stolen the snake nor had it stolen for him. He put the point to Blaney-Heaton.

"I never believed Burnaby would steal or be a party to the theft of anything," the professor answered, "and his papers convinced me of it in the case of this snake. I confess I did not think of murder, but now that you've suggested it, I can see what a very strong case for it there is."

This was the view French himself took as he walked back a little later to his hotel. Mentally he summarised his conclusions to date. First, it was extremely unlikely that Burnaby stole the snake himself. Second, the only person he could have employed was Cochrane, and Cochrane had given French the impression of innocence. Neither of these points was proven, though French was inclined to accept both. Third, Burnaby did not want a snake of the kind in question for his work.

But if these points—and particularly the third—were true, the case made by the coroner broke down. If so, was not the only explanation of the affair that of murder?

Satisfied that the investigation must be continued, French reached his hotel and turned in.

CHAPTER XVII

VENOM: THROUGH INTERROGATION

THE following morning, before returning to police headquarters, French sat down in the deserted hotel lounge to review his impressions of the case and plan his next moves.

If murder had been committed, the natural question was: Who might be guilty? He had seen at once that the heir to twenty-two thousand pounds had a pretty strong motive. That was the nephew, the solicitor, Capper. But Capper, Rankin said, had an alibi. He was forty miles away when the crime was committed.

This raised two further questions. First, had anyone else a motive for the crime? And second, was Capper's alibi water-tight?

In answer to the first question, French could think of no one. The deceased was a man of kindly disposition, liberal, friendly and generally popular. So far as French knew, he had injured no one, and as his experiments had not been successful, there was no case for jealousy among other workers. From the facts so far ascertained, it certainly seemed as if only Capper could be guilty.

The second question, whether Capper's alibi was water-tight, French hadn't enough information to answer. As a rule, he was suspicious of alibis. He had known so many which had appeared convincing at first sight, but which had proved fakes on investigation. It looked as if his first job would be to test Capper's.

Apart from the motive and the alibi, how was Capper fitted for the role of murderer? Taking out his note-book, French entered the points as they occurred to him. From Rankin's dossier he was able to supply a number.

Firstly, Capper knew Burnaby and his disposition and habits. He also knew about his experiments. He was therefore in a position to devise a scheme which fitted in with these. Secondly, he was acquainted with "Riverview" and the routine of the house, and probably was aware of the hours at which Mrs. Pertwee would be out, as well as of the deceased's weekly chess expedition. Thirdly, he could have met Burnaby on his way to Leet's without startling him or causing him to cry out. In short, apart from the alibi, he had all the needful qualifications.

Except perhaps on one point. Could Capper have stolen the snake?

There was no evidence that Capper knew anything about snakes or the Zoo. There was no suggestion that he could have procured the necessary keys or could have used them if he had. Unless Rankin had gone badly adrift, French felt convinced that Capper could not have obtained the snake.

But could someone else have obtained it for him? Cochrane had been working on and off at "Riverview" since his dismissal, and Capper had probably met him there and knew his story. Had Cochrane been the dupe? Had the money for the cleaning outfit come from Capper and not Burnaby?

French wondered whether the fact that it had been bought with single notes showed design. If the transaction had been merely charitable, would Burnaby not have used fives or tens? On the other hand, Capper would necessarily have kept to singles.

After consideration, French decided he could deduce nothing from this point. Burnaby might easily have had the singles in his cash-box.

It was unlikely, however, that Cochrane would have done anything to injure Burnaby. But if Capper had approached him, he would certainly have told him some yarn to account innocently for his action. And when Burnaby was dead and Cochrane had guessed the truth, it would be too late. He would be in Capper's trap, and for his own safety his lips would be sealed.

French was reasonably satisfied with his progress. If he had not reached any very illuminating conclusions, at least he saw his next step. He must test Capper's alibi, and if it proved sound he must find out where Cochrane was at the time of the murder.

He had the details of the alibi in the dossier, but he thought he should meet Capper, so as to obtain for himself an idea of his mentality. There was, of course, the objection that it would put the man on his guard. But this would be done in any event by the mere re-opening of the case, of which Capper was certain to learn.

After a call at police headquarters French, with a local sergeant, took a train to Bursham. It was a town of eight or ten thousand inhabitants and Capper occupied a fine old house in what had evidently once been a fashionable street. He carried on business on the ground and first floors, and lived over his office on the second and third. French sent in his civilian card to prevent discussion among the clerks, and after a short delay was admitted to Capper's room.

"I must show you my business card," he began, taking the chair to which Capper waved him. "I have been asked by the Birmington City Police to look into one or two puzzling points in connection with the recent stealing of the snake from the local Zoo: I mean the snake which caused the death of the late Professor Burnaby. I have called to ask your help."

As French spoke he unobtrusively watched the solicitor. Capper got a slight fit of coughing and efficiently blew his nose, but when presently he answered, he had himself well in hand.

"You surprise me, Chief Inspector," he returned in what French thought might be quite normal tones. "I thought the affair was over. What sort of points puzzle them?"

"Well," French answered easily, "for one thing, they don't understand how, with all the precautions that are taken at the Zoo, the snake could have been stolen. It's a serious matter, because if it happened once, it may happen a second time."

"I see that," Capper said, cautiously, "but what I don't see, is how I can help you in the matter. I only know what came out at the inquest and you probably have more information than that. All the same, of course, I shall be glad to do anything I can."

"Thank you, sir," French replied with a cheery intonation. "Then I'd better tell you something else. But I'd be obliged if you'd kindly let it go no further."

Capper nodded gravely.

"I may tell you then," French continued, with a more confidential manner, "that we've discovered that the late professor was murdered."

Once again French felt baffled. That Capper was completely taken aback at the news was obvious, but whether this was merely the reaction natural under the circumstances, or whether it indicated fear or a guilty conscience, he could not be sure.

"That's very startling news," Capper said, with an air of concern. "I'm sorry to hear it. I presume you wouldn't say it unless you are sure, but I confess it seems unlikely to me. My late uncle was popular in his quiet way, and I can hardly believe he had enemies."

"I agree," French nodded, "the same point has been puzzling us. However, there must be some explanation for it."

"Yes, if you're correct, there must be."

Naturally Capper was not going to help in what might be his own downfall. French therefore went on. "As you must know, Mr. Capper, from your professional experience, in all cases of suspected murder certain enquiries are made as a matter of routine. All those who might have benefited in any way from the death are asked to account for their movements at the time of the crime. Now you are the deceased's heir, and it therefore becomes my duty to ask that question of you. Perhaps you would kindly tell me?"

Capper smiled a little grimly. "My professional experience, as you put it, also tells me that I am not bound to answer any such question," he said drily. "However, I don't wish to stand on the letter of the law and I'll tell you everything I can. On that Wednesday evening I was here, at least in my rooms upstairs. Is that enough?"

"To be candid, sir," French said, deprecatingly, "it isn't."

"Perhaps you'd like the whole of my movements?"

"If you please, sir."

Capper took a small diary from his pocket and turned the pages. "Let's see, that Wednesday—no, I'd better go back to the Tuesday. On Tuesday I was in London: I had appointments on that afternoon and evening, and I slept there that night. I returned here shortly before lunch on Wednesday. During the visit I was troubled with toothache. It had been bothering me off and on for some time, but on Tuesday night it kept me awake and I decided I must get it seen to on the Wednesday. I go to a dentist in Birmington and in the morning I rang him up from London and asked him if he could see me that evening. He fixed six o'clock. I finished in the office about half-past four, and after a cup of tea I drove to Birmington. I had to wait a little time for my appointment, but it was worth it, for I got the aching tooth filled. I really don't remember what time I left the dentist's, but I suppose it must have been about quarter to seven. I got home here about quarter past eight or a minute or two later. Something was rattling infernally about my car, so I ran it direct to the garage which does my repairs, asking them to see to it next morning. I sat down to my evening meal just before eight-thirty. I know that because I looked at the clock. The dentist had told me I mustn't eat too soon and I remember thinking that by eight-thirty the filling would be quite hard."

"Thank you, Mr. Capper, that's all very clear. What happened then?"

"I had supper and just as I had finished Dr. Marr's message about my uncle came through."

"When was that, do you remember?"

"About ten to nine. I hurried down to the garage, got the car, and drove over as quickly as I could."

"That's just what I wanted. Thank you very much. Now, just a point or two for the routine checking. Who is your dentist?"

"Mr. Maxwell of Clovelly Street. But I gave all this information to the local inspector."

French thought he had seen enough of the man and put his note-book in his pocket. "I'm sorry, sir. Did you tell him the name of your local garage?"

"Yes."

"And where you called and stayed the night in London?"

"Yes, all of those things."

"Then I needn't trouble you any more. I'm sorry if I've repeated what you've already been asked."

If Capper's statement were true, his alibi was stronger than cast steel. French didn't see how it could possibly be faked, as every item was capable of a number of independent checks.

The crucial point, of course, was whether the man was at or near his home at ten minutes past eight, the hour at which Burnaby was bitten by the snake. For this there should be the testimony of the housekeeper, the garage proprietor and probably others in the garage and elsewhere. To set the matter beyond doubt he must obtain this testimony. But the visit to the dentist was of little moment and he need not waste time upon it.

He thanked Capper for his help and went to see the manager of the garage, whose name he got from Rankin's notes. Capper's tale, it appeared, was true. The car was an Austin Seven and was fitted with a luggage carrier at the back. The loss of a bolt from this had caused the rattle. Repairs had not been carried out at that time, as Capper had come in for the car again that night, a little before nine, the manager thought. The bolt had, however, been replaced when the car was returned next day.

French reached Birmington feeling more baffled than when he had left it. From the dossier he knew that Rankin had obtained and tested all the particulars of the alibi. The account of the inspector's investigations in London was given, and though French felt that before he gave up the case he must repeat the enquiries, he decided he need not do so at the present juncture. It certainly did seem that Capper had been in Town when the snake was stolen, and forty miles from "Riverview" at the time of the tragedy.

Could Cochrane then have been his agent, or was he, Capper, definitely innocent? French didn't see how Cochrane could have been involved, and yet he supposed it was just possible. It would be better to find out what Cochrane had to say about it.

There followed a tedious and inconclusive investigation. Cochrane said he had been at his home on both nights. His wife supported his story, though neither was able to produce further confirmation. On the other hand, French learnt nothing which threw the slightest doubt on their word. He felt that while not proven, the statement was probably true.

He went home that Saturday evening, returning to Birmington on the Sunday night. He had taken the dossier with him and in the train had plenty of time to study it. So far the results of his investigations had proved most disappointing. These provincial police had been quite as wide awake as he himself. He had suggested to them nothing which they had not already thought of for themselves, and their objections to his theories were sound; indeed, unanswerable. He felt that so far he had not shone in the affair.

But, after all, he was no fool himself, and the fact that he was puzzled simply meant that he had not yet investigated sufficiently. He was convinced that this was a case of murder. He had suspected Capper, but there he had been wrong. He must therefore find some other suspect. And vague imaginings wouldn't do it. He must get down to it and use such brains as he had till he found the solution. Similar difficulties had arisen before in his life and he had met them in the same way: by hard work and by nothing else.

On Monday, as a matter of routine, he saw all the other persons who had featured in the case, George, Colonel Kirkman, Mrs. Pertwee, Lily Cochrane, and several others. But from none of them did he learn anything helpful.

It was then that an idea leaped into his mind which made him wonder had he at last hit on the truth. He had on various occasions come across delayed action appliances. Could this murder have been carried out by something of the kind?

The idea was not new to him; indeed, he had thought of it early in the case. But all the delayed action appliances he had known had been mechanical. Bombs were favourite instruments in this connection. A bomb could be set off by clockwork, or by the opening of the parcel which contained it, or when some other movement had been made—all hours after the murderer had left the site. Cords tied to the triggers of guns indicated another form of the principle. Poison left where it would afterwards be taken, still another. In fact, there was no end to the lethal devices which fell under the heading.

But never before had French known anything to be worked with a living animal. He did not see how it could be done, and it was for this reason that he had not pursued the idea. A snake, he had realised, could easily be shut into a cage, the door of which would be opened at a given moment by some prearranged device. But nothing of this kind could have been used in the present case, for two reasons. First, the mere setting the snake at liberty would not guarantee that it would strike Burnaby, which presumably would have been the object of the device. Second, had such a device been used, it was clear that unless the murderer were there to remove it when it had done its work, it would have been found. About that he realised two points: first, if the murderer had been able to do that, there would have been no need for the apparatus, and second, neither Capper nor Cochrane could possibly have reached the house before the police.

French now wondered if he had not been premature in reaching this conclusion. He really had not sufficiently considered the question. Now it seemed to him the only possible solution of his difficulty, and he felt he must go into it exhaustively. If he could make nothing of it, he would at least be no worse off.

All that evening he worried over the problem, eventually taking it to bed with him. He lay awake with it for some hours; and then a further idea struck him, and once again he wondered if he had reached his solution.

Had a delayed action device been used, and had it been, like all he had previously known, mechanical? Had the living snake been out of the picture altogether?

French now saw that he had allowed himself to be obsessed with the idea of the living smake. Suppose the creature had been used only to supply venom, which had then been employed in some sort of mechanical striker? Suppose points had been arranged to prick the professor's hand, and suppose these points had been painted with the venom? He remembered reading of the rings used in the Middle Ages by the Borgias and like-minded gentry, and how, when shaking hands, the sharp point could be pressed into the victim's hand. Had some modern version of the Borgias' murders been committed?

French turned his thoughts to the wound on Burnaby's hand. It had been assumed that he had been bitten while trying to ward the snake off. But instead had he grasped something with poisoned points which had pricked him?

This idea was certainly promising. French grew almost excited as he pursued it. Where exactly was the injury?

On the palm of the right hand, near the base of the first and second fingers. French clasped his left hand with his right. Why, yes, that was the part of the hand which normally touched a grasped object.

What could such an object have been? Something apparently connected with Burnaby's departure from home. What did a man grasp on leaving his house? Obviously a door handle: he would pull some door after him. Could poisoned spikes have been fixed to a door handle, and when Burnaby seized it to close the door, could he have pressed the spikes into his hand?

Then French remembered that if either Capper or Cochrane was guilty, this could not have happened. The police were in charge at "Riverview" before either could have reached the house, and it was absurd to suppose that a trick handle could have been removed under their noses.

What else did a man grasp on leaving home?

In spite of careful consideration, French could think of nothing. A spiked door handle would fit the wounds on Burnaby's hand, but so far as he could see, that was the only object which would do so.

It was as a last resort, rather than as a promising line of research, that next morning he went to "Riverview" to see if he could find the required object. He put himself in Burnaby's place leaving the house. What might he pick up? A walking stick? No, if he had been injured by a walking stick he would have dropped it and it would have been found. There seemed to be nothing.

In despair he examined the door handles. They were all quite normal. None bore marks suggesting that some lethal apparatus had been attached.

French was disappointed. The idea of a delayed action appliance had seemed too promising, and now it also had proved a washout. He must be on the wrong track altogether. Someone other than Capper must be the murderer. He would have to begin the case again, looking for someone else who wished Burnaby dead.

What, he thought suddenly, about Leet? Could Leet be the man they were all looking for? No one seemed to have suspected Leet and he wondered why. Probably because Leet had no motive. But French saw that this assumption might easily be false. Leet might have had a motive. He might have had dealings with the professor that no one else knew of.

As he turned this idea over in his mind he saw how easy it would have been for Leet to commit the murder. Suppose he had got the snake, either having stolen it himself or bribed one of the Zoo attendants. He could have walked over to "Riverview" with the snake in its tongs just before Burnaby was due to start. Probably he would have disguised himself and taken the path by the Choole, which would be deserted at that hour. He could have met Burnaby as the latter was leaving his house, held out the snake to him, and as Burnaby was warding it off, he would have been bitten. Then Leet could have dropped the snake into the barrel and returned home, probably getting rid of the tongs on the way, perhaps by throwing it into the river.

French wondered why Rankin had not gone into this possibility. Then he thought he would go round and have a word with Leet and see what sort of man he was. A question about the time he had expected Burnaby would account for his visit.

He took the small footpath from the "Riverside" door which led to the north-west corner of the little estate, that nearest Leet's house. He was opening the gate on to the road, when suddenly he stopped as if shot.

Except that there was no upper lintel, it was more like a door than a gate: a close-sheeted wooden structure with a spring to keep it shut. But it was not this which had attracted French's attention. To open it you had to turn a handle!

French looked at the handle. It was pear-shaped and made of bakelite, with a small sunk screw in the neck to keep it on the turning bar. He bent down and examined the screw. Though the handle itself was old and weathered, the screw looked new.

A little thrill of excitement ran through French as he realised that here might be the solution of his problem. Burnaby would necessarily grasp this handle when going to Leet's, and it was a practical certainty that at that time of night no one else would. Moreover, the place was hidden by shrubs from the house and the murderer could easily have changed the trick handle while the police were in charge.

With the idea of Leet swept from his brain as a teacher erases a sum from a blackboard, French set his mind to considering whether Capper could have murdered his uncle by a trick door-handle.

CHAPTER XVIII

VENOM: IN THE WORKSHOP

TO think effectively French had always found he must be comfortable in body. Whether it was that physical discomfort gave him a subconscious unrest which distracted his attention, or whether a luxurious pose released energy for his brain, he did not know. But he was quite certain that the more difficult his problem, the more valuable became quiet, a bright fire, an easy chair and a pot of coffee. Bed really was the best place to think, and as he looked back over his life, he saw that more of his really heart-breaking puzzles had been solved there than in any other place.

But this particular conundrum scarcely seemed to require such heroic methods. Once given the main idea, to think out the details should be comparatively simple. He dispensed therefore with elaborate preparations, simply sitting down in a quiet corner of his hotel lounge, his pipe in his mouth and his notebook open on his knee.

Suppose Capper had designed and constructed in his workshop—he was a skilful wood and metal worker, so must have a workshop—the Borgian handle, with its venomed spikes set to puncture a grasping hand. Two further operations would be required for the full fruition of the scheme. The handle would have to be put in place before Burnaby started out for Leet's (but *after* the gate was likely to be used by anyone else) and it would have to be taken off again before the police could find it. Could Capper have carried out these operations?

Very little thought showed French that he could. "Riverview" was on the road between Birmington and Bursham, and Capper must have passed it at least twice on that evening, once before eight and once after it.

It was at this point that French, with rising excitement, saw the significance of that tale of the dentist and the filled tooth. He had wondered at the time why Capper had told it, but now he saw. The episode was clearly designed to facilitate the first of those passages, and Capper had told the story to explain his presence should he have been seen in the vicinity of "Riverview."

Simpler still was it to see how the handle might have been removed. Capper was Burnaby's only relative, at least in the district. Marr, as the old man's neighbour and doctor, would hear at once of his death and would be certain to ring Capper up. Capper would naturally come into Birmington, and on his way to Marr's would pass the very gate. Nothing easier than to stop and re-change the handles. Normally he wouldn't be seen, but if he were he could say he thought his uncle's body was at "Riverview."

Here was a satisfactory theory at last! French hugged himself with delight. He was going to get his own back on the Birmington police after all. And badly his self-respect required such a development. But he mustn't be too cocksure. Every item would have to be tested before he spoke of it. He wouldn't risk another snub. Slow and sure did it.

He turned to the question of what tests he required. Three were obvious and he would get on with them at once. Probably they would prove sufficient.

First, he would ask Rankin confidentially to go into all the notes made by patrolmen who were in the neighbourhood of "Riverview" on the night in question. Had any of these men seen a parked car, an Austin Seven for preference? Next, he would interview the dentist and check up hours; and lastly, he would see Marr and get his views about the spiked handle.

Rankin showed considerable interest when French made his request. But French did not satisfy his curiosity. "Just a notion," he said, evasively. "If there's anything in it, you'll be the first person to hear. Don't make a fuss about it, like a good fellow. Just let me have any information you get."

When French reached Clovelly Street he had to wait nearly an hour for an interview with the dentist. But he did not repine, for the information he eventually received was complete and definite. Capper's story was true—as far as Mr. Maxwell could check it. He could not, of course, tell whether Capper had been kept awake by his tooth, but he might have been. The trouble was of long standing and it was quite time that it was seen to. Capper had rung him up as he had said, and an appointment had been made for six o'clock. Owing to press of work he had been unable to see Capper till some twenty minutes later, and Capper had left about a quarter to seven. He, Maxwell, was sure of the hour, as he had himself been kept late and it had upset a dinner engagement.

From quarter to seven to quarter past eight, when Capper said he had reached home, allowed only an hour and a half for changing the handle, driving forty miles, leaving the car in Sloan's garage and walking to his house. Could Capper have done it with so small a car?

French believed he could. Austin Sevens, he knew, were capable of high speeds. He might take it then that so far his theory was watertight.

He found it impossible to see the doctor till after dinner and about nine he paid his call.

"I'm not often glad to hear of some poor wretch being taken by you fellows," Marr said, after greetings, "but this case would be an exception. If anyone murdered poor old Burnaby with that snake, I'd see him hanged with pleasure."

"I agree with you," French returned, "though, of course, we can't allow our feelings to come into our job. The deceased seems to have been a favourite?"

"I shouldn't put it exactly that way," Marr answered. "He was too quiet and retiring to be popular. But he was a really good old fellow, and no one who knew him could fail to like and respect him."

"Quite so." French paused for a moment as if to indicate that polite exchanges were now over and that business was beginning. "I should like to ask you a question, Dr. Marr," he went on, "and I should like it to be between ourselves."

Marr glanced at him questioningly. "Certainly, Chief Inspector, if you wish it."

"Thank you, sir. Assuming this was murder, which of course has not been proved, I have been trying to think out how it might have been committed. The snake, of course, might have been used directly, but I am wondering whether instead some mechanical arrangement might have been devised. Suppose, for example, the deceased gripped a door handle provided with poisoned spikes which pierced his hand? Do you consider that a possibility?"

For some seconds Marr did not answer. "I consider it a most interesting suggestion," he then said, doubtfully. "But I do not consider it a likely one. There are two reasons. The first is that Burnaby's hand was bitten, not merely pierced by something sharp. I mean that there were distinct signs of a closing mouth.

There were the two deep punctures from the venom fangs and there was also the slighter mark of the lower jaw. Now, I suppose that could be done by some design of spikes, but I don't see just how. However, the second reason I consider conclusive. The unfortunate man received more venom than could possibly have been conveyed in the way you suggest. There must have been an actual passage of fluid from the snake's sac to the hand."

This was like a slap in French's face. If the doctor was right, as of course he must be, it was the end of his delayed action theory. And if that theory were false, Capper was innocent. And if Capper were innocent, it looked as if after all Burnaby had stolen the snake and his death had been an accident: as if, in short, the local police had been right and he himself wrong.

French was cruelly disappointed; not that he wished ill to any poor creature, but because of the blow to his own prestige and that of the Yard.

"I suppose there's no possibility of doubt in all that, doctor?" he said, unhappily.

Marr shrugged. "I have none in my own mind," he answered, "but then I'm no expert. I don't mind telling you that this is the first case of snake-bite I have ever treated. But why not ask Professor Blaney-Heaton? It's his subject and he'll tell you straight away."

"I'm obliged for the hint. I'll do so."

"I'll ring him up for you if you like to go now?"

"Thank you, sir. I'd be grateful."

Half an hour later French was seated in the professor's study, hearing Dr. Marr's opinion confirmed by authority. On both points, it seemed, Marr was right. Blaney-Heaton knew of no mechanism which could produce the effects found.

Capper, therefore, was definitely innocent. Neither he nor his deputy, Cochrane—if Cochrane was his deputy—could have been present at the time Burnaby received his injury, and neither could have set any gin or trap which would have done the job in their absence.

But French's previous cogitations unquestionably suggested murder. If Capper were innocent, presumably someone else was guilty. In a sort of desperation his thoughts returned to Lect. It was, however, too late to call on Leet that night, and he decided he must do so first thing in the morning.

In the morning, however, he received some news which turned his thoughts once more off Leet and back to Capper.

Rankin had found a note in a patrolman's book, and when French read it he experienced again that little thrill which suggested a hot scent.

It appeared that the patrolman had been walking along Calshort Road just before seven on the night of the tragedy. He had turned in from Liverham Avenue and was approaching "Riverview" when he saw a car drive out of the lane in front of him. This lane, as has been mentioned, ran between Mornington's and Leet's houses, forming an approach to the footpath along the river bank. As cars were prohibited on the bank, the constable wondered where this one was coming from, and it was for this reason that he had noted the matter in his book. When he reached the lane he had flashed his torch on the ground, and in the soft mud he had seen the tracks of the car. These showed that it had simply pulled in off the road and parked. He could not tell what make the car was, but it was small and might have been an Austin Seven.

In the theory he had built up French had postulated that Capper's Austin Seven had parked somewhere near "Riverview" just before seven on the night of the tragedy. Here the very thing had been seen. Was this too remarkable to be a coincidence? French thought it was. His little thrill returned as he decided that in spite of the medical opinion, that must have been Capper's car, and Capper must have set some apparatus which had killed Burnaby.

Once again Leet was forgotten and French turned back to his former problem: how could he prove Capper's innocence or guilt?

For half an hour he pondered the matter. Then he decided he would visit Bursham again and if possible have a look into Capper's workshop. It would not be the first time he had obtained vital evidence from such an examination, but here the snag was that without a search warrant he would have no right to force an entrance. However, he could but try.

He set off presently with his attendant sergeant, and by midday they were walking down King Street in Bursham. Off this was Carlton Street, in which stood Capper's house some hundred and fifty yards down and on the opposite side.

French did not turn into Carlton Street, but passed it and went down the next road, Waverley Avenue. This thoroughfare scarcely lived up to its name. It was at the end of the town and was really laid out for posterity. Admirable as to width and grade, it was somewhat indeterminate as to boundaries. Only some half-dozen houses had been built and the vacant lots between had degenerated into a species of common, dotted with twisted shrubs and tufts of coarse grass. Across this ground French could see the backs of the Carlton Street houses, with their gardens running back to a narrow service lane between the two roads.

Strolling aimlessly, he and the sergeant presently found themselves on this lane at the edge of Capper's garden. French was pleased with what he saw. An orchard entirely hid the lane from the windows of the house. Moreover, in that hidden area was a wooden shed which had all the appearance of an amateur's workshop.

French hesitated. He was sorely tempted to enter. He would be, of course, entirely in the wrong to do so. On the other hand, the circumstances simply asked for it.

The struggle was short-lived. With "Keep an eye out, will you," to the sergeant, he slipped into the garden and crossed to the door of the hut. It was locked, but the lock looked old fashioned. He had a little tool on his ring and a moment later he inserted it in the keyhole and began twisting it round with skilful sensitive fingers.

Some slight feeling of sympathy for his hereditary enemies, the burglars and housebreakers of Britain, crept into his heart as he stood wrestling delicately with the lock. He was, he felt sure, safe. At twelve o'clock on a week day Capper would be in the throes of deeds, conveyances, torts (whatever they were) and suchlike mainstays of his profession, no doubt as regardless of the law in his own line, French thought viciously, as French himself was in his. And each evildoer doubtless justified his conscience in the same way: that the essential and admirable end justified the peccadillo in the means.

Suddenly his wandering thoughts returned to the job. There was a click as the bolt shot back. The door swung open. French entered the shed and closed the door behind him.

He had certainly struck oil. This was Capper's workshop, and not too bad a one either. Along one side ran a carpenter's bench, at the other were a lathe and a small universal slotting and planing machine. It was evident the man worked both in wood and metal. Like that of many amateurs, the shop was untidy. Tools and shavings covered the bench and the floor looked as if it had not been swept for weeks.

French did not know what exactly he hoped to find and therefore could only look about generally. Rapidly though systematically he began going over the bench and peering into the various drawers and cupboards. But nowhere could he find anything in the slightest degree suspicious.

At the end of half an hour he had been over everything. He was beginning to feel that his journey had been wasted. Also he saw that he must soon end his search, as Capper might come down to the hut at lunch-time.

As a last resort he got down on his knees and with his torch began turning over the debris on the floor. Here also he was systematic, beginning at one corner and working steadily towards that diagonally opposite.

Then unexpectedly he reaped his reward. Screened behind one of the metal standards of the lathe he found a scrap of bakelite.

It was a thin dark brown flake and very small, only about half an inch by a quarter, and was evidently broken off some article on which work had been in progress, as while three of its sides were rough fractures, the fourth showed tool marks. This worked side was cut to a radius of about half an inch. The surface was also convexly curved in both directions and was ribbed with narrow ridges and hollows.

French's thrill returned more strongly than ever as he gazed at it. He would, he told himself, eat his hat if the fragment wasn't part of a door handle! As if it were a cut diamond he put it in his wallet and turned back to his task.

Almost at once he found two more pieces. He was about to pick them up, then an idea occurred to him and he put them back. Now was the time for the search warrant. There must be something for him to find while acting under that, because he could only produce in court what he had obtained legally.

He let himself out, skilfully relocked the door, and satisfied that he was still unobserved, returned to the sergeant. A couple of hours later they were back at police headquarters in Birmington.

"I want you," he said to Rankin, "to put another enquiry in train for me, and I hope you'll be as successful as last time. Will you try and find out whether prior to Burnaby's death Capper bought any brown bakelite door handles of this size and shape?" and he handed over a dimensioned sketch he had made of that on the "Riverview" gate.

Rankin stared. "Door handles?" he repeated. "That interests me, sir, quite a lot. You can't be more explicit, I suppose?"

French felt he must take the man into his confidence. "It's only a theory," he told him. "There may be nothing in it, but I'd like to be sure," and he went on to explain his idea.

Rankin was tremendously impressed. It appeared that he and his chief constable had considered delayed action appliances, but had rejected them because of the medical evidence. "If you can prove that, sir, you've as good as got the man."

"I'm afraid," French returned, "we've some way to go before that. However, it's not so bad if we're on the right road."

French as a matter of fact was much more sanguine than his words admitted. Motive was already proved, and now it looked as if he was going to be able to prove opportunity also. Moreover, the proof he hoped to obtain would establish facts which could not be explained on any hypothesis other than that of Capper's guilt, and would therefore lead to certain conviction.

Well content with his progress, French returned to his hotel for dinner.

THAT evening French settled down to get his new theory on paper, and to divide those points which he considered proven from those which still remained surmise. This, he felt sure, would not only be intrinsically valuable, but would indicate the steps next to be taken.

First, to summarise Capper's general situation. The man no doubt wanted the £22,000 he knew was coming to him, but which delayed so exasperatingly in making its appearance. As Nature had failed in shuffling off the professor's mortal coil, Art must come to her aid. Capper knew enough about his uncle's researches to enable him to found on them his plan. The affair would look like an accident; all the same, in case of suspicion he, Capper, must have an alibi. Hence the delayed action apparatus. From the snake he would obtain venom with which to charge his trap, then drowning the creature where Burnaby might have thrown it.

So much of course was obvious and his action with the door handle was equally clear. First, he would have to buy a number of handles, as undoubtedly he would have to experiment before obtaining a satisfactory result. He would complete his apparatus, then consider how he might put it in place. His decayed tooth would give him the hint, and he would invent a night's pain and a day's engagements, so as to obtain an appointment with his dentist which would allow him to pass "Riverview" at a suitable hour. This must be a little before eight on a Wednesday evening, the hour that just before Burnaby left for Leet's, and the evening that on which Mrs. Pertwee would be out and there would be no one to whom the old man could make incriminating remarks.

French now seemed to see Capper as on that Wednesday evening he carried out his evil purpose. According to his theory,

Capper left the dentist's about 6.45 with his lethal handle in the car, driving to Calshort Road and backing his car into the lane next Leet's. Then with the handle he ran down to the river, and hurrying along its deserted bank, crossed the "Riverview" grounds to the gate. There he changed the handles, hiding the old one somewhere close by. Either at this time or on his second visit he dropped the snake, which he must have previously drowned, into the barrel. Hastening back to the car, he drove as quickly as he could to Bursham. There he took his car to the garage, as a check on the hour at which he reached home. Doubtless he had himself loosened the bolts of his carrier.

He knew that Marr would be called in and that owing to his relationship to Burnaby, Marr would ring him up if the old man died. Marr did so, and Capper took his car from the garage and drove back at his highest speed to the lane beside Leet's. A few moments would suffice to remove the trick handle and replace the old one, and one other detail dealt with, he would run on to Marr's and complete his alibi.

That detail was the disposal of the trick handle. Capper *might* of course have carried it away in his car, but French felt this was unlikely. He would be safer to get rid of it at once. How could he do so?

There was a very obvious and a very easy plan. As he ran back to the car along the bank, why not throw the handle into the river?

French was delighted with his theory. He felt sure it was what Capper had done. He would have bet long odds that on the bed of the Choole, somewhere between Burnaby's and Leet's, the trick handle was lying.

He wondered could he find it? If so, it would prove his theory and convict Capper.

By a curious coincidence it was only a few months since the search of a river bed—the Thames at Henley—had provided him with a clue which led to the clearing up of that unpleasant case of the death of Andrew Harrison. The use of a diver had proved extremely profitable. Could he hope for a similar piece of luck twice running?

He sat up till the small hours pondering the matter, and next morning he saw the Chief Constable, explained his theory, and recommended a search for the handle. At most, an area of only some hundred yards long by fifty or less wide would have to be covered, but probably this could be reduced to about ten yards square, as the handle more than likely lay in midstream opposite the "Riverview" gate. Capper's urge would undoubtedly have been to get rid of it at the first possible moment.

The Chief Constable was almost as much impressed as had been Rankin. A little to French's surprise he did not pooh-pooh the theory and try to suggest snags. Instead he was complimentary, saying he believed French had reached the truth. He was in favour of an immediate search.

"How do you propose to do it?" he asked, getting down to details. "Special drags?"

French didn't think special drags would be successful. "There would be a danger," he explained, "of pushing a small object like a door handle down into the mud. I don't know that there's mud there, of course, but I should imagine it because it's a sluggish reach. No, sir, I suggest a diver."

Mr. Stone made a grimace. "Pretty expensive, wouldn't that be? What would it run to?"

French didn't know, but he thought that considering the area to be covered, the cost would not be deadly. "You could get a man from Liverpool, I'm sure, and with luck he might do the whole thing in a day. You could get an approximate estimate, if you liked."

For answer the Chief Constable picked up his telephone and asked for the Liverpool police headquarters. He soon obtained the name of a reputable firm and in another ten minutes was discussing the affair with its manager. Finally it was arranged that a squad should be sent to Birmington by the first train next morning.

"Meantime, Rankin," went on Mr. Stone, "you see about the necessary barge and get it towed up to the place. And there are certain other things the diver will want," and he went into technical details.

The scene next morning brought back vividly to French that other day at Henley when, just as now, he had waited with anxious expectation for the confirmation or refutation of his theories. This time even more hung on the result. Then the evidence that he hoped to find, and did eventually find, was not a major clue which in itself would solve his problem. But here he was looking for something which, if he found it, would practically end his case.

The men worked quickly and soon the diver was clothed, first in his multitudinous sweaters and then in his rubbered canvas outer dress. He sat, enclosed to the neck, as the other diver had sat, consuming a last cigarette before the helmet was lifted over his head. Then slowly he moved to the side of the barge, stepped down the rope ladder, and disappeared.

French stood looking on, with that strange feeling of familiarity with the whole scene which is so often experienced. The smooth reach of the river curved gently away in each direction, to the north till it slipped behind its protruding eastern bank, and to the south till it gathered itself and passed under the three grey stone arches of the Liverham Avenue bridge. On the west bank ran the old towpath, separated by a railing and gates from the various little estates. Opposite stretched the Municipal Park with its green sward and splendid oaks and elms. And in this charming setting floated the square-nosed barge with its rust-stained tarred sides, its boiler, donkey engine and derricks, and the balks of timber and other debris on its deck. Among the varied impedimenta two men slowly rotated the windlass-like air-pump, producing a soft clacking of valves. The air-pipe led over the side into the water, and a little further away, moving slowly here and there and disturbing the mirrored surface, a rush of bubbles marked the diver's position.

Time passed slowly for French, as it always did when he was anxious. He had marked out with guide ropes the area into which he thought an object thrown from the gate of "Riverview" would fall, and the diver was slowly working backwards and forwards across this. Not till it was completely covered would he move further down stream.

By now a little knot of people had gathered along the east bank in the park. French had put out a story that the work was being done by the Corporation, who wished to find a submerged drainage sluice, but he was not surprised to hear the tale was rejected of the populace. Then when Rankin was recognised the truth was out, and the crowd increased in number and curiosity.

Suddenly French saw the diver's hand waving some object above the water, which was there only some seven feet deep. French couldn't see what it was, except that obviously it was not a door handle. But when at last it was handed to him, he breathed a sigh of intense relief. Though the find might not convince a jury, it satisfied him beyond possibility of doubt.

It was a small screwdriver, of the size which would fit the screw in the waist of a door handle, and to it was attached a tiny electric torch, arranged to light up the work in hand. It was like one of those pencils for writers or inventors whose fertile brains produce ideas which must be recorded during the dark watches of the night.

Half an hour later the trail of bubbles moved to the rope ladder, and presently the globular helmet appeared like the head of some uncouth marine monster, blowing spray as if from its mouth as it emerged. The diver reached the deck and then held out a small object to French.

It was a brown bakelite door handle.

French took it with a feeling of overwhelming satisfaction. Once again his judgment had been vindicated! He had guessed from that mere newspaper story that Burnaby's death was no accident, and in spite of the opinions of the local experts, he had trusted his own belief, he had staked his reputation on his view, and—he had won! Moreover, he had upheld the prestige of the Yard, and had shown once more that it was *the* final court of appeal in the police service.

He carried the handle gingerly, not knowing in what terrible way it might reward a careless grasp. Without changing his hold, he took it to Blaney-Heaton and gently deposited it on the scientist's desk.

"Hullo, Chief Inspector," he was greeted. "What have you got there?"

"That's what I want you to tell me, sir," French returned cheerily, his smile indicating triumph in spite of rigorous self-repression.

"You seem very pleased about it at all events," Blaney-Heaton commented, as he stretched out his hand to pick up the strange object.

"Careful, sir!" French warned him. "If you touch it carelessly, it may bite you."

The professor halted and looked searchingly at French. "Good heavens!" he said quietly. Then he crossed the room, and returning with a chemical clamp, fixed it on the waist of the handle and held it up.

"You're right," he went on grimly, pointing to two small holes some half an inch apart, with about half an inch from them a narrow slot of about the same length. "See, here are the venom fangs, and here," indicating the slot, "are the teeth of the lower jaw."

French beamed. "I thought so, sir," he admitted.

"I wonder how they work?" Blaney-Heaton slowly turned the handle over. "Ah, here you are." He pointed to a circular slot about an inch in diameter. "That disc I'm certain acts as a press. When you push it in by grasping the handle, you release some mechanism which shoots out the fangs. What do you think?"

This, it appeared, was precisely French's idea. "Will you open it," he went on, "so that we may see the mechanism?"

"Ah," returned the professor, "I'm afraid you've got me there. It seems very firmly made, and I fear I should only break it if I tried."

"Then would you advise me to send it to the Yard?"

Blaney-Heaton considered. "I suggest trying it on Major Meake," he said at last. "He's an officer in the garrison here and a very good fellow. I understand he specialises in opening live bombs, so this should be in his line."

"He sounds the very man, sir."

"Right, I'll get hold of him. I'll tell him to be careful and I'll let you know what he says."

French would have preferred to have himself taken the handle to Major Meake, but he thought it better to let Blaney-Heaton arrange the matter. After all, he would not have to wait long for the result.

Nor had he. A couple of hours later the professor rang up for him.

"This is a very ingenious little contraption," said Meake, when the necessary introductions had been made. "The professor has told me the circumstances and it's your snake all right."

Though French hadn't doubted it, this confirmation was welcome. After all, his own ideas were not evidence, but Major Meake could be taken into court to repeat his testimony. "Show me, sir," French asked.

"This disc," the major demonstrated, pointing to the surface enclosed by the circular slot, "is really the head of a press or push. Grasping the handle automatically pushes it in. I have called it the trigger. See?"

French nodded.

"Now that releases a little trip on a shaft, and the shaft, driven by a powerful spring, makes a turn, one turn through a complete circle. The arrangement is like one of those rotating camera shutters."

Again French nodded.

"At another point on that shaft there is an eccentric, or cam, if you prefer the word." He pointed. "That of course also makes a single revolution, and it works two ingeniously arranged pieces of mechanism, which I have called levers, corresponding to the upper and lower jaws of the snake."

"Very clear so far, sir."

"I've made a sketch of the idea," Meake went on, picking up a paper, "shown as a diagram rather than an actual drawing: two sketches, in fact, of the trigger and the fangs respectively. You see, the eccentric, rotating in the slots of the levers, pushes out the teeth of both jaws and draws them in again. The jaws are made to converge, so that the marks look like a genuine bite and not merely separate punctures. You follow?"

"Very clearly, sir."

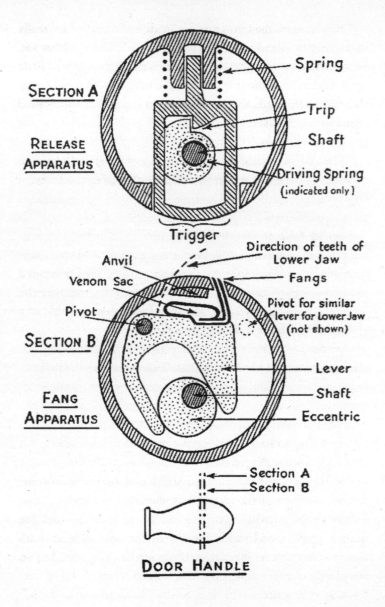

SECTION A

RELEASE APPARATUS

Spring

Trip

Shaft

Driving Spring
(indicated only)

Trigger

Direction of teeth of Lower Jaw

Anvil

Venom Sac

Fangs

Pivot for similar lever for Lower Jaw (not shown)

Pivot

SECTION B

FANG APPARATUS

Lever

Shaft

Eccentric

Section A
Section B

DOOR HANDLE

"Now you see the two fangs are made hollow: they are really tiny steel tubes; and they are connected with a little rubber sac. When the tooth is pushed out, the sac is squeezed against a little anvil, and the venom passes down the tube, through the fangs, and into the wound. The entire arrangement is of course copied from that in the snake's mouth."

"It's certainly ingenious, as you say."

"Yes, and well made. All the details, as well as the fangs, are of steel, and the fangs are sharpened at the piercing ends to a razor edge."

"Chap deserved to succeed," French smiled.

"Yes, and there's another clever point. People grasp doors in different ways and by different parts of the handles, and this machine must not be set off unless part of a hand is pressed over the fangs. Now the fangs are placed exactly opposite the trigger, and that's what I say is clever. Pressure at one side of a grasped object ninety-nine times out of a hundred involves an equal pressure at the other side to balance it—just try gripping anything and you'll find it's so. This means that the trigger won't be set off unless another part of the hand is where it's wanted."

"He deserved to succeed," French repeated, though he was sure that Capper had also taken the precaution of watching just how Burnaby did grasp handles.

"Well," Blaney-Heaton returned, "thanks I suppose to yourself, he's not going to. Have you any idea who is guilty?"

French felt this was straying on to delicate ground. He smiled again. "Don't you know, sir," he apologised, "that that's always a state secret? We can't ever answer that question, lest an occasional refusal might look as if we were baffled. I feel sure, however, that what you've done for us will help us to find out."

"Nicely put," Meake returned drily. "There's another point. I think I'm right in saying that the wound was in the right palm at the base of the first and second fingers?"

"Quite right, sir."

The major grasped an imaginary handle. "Then the teeth must have been deliberately set to project in the right direction: at about three o'clock."

"Yes," French agreed, dry in his turn. "I entered it in my book as due east, but three o'clock is certainly better."

Blaney-Heaton smiled. "I think we must both congratulate you, Chief Inspector," he said pleasantly. "I don't know how you got on to this, but its discovery shows you've done some pretty hard thinking."

French thanked him. "There's another thing, gentlemen," he went on, "though it's not so directly in your line as what we've been discussing."

As he spoke he took out his wallet and laid on the desk the scrap of bakelite he had found in Capper's workshop.

"Hullo?" Meake exclaimed, picking it up and inspecting it closely. Then he turned to French with a smile. "You're a fraud, Chief Inspector! You've been pretending ignorance as to the criminal, and now you produce evidence which will no doubt hang him. I suppose it's a secret where you found this?"

"I don't feel that I'm in a position to mention names even to you, gentlemen," French answered. "But I should like your views on the fragment."

For answer Meake turned the handle with the press disc upwards. Then he laid the fragment on the disc and pushed it about with his finger. "What ho?" he said, when he had arranged it to his satisfaction.

It was as French had expected. The scrap was identical in colour, thickness and surface finish to the handle, and the curve on its worked edge corresponded with that of the hole for the press. Its surface curvature worked in with the handle contours, and its ribs and hollows exactly registered with those on the handle. It was clear that the fragment was a part of what had been cut out to make room for the trigger, and French felt sure that with the pieces still remaining in the workshop, he would be able to build up the entire disc.

If so, it amounted to proof of Capper's guilt. Indeed, French thought there was enough evidence to secure a conviction.

Of course, the problem of how Capper had obtained the snake still remained unsolved. French felt that this could wait. The immediate essential was to get the man under lock and key. He would be growing anxious. Directly he heard that a diver had been working in the river he would realise that the police were on a hot scent. He might try to escape, either by losing himself abroad, which might give a lot of trouble, or by committing suicide and so cheating the law.

French went on to police headquarters and saw Rankin and Stone. Both were impressed with his story and both agreed as to the urgency of the arrest.

"Too late to do anything to-night, I think," Stone decided. "I'll get the warrant and so on if you and Rankin will go out and bring him in to-morrow night."

About nine the next evening a police car left Birmington for Bursham. In front with the driver sat French, and behind were Rankin and a sergeant. But it was a good sized car and there was room in the back seat for a third man.

CHAPTER XX

VENOM: THE RECKONING

WHILE French was working up his case against Capper, George Surridge was passing through a period of mental stress.

He was surprised and horrified to find that the passage of time—slow enough in all conscience—did nothing to ease the weight of fear and remorse under which he was labouring. Rather the load grew heavier. As day succeeded day he grew more and more nervy, more apprehensive, more restless, more miserable.

One of his heaviest burdens was the unceasing need for watchfulness over his every word. A careless phrase might mean disaster. Again and again he pictured himself making some chance remark which conveyed nothing untoward at the moment, but which would afterwards make his hearer think. If ever this thought produced a question such as, "How did Surridge know that?" it would be the beginning of the end. And such a remark would be fatally easy to make.

The burden grew because it was unshared. There was no one—no single individual in the entire world—in whom he could confide. He had to bottle his dreadful secret up in his own mind, and it festered there. His wife was his natural confidant. But he had long since forfeited her sympathy. If she knew the truth she would curse him even more bitterly than he believed she had. His friends in the club? *Friends!* There was not one of them who wouldn't hasten to the police if he suspected the truth. No, there was *no one* to whom he could turn for relief.

Not even Nancy. Nancy indeed had become his most dangerous acquaintance. He longed to see her, to rest in her presence, to hear her voice, to unburden his soul in her sympathy: but increasingly he realised that the possibility had gone for ever. He simply dared not risk such intimacy. The more closely he came in touch with people, the more likely they were to penetrate his defences.

Another disconcerting matter was that concentration on his business was growing more and more difficult. At one time his business had been his pleasure, but now that was changing. The mental grind which formerly he had taken in his stride was growing irksome. He was finding it more difficult to reach decisions, to keep his attention on the matter in hand and take in what was passing. More than once he found Miss Hepworth looking at him with a sort of thrilled expectation, as if she suspected a secret and believed she would worm it out. He grew to hate Miss Hepworth. He would gladly have got rid of her, but this again he could not risk.

More dangerous still, his craving for spirits grew greater and greater. Whisky, he knew, would remove all these terribly distressing feelings and leave him once more cheerful, confident and optimistic. But he dared not take it, and he grew still more nervy and irritable.

How he envied the people who had free minds and clear consciences! What would he not have given to have had his choice over again, and to be without that terrible knowledge which cut him off from his fellows! At one time he would have laughed to scorn anyone who had suggested that he had a conscience, or that the remembrance of crime could become a burden. That view, he now saw, had been due to ignorance. Now he knew differently, and as the days passed he would have given more and more to have been morally clean.

Then something happened which brought all his fears to a focus and left him face to face with sheer stark terror. He had

returned by the afternoon train from spending a couple of days
in London, and after glancing over his letters, had gone to the
club to kill time over a rubber of bridge. But he had not enjoyed
the game, and when one of the players was called away and broke
up the party, he took the opportunity to go home. It chanced
that in the porch he met Dr. Marr, also leaving.

"Going home?" Marr inquired. "Do you feel like a walk?"

Though part of George wanted to be alone, the rest of him
dreaded his own company. A walk with Marr, whom he liked
and respected, seemed an admirable suggestion. He agreed and
they set off.

For a while they chatted about various matters and then Marr
asked, "Have you seen French yet?"

"Been in London the last two days," George returned. "Who's
French?"

"You don't mean to say you haven't heard?" Marr answered,
with astonishment in his tones. "Chief Inspector French of
Scotland Yard."

George's misgivings flooded back in a great wave. "I don't
know what you're talking about," he said, as carelessly as he
could. "What's happened?"

"You surprise me," Marr declared. "Haven't you heard that
the Burnaby affair has been re-opened and that Stone has called
in Scotland Yard?"

An icy hand seemed to close slowly on George's heart. What
hideous thing was this that he was hearing? Was it—no, it
couldn't be!—the beginning of the end? What did they suspect,
these police? They couldn't surely *know* anything? Or could
they? Was he—no longer—*safe*?

His brain reeled as he fought for composure. Then he heard
himself answering, "Good heavens, Marr, you don't say so?"

"You hadn't heard?" Marr replied, still speaking casually. He hadn't noticed anything! "I should have thought they would have been to you first of all."

George struggled desperately to conceal his fear. What did those words mean? Was Marr's phrasing merely unhappy? Why should the police wish specially to see him?

"How do you mean?" he asked, with increasing thankfulness that it was dark. "I couldn't tell them anything more than they already know."

"You can tell them about the conditions under which the snake was kept," the doctor answered, "and that seems to me vital. I've always believed that if we knew who stole the snake, we'd know everything. You'll find that's what they'll go for."

George breathed more freely. Marr obviously suspected nothing. At the same time his suggestion was horribly upsetting. Suppose this Scotland Yard man did concentrate on the stealing of the snake, what would he discover?

Then George pulled himself together. He would discover nothing! How could he? He, George, had left absolutely no trace whatever. No one could possibly connect him with the affair. No one knew he had left his room that night. No one knew he had been in the snake-house. No one knew he had sent the snake to Capper. No, whatever mistake Capper might have made, he, George, was safe.

So bravely he told himself, as he strove to talk coolly to Marr. But when, after a nerve-racking walk, they parted near the Zoo gates, he knew that he didn't really believe it. Capper had somewhere made a slip. And if Capper were taken, could he escape?

For the next two days life for George was an absolute nightmare. The discussions and surmisings at the club drove him almost frantic, and yet he dared not keep away. He must know what was going on and he knew of no other way to learn.

Then on the evening of that second day matters came to a head. As after dinner he was sitting in his study, trying to whip up courage to go out, he heard a ring at the door. Before the maid came in with a card, he knew who was there.

"Chief Inspector French and another man to see you, sir," she said, with goggling eyes.

"I'll see them in a moment," he said coolly. "Just ask them to wait."

George realised that one of the major crises of his life was upon him. Now, he told himself, was the time for whisky; a carefully graded amount; enough, but not too much. He knew that the smell of whisky on his breath would be suspicious. French would guess he had been fortifying himself for the interview, and why should he do that unless he feared it?

He had foreseen the difficulty and made a plan. Quickly he poured out half a tumbler of neat spirit, and with a dash of water, tossed it off. Then he poured out a finger, added water till the glass was half full, and placed it at his hand on his desk. On the desk also he laid out certain account books, and a sheet with pencilled figurings which he had prepared. With a quick glance round he walked to the door, opened it, and looked into the hall. A rather stout, blue-eyed man bowed and advanced a step. Behind was an obvious policeman in plain clothes.

"Good evening," George said pleasantly. "Come in here, won't you? A cold evening. Won't you sit down?"

As he spoke he drew forward his arm-chair to the fire, placing another chair near by for the second man. French thanked him and sat down. "I hope we're not interrupting you," he began. "I'm afraid you're working?" He glanced deprecatingly at the desk.

This was just what George wanted. It accounted for the delay in admitting the visitors as well as for the smell of whisky. "Not at all," he answered lightly. "My business is not urgent." He took glasses from a cupboard. "Will you join me in a drink?"

French shook his head. "Very good of you, sir, I'm sure," he answered politely, "but we don't do it when we're on duty."

"Well," said George, sitting down at his desk, "you won't mind me finishing mine? And do smoke if you feel like it." He pointed vaguely to a box of cigarettes on the chimneypiece.

It appeared that police officers did not smoke either when on duty. Once again French was politely grateful, going on to explain that they had called to ask George's help in connection with their investigation into the death of the late Professor Burnaby.

"I heard that the affair had been re-opened," George answered coolly. The whisky had acted and he felt at his best, with a full grip of himself and a certainty of his competence in handling the interview. "I confess I was surprised. I thought the inquest had left everything cleared up in a satisfactory way."

"Then you think the deceased met with an accident?" French said, with a show of interest.

"I did think so," George answered judicially, "but then probably I was biased. I had myself some time earlier come to the conclusion that, owing to his breakdown in health, it was no longer safe for Professor Burnaby to handle the snakes. As you probably know, I was instrumental in getting his permission to do so withdrawn."

"So I have heard, sir. Perhaps you would tell me about that? Also I'm anxious to know just how the snakes were kept?"

George was here on safe ground, but he made a point of hesitating before each reply, so that if he were asked a difficult question, a pause should not be suspicious. However, as the interrogation advanced, he breathed more and more freely. The questions were innocuous, French's manner was respectful, and his obvious acceptance of all George said was comforting.

French was certainly thorough. He took up his various points in a logical sequence and systematically exhausted each before going to the next. If George had been guilty of any slackness in the running of the Zoo, it would have quickly stood revealed. Luckily George's conduct of his business had been impeccable.

About one thing only was George perturbed. He found he had taken a little too much whisky. Its immediate action had been just right, but later he began to feel its effects too powerfully. However, in spite of this he got through the interview creditably. After an hour the officers left, apparently completely satisfied as to his innocence.

The effect of the spirits lasted till he went to bed and then the reaction set in. His self-assurance evaporated and his fears crowded back more strongly than ever. French had seemed to accept his statements without suspicion, but wasn't that merely the police way? The mere fact that the enquiry had been re-opened showed that they had *some* theory of murder and guilt. George felt a little sick when he thought of it all.

During the next day or two his misery grew almost unsupportable. If only he knew what was happening, he told himself, it would not be so bad. But there in the background this persistent effort was in progress, an effort to ruin him, to take him to prison, to trial, and to that unthinkable thing which would follow trial. It would almost be better to know the worst than to bear this awful doubt.

Gradually the conviction that the strain was too great began to fill his mind. He simply couldn't go on like this. His mind would give way. Slowly his thoughts turned towards suicide.

What a relief, what an overwhelming relief, it would be to have done with it all! To have done with the fear, the need for acting a part, the wearing pretence of an easy mind which he didn't feel! To get rid, once and for all, of those haunting eyes which seemed fixed on his wherever he went and whatever he did: Burnaby's eyes with their maddeningly reproachful gaze. To shed for ever that load of guilt which separated him off from his fellow men. Yes, suicide would do all that.

And do it easily. What, for instance, could be simpler than to put his hand into one of the cages in the snake-house? It would be a rapid and nearly painless end. Or gas. That would stupefy and there would be no suffering. There were many ways. With his knowledge and facilities he could fade out almost without a pang.

And really he had nothing to live for. His home life was in ruins, his business was threatened: he would certainly lose his job unless he pulled up his work. His amusements, his golf, his club, his hobbies? He loathed them all! And Nancy?

He really didn't know about Nancy. He wasn't sure whether he ever wished to see her again. He knew he had lost her. Never again could he confide in her or enjoy her society. No, there was nothing for him there. If he were to fade out to-morrow there was no one and nothing that he would object to leave.

And there was nothing in those old wives' tales of life after death. Suicide would be the end: it would be forgetfulness for ever. And there was no God or any of that stuff—else he wouldn't have been allowed to do what he had. No, he was alone in the universe. No one cared any more about him, except to hound him down and take his life. He hated everyone. The thing to do was to make an end of it all.

As if in a dream he got up and examined the gas fire in his room. Yes, it could be done quite simply. He would cover the fire with bedclothes so that the gas would be concentrated, and then lie down on the floor and push his head under the clothes till it reached the gas. It would be easy and painless. He would just go to sleep, and as he did so all his troubles would fade away. He would never be conscious of anything again.

Stealthily he locked his door, and then taking some clothes from the bed, he fixed them over the fire, bringing them down to the floor all round. Then he crawled underneath, so that his head was in a sort of chamber. Setting his teeth, he seized the tap to turn on the gas. He felt sure he would feel little. There might be some choking or headache, but he was not afraid of either. They would be as nothing to the mental pain he would be rid of.

Then a sharp thrill of dismay passed through him. He couldn't do it! He simply couldn't do it! Up till now it had been different. None of the preparations he had made was irrevocable. But he couldn't reverse the tap if he afterwards wished to. He would be *dead*! He lay there trying to fight what he considered was just weakness.

At last the truth revealed itself to him. It was not the physical suffering he feared—if there would be any. It was not even physical death itself that he shrank from. It was the load he was carrying which had made life impossible for him, and now this load was adding nameless and hideous terrors to death. He could die, he told himself, easily and gladly even, if first he could clear his conscience. In spite of his reason, he knew that as he was, he couldn't face death.

Shakily he got up and went back to bed. He would postpone his decision till the morning. Perhaps then he would see some better way.

He wondered whether if he were to leave a confession, it would ease his mind. He thought it might. But he doubted whether a confession written before suicide would be enough. It was surely not the act of confession so much as the realisation that others knew his story. Must he not be there to experience that? Must he not, in fact, be there to take the consequences?

But that, he saw at once, was insane. It was arguing in a complete circle. To escape the consequences of what he had done, he must himself produce those very consequences! That at all events was not the way out.

At the same time the idea of confession took hold of his mind. It could not be an entirely mad idea, as many men had adopted it. Many who had been led into crime had found they could not carry its load, and had given themselves up to the police. George saw of course that he could not go so far as that, but he believed that some move in that direction might be helpful.

Then a wave of profound relief swept over him. He need not think about confession, because it was out of the question. To confess would be to incriminate Capper. Obviously under no circumstances could he do such a thing, even if it seemed the best for himself.

Now that he could not make it, he saw quite clearly that confession was the thing he needed: not a written statement before he committed suicide, but a giving up of himself to the police with the knowledge that he must pay for what he had done. But of course he couldn't do it. Apart from the disastrous consequences to himself, he couldn't do it because of Capper.

Some more days of misery dragged out their weary length, and then an event happened which increased his fears a hundredfold.

He heard at the club that the police had had a diver working in the Choole opposite "Riverview," and it was believed that they had made some find of importance. He was able to show the necessary mystification, for the simple reason that he had no idea what the fact portended. But his feeling that it spelled disaster became so strong that he simply could not resist an appeal to Capper.

Accordingly that evening he rang him up from a street booth. Capper was guarded in his language, though he conveyed clearly enough his opinion that George had committed the unpardonable sin in communicating with him. But when George mentioned the diver he changed his tune. Obviously he became deeply moved, and though he said little, he left George quaking with terror. "If they've got that it looks like the end," Capper answered in a voice which had become hoarse. "Look out for yourself and keep away from me."

Wondering with dismay if the blow he had so long feared was at last about to fall, George rang-off and went unhappily home.

CHAPTER XXI

VENOM: THROUGH DEATH

THE car containing French, Rankin, the sergeant and the vacant seat drove on through the darkness till it reached Bursham and drew up at the police station. It was just a little past ten. They would not be delayed long. Three or four minutes would take them to Capper's house, and another three or four would make the arrest. Then Capper had only to get his coat and hat and give parting instructions to his housekeeper, and they would be off. With the prisoner they would return slowly, so as to reduce as far as possible the chance of accident, but they should reach the Birmington headquarters before midnight. The charge and search would follow and the whole unpleasant episode should be over by half-past twelve.

For technical reasons it had been decided that the actual arrest should be carried out by Rankin as representing the local force. Nothing more was to be attempted that night, but a man from the Bursham station was to be left in charge, and next day French and Rankin would return to go through Capper's effects.

Rankin disappeared into the station, while French sat on in the car, lost in thought. This was a part of his job which he absolutely loathed. The running down of a criminal was a different matter. There was the intellectual problem, the slow search for facts with which to build up and prove a theory and the excitement of the chase, all thoroughly interesting, if occasionally somewhat exasperating. But when the affair became personal, when instead of dealing with a factual jigsaw, French found himself bringing terror and despair into human eyes, he wished he was out of it. There was no use in his reminding himself that his victims had usually done the same thing to someone else and with less cause: he was always distressed by their distress.

With the local constable who was to watch the house during the night, they now ran on through half a dozen streets and pulled up at Capper's door. The town was empty: evidently the inhabitants were early people; and this street in which Capper lived was entirely deserted.

The door was opened by an elderly woman, who proved to be the housekeeper. "Yes, gentlemen, Mr. Capper's upstairs," she told them, evidently without the slightest idea of what the call portended. "He's not engaged. Will you come up?"

With heavy, sinister steps the men passed into the hall and up the staircase. As French began to ascend he thought he heard a door close softly on the landing above, but when they reached the sitting-room Capper was in an arm-chair, reading before the fire. Beside him was a table with whisky and soda and a half-emptied glass. He put down his paper and rose to his feet as the others entered. His manner was cool and collected, and French thought he looked normal, except that his face was very pale.

"Good evening," he said shortly. "Will you sit down and tell me what I can do for you?"

Rankin waited till the door was shut. Then all three men quietly crossed the room and got beside their victim.

"We're here on unpleasant business, Mr. Capper," Rankin said stolidly. "I'm sorry to tell you that I have here a warrant for your arrest on a charge of being concerned in the death of the late Professor Matthew Burnaby, of 'Riverview,' Calshort Road, Birmingham, on the night of the 23rd of November last. I have to warn you that anything you say will be taken down and may be used in evidence."

For a moment Capper remained silent and motionless, while his face grew ghastly. Then French thought he heard a slight click and an expression of pain passed over the man's features. He said quietly: "Right! I expected this. But I want to make an immediate short statement. Sit down for a moment."

"I'm afraid this is not the time for making statements," Rankin answered gravely. "You'll have to come along with us now. But you'll have ample opportunity later to say whatever you think right."

Capper sat down slowly. The officers were standing close to him, not actually touching him, but ready to stop any slightest movement of escape or suicide. He shook his head firmly. "I'll make it now, while I can," he declared, with great resolution. "Don't be a set of fools: I know I can't get away and I'm not going to try. Take this down."

His manner was so determined that Rankin hesitated. French looked across at the inspector, while a dreadful misgiving formed in his mind. "Let him say what he wants to," he advised urgently.

Rankin shrugged. "As you will, sir," he agreed.

Capper immediately signed to the sergeant to write and began to speak.

"While I am still able," he began, confirming French's fear, "I wish to confess to the murder of my uncle, Professor Burnaby. No," he hurried on, as Rankin would have stopped him, "I'm quite determined to do it. I was short of money and I killed him with snake poison, administered through mechanical fangs. I put a special door handle on the gate of the footpath to 'Riverview,' and when he gripped the handle the fangs shot out and pierced his hand. I had wanted to kill him for a long time and I had made copies of his keys for the Zoo. With these I stole the snake and——"

Capper paused and an expression of pain once again crossed his face. He gazed straight in front of him in a helpless sort of way, then appeared to make a great effort.

"I extracted the venom and—then drowned—the snake," he went on, speaking as if with difficulty. Then he lowered his head. For some moments he sat motionless, then crumpled down in his chair. Only for the support of the officers, he would have fallen forward on the floor.

They laid him on his back on the rug while French and Rankin hastily administered such first aid as was possible, and the local constable telephoned feverishly for medical help. But nothing they could do was of any avail. He gradually grew weaker, and by the time the doctor hurried in he was only semiconscious. Rapidly he sank, and after a little time he was dead.

French and Rankin exchanged gloomy glances.

"He must have known what was coming to him," French said shortly. "Who tipped him the office?"

Rankin shook his head helplessly. "No one knew. *No one* except ourselves."

"He's heard about the diver," French suggested. He frowned, then went on: "This is a nice thing for you and me. It'll take some explaining."

Rankin did not answer and he went on. "We needn't worry about it now." His manner changed and he swung round to the doctor. "What did he die of, doctor?"

For answer the doctor pointed to Capper's left hand, which was tightly clenched. "I can see no cause so far," he answered, "but that hand looks swollen. I can't open it without using force."

"Use force then," French said, shortly.

The doctor bent down and presently the locked fingers relaxed. A spheroid about the size and shape of a bantam's egg rolled out of the limp hand.

"Don't touch it," French cried sharply as the doctor made to pick it up. "I know how it works."

French carefully lifted and examined the little ball. It contained, as he had supposed, a mechanism similar to that of the door handle. Capper had obviously made it when he was making the handle, as a precaution against disaster. Doubtless he had been told about the diver, and realised that the police must be on his track. When he had heard the ring he at once suspected that his time had come and had gone for the ball, grasping it in his left palm. There he could hold it without attracting attention. If the interview went well, no harm was done, but if he saw that disaster was inevitable, he had only to squeeze the ball, and the trigger and spring and venom would do the rest.

French's chagrin was profound, even greater, he imagined, than Rankin's. He, French, was the senior officer, and though technically the local man was making the arrest, blame for what had happened would undoubtedly fall on the superior. The episode was going to mean a very considerable loss of prestige, as well as a heavy blow to his pride. It would avail him little to have solved the mystery and identified the guilty man, if he had immediately let him slip through his fingers. It was a bad business, a very bad business, and it would be a long time before he could live it down.

"Well," he said shortly, to Rankin, "will you get on with it? Ring up the local station, tell them to bring their own doctor, and all that."

He sat in Capper's arm-chair and gave himself over to bitter thought, while Rankin busied himself with the routine operations which had become needful. So this was the end of his case. He would go back to Sir Mortimer Ellison and the Yard, having vindicated himself on all major issues, and yet having spoilt the whole thing by a failure in detail. He had allowed himself to be duped like the veriest beginner. As he had told Rankin, it would take a lot of explaining and a lot of living down.

It was true, of course, that neither he nor Rankin had actually been to blame. The ball had obviously been made for a considerable time. Almost certainly it had been constructed at the same time as the handle, and both had been charged with the venom together. Capper had heard them coming in and had then and there, before they had reached the top of the stairs, grasped it in his hand. He was thus in a position to kill himself at any moment, and without attracting attention. Even if French had deduced what the man was going to do, he could not have prevented him. Before he could have taken a single step across the room, Capper could have closed his hand, and once he did that he was as good as dead.

But the fact that French hadn't been to blame wouldn't help him. He might avoid censure, but his failure would remain.

He wondered how soon he would get back to town. Probably the inquest would be next day. Then there would be some squaring up to be done, putting the proofs of Capper's guilt on paper and leaving all tidy. Three or four days should see him once more at the Yard: starting to live the affair down.

Then suddenly, with a shock, he remembered a fact which in the upset of the moment he had overlooked. The case was not over! Capper had not stolen the snake!

"Rankin!" French called sharply.

The young man at the moment was engaged in laboriously taking down the doctor's statement, but he excused himself and came over. French drew him into a corner.

"Didn't Capper tell you he was in London on the night the snake was stolen?" he asked.

"Yes, sir," Rankin answered, in his smart, competent way. Then the true import of the question struck him and he stopped and stared helplessly at French.

"You checked up on the alibi?" French went on, tensely.

Rankin gulped. "Yes, sir," he said, with a noticeable absence of his usual precision. "I called on the solicitor he had been with and saw the manager of the hotel he had stayed at."

"And you were satisfied?"

"Absolutely, sir."

Capper's last statement must therefore have been an attempt to save his accomplice. Excitement was once again rising in French's mind. He repressed it carefully. "You see what that means?" he demanded. Then, without waiting for a reply, he went on: "Never mind; keep it to yourself for the present. Finish up with that doctor. We'll get away as soon as we can. Then we'll come out in the morning and with the place to ourselves we'll have a proper search through the man's papers. Your warrant will cover that."

A local inspector had arrived, and while the matter of the suicide was handed over to him French said that, to square up the original case, he would have to go through the man's effects next day. In the meantime would the officer please see that the place was guarded continuously.

It was a rejuvenated French that drove back next morning to Bursham. He had—through no fault of his own—come a cropper on the previous night, but the case wasn't ended. He now had the opportunity to retrieve his misfortune. The capture of the accomplice would go far towards wiping out the loss of the principal. He must be particularly careful this time, so as to run no risk of a second disaster.

He wondered if he should have gone more deeply into the matter of the accomplice, because, of course, he had known that there must have been an accomplice. But he had been so fully occupied in proving Capper's guilt, that he had not had time for more. Concentration on the accomplice would have been the next step in any case. He saw that he had not been to blame.

The search of Capper's effects was soon in progress, and before lunch-time French had found enough to assure him that at last he had reached the full truth of the affair. First, he had learnt that Capper had been extremely hard up. In his desk was a private account book which showed that for years he had been gambling on the Stock Exchange. The amount of the sums he had staked—and usually lost—amazed French. French could not believe it had all come out of the practice. In this alone he believed that there was an entirely adequate motive for the crime.

His next discovery was not so immediately promising, but it led to an even more satisfactory conclusion. Another stack of papers showed that Capper had been solicitor to a Miss Lucy Pentland, and when French learned who this lady was, he realised that he need go no further. Here was a connection, hitherto unsuspected, with the Zoo, and more than that, with the one member of its staff who could most easily have stolen the snake! French was thrilled, and dropped everything to follow up this line of research. The correspondence shewed, first, that though Capper had been employed by George on Miss Pentland's death, he had not yet applied for probate. Whether or not this was suspicious, French didn't know, but when at last he learnt that Capper had held the deceased's securities, he felt like a ship master when in tricky waters a fog suddenly lifts.

The next enquiry was obvious. The securities must be produced and checked over. The office records showed that these were not in the bank, but in a safe deposit in Birmington. With Capper's keys French and Rankin returned to the city.

Then suspicion became certainty. Not a single one of the securities remained, and French's examination of the deceased's books showed that they had been sold at various times during the previous ten years.

It took a little time to calculate their present worth, but eventually French found that George's loss amounted to over eight thousand pounds. Here, he realised, was an entirely adequate motive for the accomplice also.

He sat thinking over what George must have done, but nowhere could he see how any of his actions could be established in court. However, it was inconceivable that the man had *nowhere* made a slip. All that was necessary was to trace his probable movements, and he would surely come on the required evidence.

One obvious line of research would be into his finances. Rankin's routine inquiries showed that George was living on the scale which might naturally be expected from a man in his position. It might, however, be that in his life there was some secret expenditure corresponding to Capper's gambling. The turf, cards, an expensive hobby, women: there were innumerable ways of getting rid of money, and it would be French's duty to see if he could find any such financial leakage in Surridge's life.

There were two avenues of research therefore—into Surridge's movements on the night of the theft of the snake, and into his life in general. Were there any other lines?

Suddenly, it occurred to French, that one episode which Rankin had noted without comment was really highly suspicious: George's story of leaving his keys in the side door of the Zoo.

Was it likely, French now asked himself, that a man who had the custody of such vitally important keys would neglect to wear them on a chain? But if George had worn them on a chain, he could not have stepped over to a car, leaving them in the lock. Then French saw that the whole episode of the car was improbable. The driver had stopped to ask if this were the way to Bursham, but French remembered having seen a quite adequate direction board to Bursham at the end of that very street. A driver turning into Calshort Road would have seen the notice, and therefore the question would have been superfluous.

On the other hand, if a snake were to be stolen in the early future by the use of just those keys, what more likely than that George would try to account for their having got into other hands for a long enough period to enable impressions to be taken?

French returned to his hotel determined that before he went to bed that night he would re-read the dossier in the light of his new discoveries. He believed that with this fresh outlook he would find some further lines of investigation, one of which would give him what he wanted.

CHAPTER XXII

VENOM: THROUGH THE TONGUE

FRENCH found his study of the dossier disappointing. He came on no facts from which by a brilliant *tour de force* of deductive reasoning he could prove George's guilt to an admiring court. The man seemed to have been distressingly efficient in his actions. Apparently he had left no clues for investigating detectives to pick up. French might himself be sure of what had happened, but to prove it was going to be troublesome.

The chief difficulty was to carry on an investigation without letting the subject know what was in progress, and thus enabling him to follow Capper's distressing example. This, it occurred to French—the one crumb of comfort in the affair—would be better done by local men who knew the place, and he decided his first step must be to see the Chief Constable and discuss with him a plan of campaign.

French had, of course, reported his discoveries after the search into Capper's papers, but Stone had left to him the further conduct of the case. Now he was surprised to find Stone a little embarrassed.

"I heard quite incidentally something of which I thought nothing at the time, but which in the light of all you say becomes suggestive. As a matter of fact, it was a bit of gossip my wife repeated in an idle moment. She shouldn't have done it, of course, and I rather hesitate to use anything so obtained, but there it is, I think I must give you the hint. There's a Miss Corrin who lives out near the Zoo. She's one of those women with brains and energy and no outlet for either, who minds everybody else's business, and to whom spiteful gossip is the breath of life."

He glanced at French, who nodded appreciatively. He knew those women. They were what used to be called "dangerous." They came to the Yard with tales against their neighbours and you had to be extraordinarily careful not to act on them rashly, or you might find yourself sustaining an action for wrongful arrest.

"She had been full of a story of going off to some God-forsaken hole to look for a maid—it was a place called Bramford, with a rather decent old inn—and seeing Surridge drive up in a sports car with a pretty stranger. She told the story with all due suggestion and innuendo when Mrs. Surridge was present—my wife was there, too, as a matter of fact—and Mrs. Surridge turned it off with some tale about a friend who was house-hunting. But my wife thought it was a true bill."

French listened to this story with profound satisfaction. "That may be just the hint we want, sir," he declared. "Did Miss Corrin give the date when it happened?"

"No, I've told you everything I know. If you want more you'll have to go to the lady herself."

"I'd rather avoid it if I could. The inn people might recognise a photograph, or we might get something else there. Or perhaps from the car. Any of your men know what kind of car Surridge drives?"

Stone made an inquiry on his desk telephone. Presently a constable entered.

"Doesn't Mr. Surridge of the Zoo live on your beat?"

"Yes, sir."

"What kind of car does he drive?"

"A Mortin, sir, an old model. Looks about twelve or fourteen horse, and about five years old, but I don't know exactly."

"Ever seen any of them in a sports car?"

"No, sir."

"Looks as if the car wasn't Surridge's," Stone went on, when the constable had withdrawn. "He might have hired it."

"He might have hired it, yes," French agreed, "or it might have been the woman's, or one or other might have borrowed it. Perhaps we should try round the city garages before we go any further."

"It's a chance. I agree it's worth taking."

A number of constables were enlisted and sent out to work various areas, while French sat considering what further steps he must take if the inquiry drew blank. However, before an hour had passed, one of the men rang up.

"Speaking from Bailey's Garage in Norfolk Street, sir," came the voice. "Mr. Surridge ran an account here for the occasional hire of an N. J. Gnat sports car. Is that what you require?"

"Sounds like it," French answered, with satisfaction. "Just stay where you are, and I'll be with you directly."

French called Rankin and in a few minutes the two men reached the garage. There recourse to the books showed all the occasions on which Surridge had taken out the Gnat. French noted the dates and hours, and then minutely examined the car, this latter unhappily being without result.

"Was the car used by others than Mr. Surridge?" he asked the manager.

Another book was turned up. "Only on one other occasion during the period," the manager returned. "That type of car hires better in summer than winter."

This made it easier for French. Within an hour a general call had gone out to all neighbouring stations, asking whether during the previous few months a car of such and such details had been seen.

While waiting for a reply, French and Rankin set off for Bramford, and drawing up at the inn, asked to see the manager.

He proved a fussy little man of the self important type. He declared that it was impossible for either himself or any of his staff to identify a call from a man and woman on some unknown date several weeks earlier, and thought the officers were unreasonable to expect it. While admittedly they had not a great many for tea in the winter—making their money in the bar—they still had too many to recall individuals.

Without comment, French handed over his batch of photographs.

The manager didn't recognise any of them, but when the waitress was called, she picked out George. "That gentleman was in some time ago for tea," she declared. "He sat there in the window, and there was a lady with him."

"You didn't recognise the lady?"

The waitress had never seen the lady before. But she was an observant girl and had noticed a good deal about her. Presently French had obtained a vaguely sketched portrait of Nancy herself, a rough description of her clothes, and a detailed and highly technical specification of her red hat. The waitress, it appeared, trimmed her own hats and she had approved Nancy's and decided to have one like it.

This was more than French could have hoped for, and when he returned to Birmington and found that a reply had been received to the general call about the car, he felt that his progress was almost uncanny.

The sergeant in charge of the small station at Neverton reported that one of his patrols had on three separate occasions noticed a car of the type and number standing on the road at various places near the village. In each case a man was sitting in it reading a book. On the first occasion the constable had seen nothing unusual in the matter and had simply passed on. But on the second and third he remembered having seen the car before, and on general principles he noted its particulars in his book. There was, of course, no reason why he should have interfered, and he had not done so.

French next morning set off for Neverton and saw the sergeant and constable.

"Now, another matter," he went on, after discussing the car. "I have the description of a lady here. Can you identify her?"

The officers looked at each other, and the sergeant called in the remaining members of his force. One of them, a young man whom French at once imagined might have an eye for the fair sex, somewhat sheepishly propounded a query. "What about Mrs. Weymore?" he asked. "She's something like that and she had a hat of that colour."

"Good looking?" asked French, drily.

On this point the young constable was not to be drawn. He thought, however, she might please some people.

"She live on your beat?" asked French again.

"She did, sir. But she's left the village."

"Tell me what you know about her."

Mrs. Weymore, it appeared, had been companion to an old lady, a Mrs. Sherwin, who had died some six months earlier. The house had then been closed and was still empty. Mrs. Weymore had left the district and the constable did not know where she had gone.

"Go and see if she left an address anywhere," the sergeant directed, with an inquiring look at French.

"Good thought," French approved. "He might get a photograph of her also, if he can. I need scarcely wait," he went on. "If you get any information let me know at Birmington."

As Rankin drove him back to the city, French again examined the list of George's car hirings. There was a suggestive gap towards the end of June, then the trips had begun again about the second week in July. Did this, French wondered, mean that Mrs. Weymore, if she were really the woman, had left the district on her employer's death, returning to some other job a fortnight later? It would at least, he felt, be worth acting on this assumption.

At police headquarters he drafted a circular giving the lady's description, and saying she was believed to have taken a house, a flat, rooms or a job somewhere about the second week in the preceding July.

Two days later there was a reply from the sergeant in the little village of Cleerby. A cottage in the neighbourhood, which had been lying vacant for some time, had been taken about the time mentioned by a lady who answered very well the description. She was still in occupation. In accordance with the terms of the circular the police had not approached her, and they could not say, therefore, whether or not she had come from Neverton.

Two hours later French and the local sergeant were discreetly observing Rose Cottage. They presently saw Nancy take her car from the garage and drive slowly off. French had intended, if this occurred, to try to search the cottage, but now he thought he might do better.

"Who's the agent of the place?" he asked the sergeant, and when he heard it was a firm in Cleerby, he drove there at once.

"My inquiries are connected with an entirely separate affair," he told the agent. "I have nothing whatever against Mrs. Southern," as the lady's name appeared to be. "All I am interested in is the negotiations about the taking of the house."

The agent hummed and hawed. The chief inspector would understand that his clients' business was confidential. However, when French promised that nothing he said would be repeated unnecessarily, he somewhat reluctantly told what he knew.

French was interested to find that the cottage had been bought by Messrs. Abraham & Co. In the evening he went to London and early the following day he called on the senior partner.

That call gave him the evidence he required. It was George Surridge, he found, who had tried to borrow, and who was therefore hard up. It was George Surridge for whom the cottage had been bought. It was George Surridge who had been carrying on this intrigue, which had run him into a heavy expenditure. Doubtless he had been depending on his inheritance to square his account. And when the inheritance proved non-existant the temptation to join with Capper in the murder of Burnaby would be overwhelming. All this, French was satisfied, could be substantiated by an examination of the man's papers. He felt indeed that already he had obtained sufficient evidence for a conviction.

At the same time it would be better if he could connect his suspect more directly with the crime. He had felt this all through and had been working on other lines of inquiry. It happened that one of these produced its fruit at about the same time.

It had occurred to him that if Surridge really was accomplice of Capper's, they must have met to discuss the plot. Could he trace these meetings?

When would they have taken place? Probably not till after Miss Pentland's death, as this was doubtless the event which brought the whole matter to a head. And as soon after that as possible, as the question of the inheritance would arise with the reading of the will after the funeral. The funeral was on the 27th October.

French turned up the list of dates on which George had hired the Gnat. Two following the 27th October, on the 7th and 10th November respectively, interested him, because while most of the hirings were in the afternoon between lunch and dinner, these two were in the evening between 8.0 p.m. and 12.30 a.m. On no other occasion had George been so late.

Could these hirings, French wondered, represent visits to Capper? With this in mind he went back to Bursham and consulted the local officers. An intensive search was made for traces of parking, and eventually some valuable evidence was obtained.

At about ten o'clock on the evening of the 10th November, the second of the two dates French had queried, a lad named James Grant had observed an N.J. Gnat car parked down a side street some forty yards from Capper's door. This lad lived at the farther end of this side street, and he was returning from a Boy Scout entertainment. It happened that he was a car fan and this particular model had always represented to him the *ne plus ultra* of two-seater design, that which he would himself buy had he the wherewithal. He even remembered the number, as he had wondered from where the car had come. The constable who made this discovery at once checked up the information. An appeal to the Secretary of the Scouts' organisation confirmed the date and the probable time at which Grant would be passing Capper's.

George then had undoubtedly called on Capper on the evening of the 10th November. And what had immediately followed? On the 11th November, the very next day, George had left his keys in the side door. Surely here was cause and effect? French was positive that the key episode was the first item of the scheme which had been arranged at that evening meeting, and he was equally certain that a jury would take the same view. Further, was there not an element of design in parking the car out of sight of Capper's door? French felt he was getting on.

Indeed, he thought he had now a sufficient case to justify an arrest. Once again he summarised it, as he would present it to the public prosecutor.

George Surridge had for some time been carrying on an intrigue which involved the frequent hire of an expensive car, and doubtless he gave the woman presents, and there was other outlay on various matters. He had bought her a cottage and had got Messrs. Abraham to advance the money. He had also tried to borrow from them for other purposes. He was therefore definitely short of cash.

He was expecting to recoup himself from a legacy of some eight thousand pounds on the death of his aunt, who was then incurably ill. The aunt died and he then learned that her solicitor, Capper, had embezzled his whole inheritance and that he therefore would not get a penny. His debt and the threatened break-up of his illicit establishment made him desperate.

Faced with such a situation, George was doubtless tempted by Capper. He could recover his money by helping in a certain scheme. His part would be to steal and send to Capper a venomous snake. Possibly he had to "milk" the snake first and send on the venom separately. Possibly he had to drown the snake before sending it. But in some form or other he had to supply Capper with snake and venom. Capper would do the rest. Probably George hesitated before agreeing. French had no doubt he did agree in the end.

This view was supported by several other facts. First, Capper could not himself have obtained the snake, as on the night of its theft he was in London. Someone, therefore, stole it for him. Of those with the necessary knowledge, George was in by far the best position to do so. Further, careful inquiry had eliminated every other possible person.

If, thought French finally, a job has been done, and if the only person who could have done it has an overwhelming motive for doing it, the case is strong. But if, in addition, all the remaining facts in the affair harmonise with this explanation, and with it only, the conclusion becomes overwhelming. Cumulative evidence again!

Well pleased with the results of his cogitations, French drafted his conclusions in the form of a report and took it to the Chief Constable. Mr. Stone read it carefully, but without showing much surprise.

"This is very able, if I may say so, Chief Inspector," he commented, laying down the sheets, "I congratulate you. I think there's no doubt you've reached the truth at last. What do you propose now?"

"I thought, sir, we had enough to justify an arrest?"

Stone nodded heavily. "I agree, and I suppose we needn't delay. What about at his house this evening?"

French sat forward. "I thought of that, sir, and normally I should entirely agree," he said. "But in this case I advocate an unexpected arrest. We must prevent what happened in Capper's case. For all we know to the contrary, Surridge has one of those oval balls in his pocket. We must take him so suddenly that he can't use it."

Stone sat silent for some moments. "I agree," he said at last. "It wouldn't do to risk a second suicide. How do you propose to make the arrest?"

"He leaves his office every evening about half-past five. I suggest we should wait for him on the private path to his house and seize him as he is walking home. It'll be dark, but there's enough moon to see by."

"Very well. To-night?"

"Yes, sir, if you can get the warrant."

"Right. We'll let Rankin do the job, but I'd be glad if you'd be present."

That evening three men slipped one by one through the gates of George's drive, and passing as much as possible behind shrubs, worked their respective ways round the house and along the private path leading to the Zoo office. There, behind bushes, they took up their positions.

"When I hear him coming I'll walk to meet him," French explained. "I'll say, 'Good evening, Mr. Surridge. Can I have a word with you?' Then you both close in and catch hold of his arms."

"Suppose he has the ball in his hand?"

"He won't have; he won't be expecting anything, and we won't give him time to get it out of his pocket."

They lapsed into silence, waiting. The night was raw and cold, and a faint breeze stirred uneasily among the trees. Otherwise it was still, save for an occasional hoot from a car. They were too far from the city to hear its roar. French found it hard entirely to control his excitement.

They waited till long after half-past five. But George didn't come.

CHAPTER XXIII

VENOM: THE ANTIDOTE

GEORGE'S sense of approaching crisis continued to grow more and more intense during the day and night which followed his telephone conversation with Capper. The latter's phrases, "If they've got that, it looks like the end," and "Look out for yourself and keep away from me," rang continuously in his ears, with their heavy portent of disaster.

He would have given half his inheritance merely to know what was going on. He had the impression of being surrounded by inimical forces working secretly and relentlessly to destroy him, forces from which there was no escape, and against which he couldn't strike back. Sometimes the loneliness and the moral weight of his crime drove him nearly mad, at others his fear increased till it crowded every thought and feeling from his mind.

At lunch at the club on the second day a terrible blow fell. The police had discovered the truth and Capper—was dead.

If it hadn't been for the whisky he drank nearly neat, George felt he could never have got through lunch without giving himself away. As it was, he almost feared he had given himself away. He imagined a number of the men had looked at him strangely. They had said nothing: though of course they would say nothing. But when he had gone what would they say? What would they do?

That afternoon George could not force himself to attend to business. He wanted desperately to get away from the office, and the questioning stare of Miss Hepworth's shrewd eyes. He felt increasingly certain that it was his guilt that was his real trouble. It was his guilt that had cut him off from his friends, and made him feel this desperate loneliness. It was his guilt that had prevented him from taking refuge in suicide, and now he saw that it was his guilt that gave him his real fear of arrest and what might follow. If only he could be rid of this feeling of guilt; if only he could feel clean and honest with people he could face anything. Even that dreadful end which might be in front of him would be robbed of half its terrors.

How he got through the remainder of the day George did not know. Had it not been for a frequent recourse to the whisky bottle he felt he could not have done it. It was with a feeling of overwhelming thankfulness that at last bedtime came and he was able once more to be alone.

But his relief was short-lived. He could not sleep and solitude he found was no ease to his mind, but rather another kind of torment. Again he played with the idea of suicide. If he were only *sure* that suicide was the end. ...

For nearly a fortnight George suffered intolerable misery and distress. Then one night, when he was at his very lowest, his thoughts went back to his childhood and his childhood's teaching. Some old words that he had then learnt recurred to him, about going to Someone and being given rest. And as these echoed in his mind he knew beyond doubt or question that he had been deceiving himself: that there *was* a God, that good and evil in his life *did* matter, and that if there was hope for him at all, it was through the Divine Man who had spoken these words.

Without any conscious intention, George suddenly found himself doing something he had not done for perhaps thirty years. He was praying.

But his prayer brought him little relief. Rather the reverse, for once again the hideous idea of confession had filled his mind. And now with a shock he saw that confession had become a possibility. The argument about incriminating Capper no longer held. Capper was dead, and nothing that he could say could injure him. Now George realised that confession was a vital issue and that at last he was face to face with his destiny.

Presently from sheer weariness he fell asleep, and when he woke he knew somehow that he had taken his decision. Cost what it might, he would confess and be done with the struggle.

Next morning he spent putting his affairs in order, and in the afternoon he went home to carry through what he knew would be the bitterest part of his whole action, the telling of his resolve to his wife.

It proved so at first. She was not helpful and he found it desperately hard to begin. And when at last, with a sort of freezing horror, she grasped his meaning, she railed on him. If he had no thought for himself, had he none for her? Did he want, because of some ease to his own mind, to ruin her life also? What sort of a future would she have if he persisted in this madness?

George, if the truth be told, had not realised fully what his action would mean to Clarissa. But he saw that, while she would have to pay for what he had done in any case, probably payment would be less in this way than in any other.

He felt that he should never see his wife again, and that he must therefore tell her everything. With hesitations and pauses he spoke of Nancy. He said that he had turned to Nancy because of the failure of their married life, and admitted to her that this failure had been his fault. He mentioned other things which he had done and which had come between them.

Clarissa, as soon as she realised his action was irrevocable, seemed turned to stone. She heard him in a freezing silence. Nor did she break that silence when, after asking her if she would not say good-bye to him, he turned and stumbled from the house.

When French and Rankin were waiting on the office pathway to take him, he was striding blindly into the city. He reached police headquarters, knocked at the charge-room door, pushed it open and disappeared within.

*   *   *   *   *

George lay on his bed with his eyes closed. His time was nearly over. Another week would see the end.

Events had moved quickly since that evening some two months earlier, when he had pushed open the charge-room door and told the sergeant behind the little desk that he had come to give himself up. He had been charged with the murder, brought before the magistrates, committed for trial, had waited for nearly six weeks for the assizes, had pleaded guilty, had been sentenced and—here he was, just waiting—waiting for this last week to pass. Everyone was extraordinarily kind. Popular sympathy was with him. An enormous petition for reprieve had been presented, but had been rejected by the Home Secretary on the grounds that if it were known that reprieve followed confession, every murderer who felt cornered would know how to escape.

George himself, though at times he grew a little sick as he looked forward, was more thankful than he could say for his decision. His prayer and confession had been the first steps to a vital contact with the Divine. Though his sorrow for what he had done remained, he now knew himself to be forgiven, cleaned from his load of guilt, and with a power and confidence to face the future to which he was moving, such as he had never before experienced.

How to make such restitution for the past as still remained possible had been his greatest problem. With regard to Nancy he could do little. His confession had at least shielded her from publicity—only the police knew of their association. He had written to her begging forgiveness for the way in which he had injured her, but he felt this was insufficient. He longed to restore her financial position, made precarious through his action.

The means came in a way he had least expected—through Clarissa's generosity in agreeing to allow Nancy a part of the Pentland legacy, which Capper's heir insisted on paying her.

Overwhelmingly thankful was George about Clarissa. A day or two earlier she had been to see him. Their previous interview had impressed her profoundly. It had started a train of thought which during these weeks of waiting had led her also to find a contact with the Divine, She had reviewed in a different way her own past life, and had realised that she also was not without responsibility for their unhappy relations. Disregarding the cost to herself, she had told him so. At that the barrier between them had broken down, and both had glimpsed what life on such a basis of honesty and love might have been, if only they had found it earlier.

But though he was going to pay for the results of that failure, a satisfaction and a peace he had never known before had grown up in his mind. In spite of what was coming, for the first time in his life he was really happy. Presently he slept, peacefully.

THE END